PENGUIN C

THE BOOK OF T

ROWAN WILLIAMS is the former Archbishop of Canterbury and currently Master of Magdalene College, Cambridge. The author of many books from *The Wound of Knowledge* to *The Tragic Imagination*, he has published several poetry collections and is a contributor to the *New Statesman*.

GWYNETH LEWIS is an award-winning poet and was the National Poet of Wales from 2005 to 2006. Her books of poetry in Welsh and English include *Chaotic Angels*, *Sparrow Tree* and *Treiglo (Mutating)* and, in prose, *The Meat Tree: New Stories from the Mabinogion*. She is freelance and teaches at Middlebury College's Bread Loaf School of English in Vermont.

To Marged Haycock,
in gratitude and admiration

The Book of Taliesin

*Poems of Warfare and Praise
in an Enchanted Britain*

Translated by GWYNETH LEWIS
and ROWAN WILLIAMS

PENGUIN CLASSICS
an imprint of
PENGUIN BOOKS

PENGUIN CLASSICS

UK | USA | Canada | Ireland | Australia
India | New Zealand | South Africa

Penguin Books is part of the Penguin Random House group of companies whose addresses can be found
at global.penguinrandomhouse.com.

Penguin
Random House
UK

First published in hardback Penguin Classics 2019
Published in paperback 2020

003

Set in Sabon LT Std
Typeset by Dinah Drazin
Printed and bound in Great Britain by Clays Ltd, Elcograf S.p.A.

A CIP catalogue record for this book is available from the British Library
ISBN: 978-0-141-39693-4

www.greenpenguin.co.uk

Contents

HEROIC POEMS

LEGENDARY POEMS

PROPHETIC POEMS

DEVOTIONAL POEMS

UNGROUPED POEMS

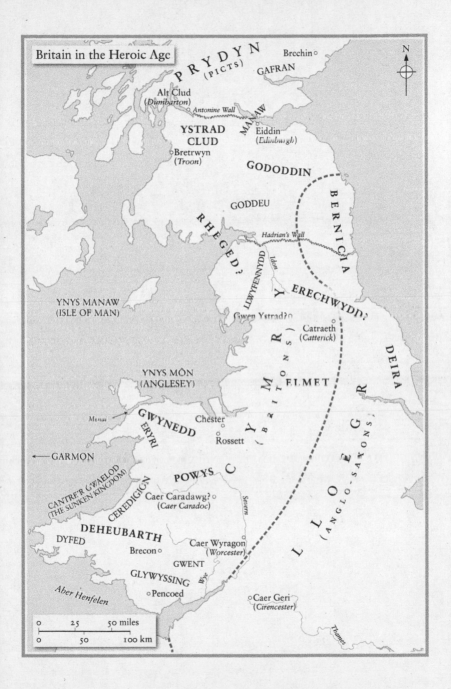

Britain in the Heroic Age

N

PRYDYN
(PICTS)

Brechin ○

GAFRAN

Alt Clud
(Dumbarton)

Antonine Wall

MANAW

YSTRAD
CLUD

Eiddin
(Edinburgh)

Bretrwyn
(Troon)

GODODDIN

GODDEU

BERNICIA

RHEGED ?

Hadrian's Wall

YNYS MANAW
(ISLE OF MAN)

LLWYFENNYDD

Idon

Y ERECHWYDD ?

Gwen Ystrad? ○

Catraeth
(Catterick)

DEIRA

YNYS MÔN
(ANGLESEY)

C Y M R Y

(B R I T O N S)

ELMET

GWYNEDD

Chester

Menai

Rossett

ERYRI

L L O E G R

(A N G L O - S A X O N S)

GARMON

POWYS

CANTRE'R GWAELOD
(THE SUNKEN KINGDOM)

CEREDIGION

Caer Caradawg ?
(Caer Caradoc)

Severn

DEHEUBARTH

DYFED

Brecon ○

Caer Wyragon
(Worcester)

GWENT

GLYWYSSING

Wye

Aber Henfelen

○ Pencoed

○ Caer Geri
(Cirencester)

Thames

0   25   50 miles

0   50   100 km

Acknowledgements

It would have been impossible to conceive of undertaking this translation without the scholarship of Ifor Williams and Marged Haycock. Their critical editions of the poems in *Llyvyr Taliessin* have provided the foundation for this version, and Marged Haycock's achievement in giving an exhaustive scholarly account of the corpus has enabled us to see this work in its full contemporary poetic and political context for the first time. Haycock's aural memory for the pairings of words in the mediaeval canon allows her to give sense to poems which present formidable difficulties. Without her work, we would have been lost; hence the dedication to her of this book, with our grateful appreciation. We should also like to put on record our appreciation for the rigorous and constructive editorial contributions of Donald Futers at Penguin, and the encouragement we have received from him and from Stuart Proffitt in the production of this book

GL/RW

Introduction

I. OVERVIEW

The fourteenth-century manuscript known as *Llyvyr Taliessin* ('The Book of Taliesin') is a hidden gem of mediaeval British poetry. Its pages include classic praise songs to the warring kings of early post-Roman Britain, as well as exhilarating poems, full of riddles and sparkling images, composed in mediaeval Wales. There are poems here that offer glimpses into fierce battles and the lavish spoils of war, poems to consolidate the poet's fame and status at the royal courts he serves; poems in a very distinctive voice that shifts unpredictably through time and space, the voice of a poet who writes as though he literally shared the life of the things he celebrates and had witnessed the distant events he recalls; and poems of a fierce national pride and lively religious devotion.

Containing compositions ranging in date from the ninth possibly even the sixth – to the thirteenth century, the *Llyvyr Taliessin* brings vividly into focus the history and culture of more than one unfamiliar world. It gathers together the kind of songs that might have been sung in the Northern British courts of the sixth century with the poems of Taliesin's various anonymous successors in an ongoing bardic tradition, which transformed him into a North Welsh prophet, a kind of Christian shaman – and, eventually, an honorary laureate of Llywelyn the Great, the first mediaeval ruler to control practically the whole of an independent Wales.

The poems of the later centuries show how substantial-
ly the half-mythical identity of Taliesin could be reworked
in new contexts. Sometimes it becomes a 'persona' for later
poets of the Middle Ages who need a mask from behind which
they can comment on and intervene in contemporary poli-
tics; sometimes it is the focus for a complex world of legend,
enchantment and riddling traditional wisdom. These later
'legendary' poems dazzle, mystify and fascinate. The voice
that utters them, Taliesin-as-seer, is one of the most mercuri-
al and tantalizing figures in the whole of Celtic literature. In
these texts, he is a shape-shifter and time-traveller, a witness
of ancient events and a prophet of future ones, boasting of his
knowledge of occult bardic and spiritual lore. His journeys
and adventures in this universe of mediaeval science fiction
shed light on elements of bardic and mythological lore as well
as mediaeval Christian arcana, filtered through the beauties
and subtleties of the mediaeval Welsh poetic tradition. To read
these poems is to see how a figure from the very beginnings of
Welsh poetry is transformed to serve a variety of new creative
agendas, through the mediaeval imagining and appropriation
of that history; and what emerges from this process is a pow-
erful body of song, a poetry of secrets, prophecy, death and
resurrection.

But also among the pieces in the collection are poems by
mediaeval writers who use the name and mythic persona of
Taliesin as a mouthpiece for some very specific contemporary
political preoccupations. There are poems here that are effect-
ively coded manifestos for political resistance and strategic
alliances against the English invaders. Along with these we find
carefully crafted religious meditations, as if the writers and
the final editor of the collection wanted to make it clear to
suspicious mediaeval authorities that bardic wisdom was not
in competition with Christian doctrine – even though many
poems are scathing about the clergy's ignorance of traditional
lore. Altogether, it is a strikingly broad range of material. The
only major subject not found here is anything that could be
called love poetry: apart from a couple of glancing references,

sexual passion is not on the poetic radar, and women are generally absent, except for the enigmatic figure of Ceridwen, the sorceress who owns the cauldron of poetic inspiration. There is no shortage of love poems in the Welsh mediaeval repertoire overall, so we have to conclude that this topic was simply not one of those associated with the particular poetic register of the 'Taliesin' voice.

The oldest poems in the anthology, which we have placed at the beginning of our translation, are associated with a figure mentioned in chronicles of the early Middle Ages, a Taliesin who praises the courage and generosity of his warlord patrons. These poems portray the 'heroic age' of Britain a century or so after the end of Roman rule in the early fifth century CE – a period of intermittent warfare between British rulers as well as struggles against the Saxon settlers. We see swords glinting, blood spilt and javelins falling like rain on the enemy; cattle raids and victory feasts are evoked alongside the heady memories of battle. The patrons of these poems are idealized figures, larger than life in their strength, virtue, wisdom and open-handedness. They are the superheroes of early Welsh history. The poems provide a vivid, almost cinematic picture of dynastic and tribal conflict and of the life of the kingly British households of the period. This is a world in which a leader keeps a poet in his court as something rather like a PR specialist: his job is to celebrate martial victories and to ensure that an idealized account of a battle or leader survives as official history. The poet depicts the glamour of court life, its drinking and feasting, and the luxury that a favoured poet can enjoy: Taliesin describes with relish the gifts of horses and fine clothes with which his songs are rewarded. Only the poetry attributed to Neirin, Taliesin's rival and approximate contemporary, can equal him in the vigour and freshness of his descriptions of that early mediaeval world of fierce courage, bloodshed, imaginative energy and intoxication (both physical and emotional).

From its oldest strata in the praise poetry of the British courts to the later material that engages with the mainstream themes of European faith and culture, whether the legends of

Alexander the Great or assorted bits of Christian apocrypha, the *Llyvyr Taliessin* prompts all sorts of insights and questions about social and imaginative life in an unfamiliar stretch of British history, the world of the Welsh-speaking communities of Western Britain from 600 to 1300 – a collective imagination conveyed in a unique body of poetry. But these poems have not only preserved historical memories; the more developed figure of the prophetic and 'shamanistic' Taliesin, ranging through the natural world and penetrating the mysteries of the past, has had a huge impact on modern English poetry, including the work of the war poets David Jones and Robert Graves, the critic and novelist Charles Williams and that unusual and brilliant philosophical poet, Vernon Watkins. Taliesin, explosive, surprising and consistently teasing and mysterious, still speaks to a variety of modern audiences.

Writers and scholars have been familiar with this manuscript for a long time. A new and accessible translation is, however, long overdue, and this is the first complete version of the poems in English for over a century. There are a number of nineteenth- and twentieth-century versions of the material, but they suffer from the lack of a solid scholarly edition of the original texts; our understanding of the development and workings of mediaeval Welsh has advanced a good deal in the last hundred years, and it is possible now to make far better guesses at the meaning of obscure passages. Many earlier renderings are misleading, some wildly fanciful. The earlier 'heroic' poems were admirably edited in the mid-twentieth century by the great Celtic scholar Sir Ifor Williams,[1] but a full critical text of the later poems has only existed since Marged Haycock's editions, especially in her *Legendary Poems from the Book of Taliesin*[2] and *Prophecies from the Book of Taliesin*,[3] published in 2007 and 2013 respectively. This monument of recent scholarship means that it is possible to approach the sometimes formidable challenges of translating the *Llyvyr Taliessin* with greater confidence than hitherto. But while we have aimed at a translation marked by accuracy and intelligibility, we have also tried to convey some of the real flavour of the rhythm and music of the Welsh originals: if these versions do not give a sense of the sheer poetic energy of the texts – of their verbal 'spring' – they will have failed.

The figure of Taliesin and the wildly diverse poetic material of the *Llyvyr Taliessin* continue to be of persistent and compelling interest as we try to imagine the nature of imagination itself. We are regularly reminded that we currently live in a 'disenchanted' age – which seems to mean that we are condemned to see the world around us as a storehouse of raw material for self-gratifying human projects, and the remote history and residually remembered myths we inherit as, at best, decorative fancies and, at worst, hangovers from an embarrassingly unsophisticated past. The Taliesin poems insist, in a voice that is passionate, sometimes derisively challenging, sometimes breathtakingly fresh, adventurous and musical, that such disenchantment is simply a way of settling down into a drab and reductive version of who we are and what our world is. We hardly need these days to underline the practical effects of this reductive approach, in the devastation of our environment, the brutal erosion of the rights and dignities of indigenous peoples and the sheer frantic hollowness at the heart of the so-called developed world. In such a world, poetic imagination is no idle luxury: the poet is the person who is most intensely and fully aligned with the hidden energy and spirit that pervades our world, and we are poorer and less human if we try to sideline or ignore this truth.

Today, words inspired by the Taliesin poetry stand on the main facade of the Wales Millennium Centre in Cardiff. The inscription is bilingual, with the Welsh justified left, and the English – a different phrase, not a translation – justified right. Spelled out in six-foot-tall letters, each forming its own stained-glass window in a single, subtle hue, are the lines, *CREU GWIR / FEL GWYDR / O FFWRNAIS AWEN*: 'creating truth like glass in inspiration's furnace'. Written by Gwyneth Lewis, the words suggest that the dome of the building is Ceridwen's inverted cauldron, as if the gifts of *awen* were spilling over into the work of the resident artistic companies. It is a powerful image for the continuing energy of these poems, and their resonance for today's readers.

II. THE FIGURE OF TALIESIN

The 'Historical' Taliesin

The name Taliesin is a combination of the word 'tal', meaning 'top' or 'gable end' (as in a house or forehead) with 'iesin', meaning 'beautiful', 'shimmering' or 'gleaming' – hence the name's common English translation, 'Shining Brow'. (Why the poet's brow should be radiant isn't clear.) It is possible to read certain passages as implying that the name designates the water into which the legendary poet was cast as a baby, referring in those cases to the shining horizon of a river or sea. In her literal translation of the poem 'Taliesin's Sweetnesses' (p. 42), Haycock glosses 'tal' as 'countenance'.[4] This might suggest an echo of Moses' radiant face after he saw God.[5] 'Tal' may also mean 'value', which could indicate a name meaning something like 'surpassing worth' or 'shining excellence'.

Although the poems in the *Llyvyr Taliessin* are implicitly grouped under this one name, it has long been clear that the anthology is the work of several hands. But at the beginning of the story is the individual writer who appears in chronicles and other early texts as a sixth-century bard, a court poet of the heroic age, celebrating the material and military exploits of a number of patrons, and enjoying the rich rewards of his work. We first meet this Taliesin in the early-ninth-century *History of the Britons* (*historia Brittonum*), composed in North Wales and traditionally but unreliably attributed to a Welsh cleric named Nennius on the basis of one set of manuscripts of the text. It relates the story of the British from the first arrival of the island's namesake, Brutus (a descendant of the Trojan hero, Aeneas, the legendary founder of Rome) up to the time of the sixth- and seventh-century conflicts between the British and the Germanic settlers – the people we now call the Anglo-Saxons –

who by then were establishing their rule over most of what is now England. The *History* shows an interest in the struggles of various British rulers, some apparently from Cumbria and the Pennine regions, some from North Wales, against the Angles of the territories that would by the later seventh century become the kingdom of Northumbria, then known as Deira and Bernicia.

Embedded in the narratives about this conflict, but with no very clear connection to what comes before or after, there is a short list of the great poets of Britain around the time of the consolidation of Anglian territories under King Ida (who died *c.*559). Five names are mentioned: Talhaearn, called 'father of *awen*', the usual word for poetic inspiration in Welsh poetry; Neirin, whose name appears elsewhere as Aneirin; Taliesin; Blwchfardd; and Cian Guenith Guaut, literally 'Cian, wheat-harvest of song'.[6] It seems a reasonable inference that these figures were based primarily in what later Welsh writers call the 'Old North', the British territories of Northern England lost to the Anglian settlers between the sixth and eighth centuries. Neirin certainly belongs in the North, as he is credited with the authorship of the *Gododdin*, a loose cycle of poems commemorating and lamenting the failed attempt of a British king from Edinburgh, in or around the last decade of the sixth century, to defend or recapture territory from the Northumbrian Angles – the climax of which campaign is a disastrous battle at 'Catraeth', possibly the modern Catterick in North Yorkshire.[7]

The *Gododdin* mentions Taliesin's name in passing, as if alluding to a well-known personage of the period, but this tells us little beyond the fact that, at some point in the composition of the *Gododdin* text as we now have it, Neirin and Taliesin were thought of as roughly contemporary with each other.

Thus, the earliest traditions suggest that Taliesin was active in the late sixth century in the British kingdoms of the North. But there is very little secure evidence – independent of the *Llyvyr Taliessin* poems themselves – for any more exact details of a date and place of composition. It is quite likely that the listing of the names of famous bards in the *History* is one aspect of its author's attempt to present ninth-century North Wales as the natural inheritor of the literary and military glories of the lost Northern kingdoms that had been at the forefront of resistance to the pagan Germanic invaders.

The name of Taliesin next appears in Brittany in a saint's life possibly dating from the eleventh century.[8] Here, we are told of his visit to a monastery in Brittany founded by the celebrated sixth-century British writer, Gildas, and Taliesin is presented primarily not as a poet, but rather as a sage and prophet: a seer who predicts the birth of the saint, Iudicael, King of Brittany in the early seventh century. This text would then agree with the *History* in placing Taliesin in the mid- to late sixth century; and the association with Gildas is an interesting detail. Gildas wrote a savagely polemical open letter attacking a number of sixth-century Western British rulers, among them the formidable North Welsh king, Maelgwn of Gwynedd, who appears in the later Taliesin tradition as a menacing figure, the enemy of Taliesin's own royal patron.

The Breton link is likewise to be found in the *Life of Merlin*, written in the mid-twelfth century by Geoffrey of Monmouth (best known as the author of a *History of the Kings of Britain*, which contains the first full-length version of the story of King Arthur). The *Life of Merlin* includes several dialogues between Merlin and 'Telgesinus' – a slightly archaic form of Taliesin's name – who is said to have studied in Brittany with Gildas. Geoffrey's Taliesin is again a sage and seer who meditates on the mysteries of creation, the movements of the heavenly bodies, the winds and the waters, and so on, as well as claiming to have sailed with the wounded King Arthur to the 'Island of Apples', where he was to be healed of his injuries.

Around the same time as Geoffrey's work appears, Taliesin also begins to surface again in Wales: he is referred to by one poet of the twelfth century as a bard to one of the leading royal houses of the Old North, the family of Cynfarch, father of Urien, whose battles are mentioned in the *History of the Britons*; and within the next half century or so we find two dialogues involving Taliesin in the poetic anthology known as *The Black Book of Carmarthen*, one with Myrddin (Merlin) and one with an otherwise unknown Ugnach. The former dialogue seems quite independent of the material in Geoffrey's *Life of Merlin*, as it focuses on conflicts of the sixth century which were long remembered in Welsh legend, especially the Battle of Arfderydd (the modern Arthuret in Cumberland), traditionally dated to 573; the latter text is hard to characterize, but seems to represent Taliesin, here perhaps in the role of a crusader of some sort, being invited midway through a journey to the Holy Land to break his journey at Ugnach's home.

Any reader of the *Llyvyr Taliessin* collection will rapidly see how diverse the material is – including the material directly ascribed to the great poet. Since the mid-twentieth century, scholars have acknowledged the distinctiveness of the core of poems, quite different in style and vocabulary from the rest, relating to the heroic memories of the 'Old North'. This group, which makes up the first section of our translation, the 'Heroic Poems', includes laments for rulers, descriptions of battles against various enemies (often, but not always, the Angles of Northumbria), and celebrations of the courage and generosity of the poet's royal patrons.

The consistent evidence of these poems supports the Northern connection, especially the poems about or addressed to Urien son of Cynfarch: clearly a significant figure in this world, he is described as Lord of 'Rheged', which seems to be a kingdom taking in large tracts of Cumbria and southern Scotland, and possibly at some periods also including territories in North Yorkshire.[9] Urien is variously associated with Catraeth (which, as already noted, may be Catterick), Aeron (Airedale or Ayrshire[10]), Llwyfennydd (usually identified as the Lyvennet valley in Cumbria) and Erechwydd, or perhaps Yr Echwydd – 'the clear/fresh waters'. Erechwydd may be the Solway Firth, as has sometimes been proposed – but not if 'fresh water' is to be taken literally as non-salt water. It could be, as Sir Ifor Williams tentatively suggested, the Yorkshire Swale with its falls at Richmond, not very far from Catterick, which would chime with the traditional identification of Catraeth with Catterick;[11] more recently, Andrew Breeze has argued that it may be a generic term for the low-lying wetlands of East Yorkshire.[12] Other place names in these poems, including a possible reference to the Cumbrian River Eden, can credibly be located in Cumbria and North Yorkshire. There are also poems about a ruler named Gwallawg who is associated with the West Yorkshire kingdom of Elmet. He appears as a contemporary of Urien in the *History of the Britons*, where he is involved, like Urien, in battle against the Northumbrian Angles, but apparently is not otherwise an ally of Rheged. Another poem celebrates a king of Powys in mid-Wales.

For a long time, these 'heroic' poems were accepted at face value as authentic compositions of the sixth century which had perhaps been reworked in less archaic language as time went on. The position suggested by more recent scholarship is, as we shall see, not quite so simple; but these compositions do undoubtedly constitute the oldest category of poems in the *Llyvyr Taliessin* – specifically, those which have some claim to be connected with a fairly definite historical time and place. Their mention of and association with a single figure named Taliesin is the first step in the creation of the complex and varied collection contained in the single fourteenth-century manuscript we are translating here, a collection which probably reached its present form in the thirteenth century.[13] We do not know whether the title is mediaeval (it is not part of the original mediaeval text); it is rather more likely to have been given by the owner of the manuscript in the sixteenth or seventeenth century, in recognition of the substantial number of items it contains which are associated with the figure of Taliesin.

What the poems in the collection show very clearly is how multifaceted this figure had become by the Middle Ages. Many of the later poems in the collection make reference to the characters of the *Mabinogion* stories, the well-known series of mediaeval Welsh prose tales narrating the doings of early Welsh heroes and of King Arthur and his followers. These references link Taliesin especially with stories involving the figure of the

sorcerer Gwydion and the 'children of Dôn';[14] but it is notice-
able that, even with these strong (and ultimately pre-Christian)
associations, Taliesin is also shown as dutifully commending
his work to God and as being familiar both with theological
questions, most notably those relating to the Incarnation, and
with apocryphal traditions surrounding the biblical narratives.
In other words, this later Taliesin becomes a bridge figure be-
tween traditional Welsh lore and the cosmopolitan world of
early mediaeval ecclesiastical learning.

This is the picture built up in the most elaborate of the
second group of poems in this book, those which have been
brilliantly edited by Marged Haycock under the designation
'Legendary Poems',[15] and it is not too difficult to discern its
historical context. The sharp anti-clerical animus in many of
them, notably 'The Spoils of Annwfn' (p. 98), reflects not so
much a global hostility to the clergy as a resentment of the new
monastic foundations of the period after the Norman Con-
quest, the Benedictine houses that sprang up in proximity to
the new castles and settlements in the Welsh Marches. Monks
from continental Europe are unlikely by this date to have been
familiar with or sympathetic to the rather older style of cleri-
cal learning represented by the riddling and legendary elabor-
ations of the Christian story found in the Irish or Anglo-Saxon
texts of the early Middle Ages; Taliesin thus becomes a mouth-
piece for this archaic Christian lore as well as the archetypal
bard and seer, so that it would not have seemed strange to
ascribe to him the cluster of religious poems included in the
Llyfyr Taliessin.

Taliesin the Shape-Shifter

So the Taliesin persona changed significantly between the ninth
and the eleventh century. Initially a straightforward court bard,
Taliesin mutates in later poems into a more mysterious, charis-
matic, riddling figure. The legendary poems present a Taliesin
whose status as sage or sorcerer – *dewin*, or occasionally even
derwyd, 'druid' – is so equal in importance to his standing as

a poet that the two might more accurately be said to become inseparable.

The gift of *awen*, poetic inspiration, involves both technical skill in the bardic craft on the one hand – including metrical ingenuity and familiarity with a huge range of traditional lore, from archaic British narratives and characters to natural history, geography and theology – and, on the other, what is often called the shamanic gift of inhabiting a life other than the poet's own. In the poems, the latter manifests itself in reports of the poet's shape-shifting and reincarnation, and in his claims to have been contemporary with various heroes of the remote past. The early Irish 'Song of Amergin' is often quoted as a parallel to this material:

> I am the wind on the sea.
> I am the wave of the sea [. . .]
> I am a strong wild boar.
> I am a salmon in the water.[16]

The relation between this and the Taliesin poems is hard to determine, given that the 'Song of Amergin' cannot be dated with any accuracy; but it makes sense to think that both Taliesin and Amergin (who in legend is an 'Archpoet' of ancient pre-Christian Ireland) represent a recognized convention of poetic composition. The context for the Taliesin texts, however, is distinctive: it is often an imagined contest with rival bards, in which the Taliesin figure demonstrates his superiority to his competitors by spelling out at triumphant length the questions he can answer about which his rivals are ignorant, and by listing the various embodiments he has experienced, as in the opening of 'The Battle of the Trees' (p. 54):

> I was in many forms
> Before my release:
> I was a slim enchanted sword,
> I believe in its play.
> I was a drop in air,

> The sparkling of stars,
> A word inscribed,
> A book in priest's hands,
> A lantern shining
> For a year and a half.
> A bridge for crossing
> Over threescore *abers*.[17]
> I was path, I was eagle,
> I was a coracle at sea.
> I was bubbles in beer,
> I was a raindrop in a shower.
> I was a sword in the hand;
> I was a shield in battle.
> I was a harp string,
> Enchanted nine years
> In water, foaming.
> I was tinder in fire,
> I was a forest ablaze.
>
> (ll. 1–23)

Extravagant claims have been made for reading this material as surviving evidence for ancient druidic lore.[18] This is speculative, to put it mildly; but it cannot be denied that these extraordinary poems reflect a sophisticated and complex understanding of poetic composition in which the concept of *awen* is central. It would be misleading to translate this idea of inspiration as 'Muse': it is better thought of as a state of altered consciousness in which the poet receives knowledge of matters beyond what can be routinely learned. According to Gerald of Wales's description of the *awenyddion*, or inspired soothsayers, of the twelfth century,[19] the gift of *awen* produces the same kinds of extreme behaviour as are associated with spirit possession: loud shouting, trance and catalepsy, disconnected but also very elaborate speech, narrated experiences of supernatural encounters which trigger the exercise of the gift, and a subsequent inability to remember what was said under its influence. Those who have encountered traditional praise singers in contemporary settings – they will still be found in tribal settings in parts of Africa, for example – will recognize these or similar manifestations.[20]

The allusiveness, disconnectedness and extravagance of many of these poems may, then, be an attempt to reflect the style or register of such ecstatic states of consciousness. This need not mean that the poems are direct transcriptions of specific compositions originating in altered states. As with all ecstatic phenomena which have a routine ritual place in a culture, the irruption of the supernatural will follow a traditional pattern, and there will be expectations about both the actual expression and the transmission of what has been delivered. A poet deliberately composing in this turbulently allusive and mystifying mode is acknowledging that if poetry is to be recognized as the authentic voice of some kind of ecstatic perception, it must follow certain classical, normative exemplars of poetic ecstasy. The compositions of lesser mortals must at least reflect something of the character of primary and very significant examples of the ecstatic voice; conventions grow up as to how the effect of *awen* can be represented in poetry. And it is clear that the composite figure of Taliesin has become such a primary and significant example of ecstatic utterance – one comparable to the Greek Orpheus: a figure to whom poems can be ascribed on the basis that they illustrate, or even teach, a particular way of *being* a poet and *sounding like* a poet. He is the model for bards aiming to produce a poetry that claims its origins in ecstasy (the transported state of being beside or outside of oneself) and supernatural visitation; and it seems likely, in fact, that the legendary poems were first collected with the aim of providing an educational template for such productions.

Exactly why Taliesin's name should be associated with this in so specific a way is not clear; but it has been convincingly argued that the tradition linking Taliesin with the Christian polemicist Gildas[21] is meant to show that Taliesin is a reputable Christian poet, who, while being endowed with the charismatic gifts of a traditional bard, does not waste them on frivolity and sycophancy, like the court poets of Maelgwn Gwynedd who

are so fiercely castigated by Gildas. He is both an exponent of
a tradition that has genuinely 'shamanistic' features – journeys
across time and space, ecstatic participation in the life of the
natural world – and a Christian scholar of a somewhat archaic
variety.

Taliesin the Prophet

Taliesin's status as an inspired seer means that it is not at all
surprising to find a collection of 'prophetic' poems alongside
the pieces we have noted so far. *Armes Prydein* ('The Great
Prophecy of Britain', p. 121) is the oldest and most extended
instance; we cannot be certain whether it was originally asso-
ciated with Taliesin's name, but it establishes what was to be
one of the unmistakeable 'Taliesin' voices in the generations to
come. Its themes, and a good deal of its phraseology, are recy-
cled in several later poems looking forward to a unification of
the British – usually under the leadership of Gwynedd – and the
advent of a heroic deliverer.

The latter, often called *mab darogan* ('son of prophecy') or
Lleminog ('the Leaper'), is a sort of reincarnation of one or
another of the great warrior kings of the sixth and seventh cen-
turies. There are many references to Cadwallon of Gwynedd,
the most prominent among these warlords, who, for a short pe-
riod in the early 630s, conquered and occupied Northumbria.
His son, Cadwaladr, likewise appears regularly; and there are
also allusions to another messianic figure, 'Cynan', who may be
the Cynan Garwyn of Powys celebrated in one of the early he-
roic poems of Taliesin, or Conan Meriadoc, who was credited
with leading the British migration to Brittany in the fifth cen-
tury and establishing the line of independent kings there. Quite
possibly these figures came to be fused in popular imagination.
The hoped-for leader is imagined as someone returning from
exile (as did Cadwallon, according to mediaeval traditions), or
arriving from over the sea, or both; on their return they can be
guaranteed to overthrow corrupt or alien rulers within Wales,
and rally the other Welsh kingdoms to resistance and ultimate

victory over the English.

In fact, this group of prophetic poems may help us understand what might have prompted the compilation of something like the *Llyvyr Taliessin* in the first place. The figure of the victorious leader who establishes a new order in Gwynedd and invites other rulers to follow him in a campaign of liberation is an obvious fit for the greatest of mediaeval Welsh rulers, the thirteenth-century Llywelyn ap Gruffydd, known as Llywelyn the Great, and it is not difficult to read most of these pieces as, in effect, propaganda on behalf of Llywelyn and the court of Gwynedd. A direct connection with that court can be established, if Marged Haycock is right in identifying the hand of one of Llywelyn's own bards, Llywarch ap Llywelyn, known for some reason as *Prydydd y Moch* ('The Poet of the Pigs') in a significant number of the legendary poems.[22] Haycock notes a large number of verbal convergences between Llywarch's works and the riddling, shamanic songs of Taliesin in the role of *dewin* (sage and magician). A natural inference is that the bulk of the legendary and prophetic pieces represent a careful weaving together of two kinds of poem: those which underline the unique status of Taliesin as bard and visionary, and those in which this particular supernaturally authoritative figure foretells Welsh victories under the leadership of the royal house of Gwynedd.

We have indicated that the corpus of legendary poems had probably already formed part of a bardic educational programme, illustrating how the ecstatic and magical 'Taliesin' voice could be credibly evoked and represented, long before their incorporation in *Llyvyr Taliessin*. Edited, elaborated and to some extent homogenized by Prydydd y Moch, this preexisting corpus of legendary poetry, along with the more archaic heroic pieces, was then attached to a group of more recent (perhaps early-thirteenth-century) variations on the themes of the *Armes Prydein* to produce a collection that appropriates the Taliesin tradition, with its deep historical and quasi-mythological roots, for the glory of the North Welsh kingdom. We noted earlier that the original author of the *History of the Britons* aimed to incorporate the legacy (literary and political) of the Old North into the prehistory of Gwynedd, so as to enhance the prestige of the North Welsh kingdom. In a very similar way, the final compiler of the *Llyvyr Taliessin* is co-opting the great prophetic sorcerer and singer into Llywelyn the Great's court.

The other main group of poems in the *Llyvyr* is the handful of devotional pieces, some quite lengthy, many of them in a state of serious textual confusion. On the face of it, it is not at all clear what they are doing alongside the other pieces in the collection. But we have already noted that part of the authority assigned to the figure of Taliesin is rooted in his expertise in ecclesiastical learning of a certain kind; and the presence of these poems in the *Llyvyr* may have been an attempt to set out the sort of thing a Christian bard, familiar with traditional techniques but also literate in a clerical way, might be expected to know. They are not on the whole particularly striking compositions, though the dramatic sections of 'A Prophecy of Judgement Day' (p. 163) show some vigour and imagination, and 'The Stem of Jesse' (p. 178) is a stylistically elegant piece which sustains a consistent flow of devotionally intense address and imagery. The texts in this group, likewise gathered together in this edition under the heading 'Devotional Poems', show a high level of corruption – especially in the often incomprehensible place names of the 'Saints and Martyrs of the Faith' poem (p. 169), where any translation is bound to depend on a lot of informed guesswork.[23]

Marged Haycock's edition places the handful of poems about classical heroes (Hercules and Alexander) alongside the compositions of Taliesin as legendary seer, and we have followed her editorial judgement on this; but they might equally well have been set alongside the devotional compositions, insofar as they reflect a degree of 'non-traditional' learning and a moral and religious perspective on the heroes of the remote past. Neither the classical nor the devotional poems are likely to date from before 1200.

The *Llyvyr Taliessin* contains two other substantial poems marking the death of a ruler but not associated with either the

Old North or with any familiar historical or legendary figures: 'Disaster for the Island' (p. 187) and 'In Praise of Tenby' (p. 190). Neither is a formal 'death song', a *marwnad*, but both lament the passing of a generous prince and express anxiety about the political future. Nothing is known of Bleiddudd, the ruler who is mentioned in the Tenby poem, and the presence of this piece in the collection is a bit odd, as it seems to express hostility to Gwynedd. The other poem, with its focus on Anglesey, is less puzzling, and it may well have found its place here because of the allusions to Gwynedd-based episodes in the *Mabinogion* stories, a feature that can also be observed in many of the 'legendary' poems. Both of the poems are likely to be earlier compositions than most of the rest of the collection, with the exception of the 'heroic' group associated with the Old North. The Tenby poem may go back to the tenth or even the ninth century, and a date in the neighbourhood of 1100 sounds plausible for the Anglesey elegy.

Llyvyr Taliessin, then, contains in itself a complex literary and political history. As we have seen, the court bard of the post-Roman period is transformed into a shaman, prophet and sage and eventually an apologist for Llywelyn the Great. But this does not imply a simple division between an historical and a legendary Taliesin. The heroic poems are clearly a coherent group with a distinctive style, and it is not hard to see them as coming from a single milieu, even if not necessarily a single hand. But they are already associated with three diverse geographical settings, namely mid-Wales, Yorkshire and the kingdom of Rheged. Despite efforts to see this as providing material for some sort of biography of a poet travelling between different courts, as Ifor Williams proposed,[24] it could just as well be read as showing that, by the time these poems reached their present form, 'Taliesin' was already the name of a fluid persona, an archetypal court poet of the heroic age, whose identity could be adopted by or associated with different living bards and who could thus be imagined as singing the praises of various great figures of the period, whether in Cumbria or on the borders of Mercia.

It is probably over-optimistic to look in these poems for straightforward evidence of events in the sixth century – and it is important to remember that their *language* dates to a much later time. It may make more sense to think of a continuing process of development and refinement in what was initially a tradition of oral performance, culminating in the 'heroic' poems in their existing shape in the ninth century at the earliest. We know from other evidence that some texts – including the *Gododdin* – were unobtrusively revised and modernized in their language over the generations; and the history of the early Taliesin poems can be understood in just this way, with traditional compositions being recycled and reworked so that new generations of poets would know what a praise poem for a local ruler would sound like if composed according to the best traditional models. But this does not rule out the possibility that there really was a famous Taliesin active in the Old North, nor that elements of his compositions may have survived through the processes of 'modernization' and transmission which produced the texts in this collection. Various features of these poems, including the specificity of the place names, strongly suggest that archaic elements belonging to the Old North and reflecting the overall course of the history of the sixth century *have* in fact been preserved. We nonetheless cannot take it for granted, as so many scholars of the nineteenth and twentieth centuries did, that we are dealing with a self-contained corpus of work from one poet of the sixth century.

Recent discussions of this question by John Koch and others have stressed that we do not have to think in terms of an 'authentic or inauthentic', 'historical or fabulous' polarity in approaching these poems. Taliesin's original location and associations are flexible, and this flexibility is accentuated and extended as the tradition develops, with Taliesin being co-opted into a variety of legendary settings in other mediaeval Welsh texts. He appears in the retinue of Arthur, both in the early mediaeval Welsh tale of 'Culhwch and Olwen', included in the *Mabinogion*[25] and later in the famous lists of notables that make up the mediaeval Welsh 'Triads', the brief mnemonic summaries of legendary material which first appear in manuscripts of the thirteenth century. The same fluidity of location for Taliesin is evident in the *Mabinogion* story of 'Branwen, Daughter of Llyr', which also has its literary origins around the eleventh century. Taliesin is listed there among those who followed the mythical Bendigeidfran to the war in Ireland – a detail which echoes the boasts made in two of the legendary poems in our collection,[26] also likely to be from the eleventh century. All of this implies that by around 1000, Taliesin had already been established as a 'floating' figure, available for use in connection with all sorts of different historical and legendary settings.

The Taliesin Legend

A final development of the Taliesin persona can be seen in the folkloric narrative that evolved during the Middle Ages and came to be recorded in its fullest form in various prose texts of the sixteenth century and later, usually under the title of *Hanes Taliesin* or *Ystoria Taliesin* ('Taliesin's History'). The oldest surviving transcription of the legend in its entirety links the bard to a number of widespread folkloric themes and locates him firmly in the West and North Wales of the sixth century.[27]

In this story, Ceridwen (whose name may mean 'the woman of the cauldron') is the wife of Tegid Voel (Tegid 'the Bald'; the story begins near Llyn Tegid – Lake Bala – in North Wales). She is mother to Morfran Afagddu ('pitch-black sea-raven', i.e. 'cormorant'), who is spectacularly ugly. In order to compensate Morfran for his ugly appearance, Ceridwen prepares a magical brew designed to endow her son with poetic inspiration. She employs Gwion Bach ('Little Gwion') to feed the fire under the cauldron, as the potion has to simmer for a year and a day; but just as it is ready for drinking, three drops from the cauldron fly out and scald Gwion's hand. He puts it his mouth and so receives the inspiration meant for Morfran.[28] He is pursued by the furious Ceridwen through a protracted shape-shifting contest, in which Gwion turns himself into a hare and she pursues him as a greyhound, he becomes a fish and she an otter, he transforms into a bird and she into a hawk. The chase ends when Gwion, in the form of a grain of wheat, is swallowed by Ceridwen in the form of a hen. She subsequently gives birth to him, and abandons the child to the river in a leather bag; he is rescued and renamed *Taliesin* ('Shining Brow' – see p. xviii) by Elffin, son of the Western Welsh king Gwyddno, and goes on to grow into a uniquely skilful poet. Later, Taliesin rescues Elffin from imprisonment at the hands of Maelgwn Gwynedd by means of dramatic victory in a bardic contest in which he magically reduces Maelgwn's court bards to babbling nonsense.

In some versions of this text, material from the *Llyvyr Taliessin* figures among the songs Taliesin sings at Maelgwn's court, providing clear evidence of a conscious continuity of tradition following on from the poems gathered in the present collection. Other songs included in the story develop – quite extravagantly – the theme of Taliesin's ageless wisdom, making him contemporary now with Alexander the Great, now with Moses, now with Noah and now with Lucifer at his fall.

Certain of the *Llyvyr Taliessin* poems show possible traces of the Gwion story's development over the centuries leading up to the *Ystoria*. Elffin, for instance, is named as Taliesin's patron several times in these pages,[29] and his rescue from the hands of Maelgwn by means of Taliesin's bardic triumph is mentioned. We have mention, too, of Ceridwen or Ceridfen, in connection with a cauldron of inspiration and the gift of *awen*, as well as what reads like a version of the shape-shifting chase in the long poem 'An Unfriendly Crowd' (p. 45) – though it has also been argued that this is originally an extended metaphor for the brewing of liquor, subsequently misread or deliberately reworked as magical narrative.[30]

Taliesin is indeed a shape-shifter, an elusive and teasing figure who slips away from any exact historical identity or even any fixed literary context. Both the texts associated with his name and the various stories told in his voice, or told about him, present him as an archetypal bardic persona, initially celebrating the victories and generosity of tribal warlords, then in-

creasingly speaking for the disturbing interconnections of the
world as seen and sensed by poets, and for the aspirations of a
marginal and fragile Welsh nationhood. In his book *The Talies-
in Tradition: A Quest for Welsh Identity*[31] the Welsh novelist
Emyr Humphreys uses the Taliesin corpus as a way of describ-
ing the whole of both the Welsh-language and the Anglo-Welsh
literary traditions of Wales, arguing that the poet's shape-shift-
ing is a model for a coherent but diverse roster of imaginative
strategies that can be used to respond to and cope with the
powerful external forces which have caused a series of crises
for Welsh society considered as a nation, from the sixth to the
twentieth centuries.

It is no doubt true that literary and poetic culture, rather
than distinctive political institutions or economic practices, has
regularly been the dominant force shaping a sense of Welsh
national identity; but Humphreys' case is perhaps rather too
generalized a scheme to be entirely convincing. Regardless of
this, however, the figure we encounter in *Llyvyr Taliessin* has
remained a powerful mythical focus – not only in Wales – for
thinking about what poetry is. 'Taliesin's' is a voice that is out-
rageous, arrogant, allusive, satirical, empathetic and joyful: a
paradigm of bardic perspective. It is fitting enough that the
name of Taliesin should surface again in more recent times as
the persona of very diverse poets trying to understand their art,
both in Wales and well beyond.

Taliesin in the Modern World

Although the *Ystoria Taliesin* was in circulation in the sixteenth
and seventeenth centuries, and the plurality of texts suggests
that there were many local oral transmissions and elaborations
of the story as well, there was not a lot of scholarly interest
in the Taliesin tradition before the beginning of the nineteenth
century. The seventeenth-century antiquarian Edward Lhuyd
noted a monument called 'Taliesin's Stone' – still to be seen
some nine miles north of Aberystwyth near Tre Taliesin (lit-
erally, 'Taliesin's Town'). The legend associated with that site

asserts that sleeping with your head on the stone either makes you a poet or sends you mad. Any connection with an 'historical' Taliesin is extremely unlikely, though it is possible that the tradition preserves the memory of an ancient site of ritual ordeal; similar folklore is attached to the peak of Cader Idris and other Welsh locations. A century later, Rhys Jones of Tyddyn Mawr published in 1773 an important anthology, *Gorchestion Beirdd Cymru: neu Flodau Godidogrwydd Awen* (*The Accomplishments of the Welsh Poets: or The Muse's Flowers of Excellence*), the first serious printed gathering of early and mediaeval Welsh poetry, and included three pieces ascribed to Taliesin; though one is associated with the comparatively recent *Hanes/ Ystoria* texts, none of these come from the *Llyvyr*.

But it was the work of Edward Williams, better known by his self-chosen bardic style, 'Iolo Morganwg' (1747–1826), which brought Taliesin's name back into currency; indeed, Iolo quite literally revived the name for his own son. Iolo Morganwg's antiquarian enthusiasm was not confined to the editing and translation of genuine historic Welsh texts, but extended to the manufacture of spurious documents claiming ancient provenance – some of which later provided the raw material for the distinctive ceremonies and vocabulary of the National Eisteddfod of Wales, the annual cultural festival whose modern form, as it evolved through the nineteenth century, was heavily influenced by Iolo's ideas of primitive British myth and religion. Some of these newly composed texts were written under the name of Taliesin; Iolo developed the early mediaeval image of Taliesin as sage and prophet, making him an exponent of the ancient druidic lore which he claimed to have rediscovered. As Marilyn Butler points out,[32] Iolo's conception of Taliesin as an avatar, especially as a witness to the Creation, may well have influenced William Blake; they knew of each other through connections with radical Unitarian circles in London. And when, in 1801, the Gwyneddigion Society of London published the first of its three volumes of Welsh literary antiquities (the series entitled *The Myvyrian Archaiology of Wales*), with Iolo Morganwg among its editors, the contents of *Llyvyr Taliessin* as well as the *Ystoria* were included, with a few poems translated into English; later volumes incorporated some of Iolo's own creations.

This was to be the main published source for Taliesin material for a good deal of the nineteenth century, and its influence was important in a number of ways. The scattered allusions to Arthur in some of the Taliesin poems collected in the *Myvyrian Archaiology* provided some basis for later writers (such as Tennyson) to locate Taliesin as a figure in the Arthurian world (as we have noted, he is treated as a contemporary or even courtier of Arthur in some mediaeval Welsh sources). The fact of being included among the *Archaiology* texts, moreover, associated Taliesin with the wider project of establishing the pseudo-antique philosophy of Iolo's 'druidic' fantasies, embodied in the nineteenth-century development of the Welsh National Eisteddfod.[33] Thomas Love Peacock's satirical novel, *The Misfortunes of Elphin*, published in 1829, made extensive use of this philosophical material, both in his retelling of the *Ystoria* legends and in his chapter on 'The Education of Taliesin', which depends heavily on Iolo's system and terminology. A couple of Peacock's poems in the novel reflect knowledge of *Llyvyr Taliessin* pieces (almost certainly by way of Iolo's texts): one is a very loose translation of 'A Song about Mead' (p. 83), and Peacock notes that another of his compositions was prompted by, but not a translation of, the 'Song of the Wind' (p. 79).

Lady Charlotte Guest's inclusion of the *Ystoria* in her *Mabinogion* (1838–45) guaranteed that the legend of Taliesin's birth and his connection with Elffin and Maelgwn Gwynedd became part of the common store of 'Celtic' material available to English writers in the later nineteenth and early twentieth centuries. Tennyson's *Idylls of the King* (published from 1859 to 1885) mentions 'Taliessin' (the spelling survives in several later writers)[34] as a bard at Arthur's court, and this motif is further developed in twentieth-century fiction and poetry. Tennyson also used the name on one occasion as a pseudonym when publishing a poem with contemporary content.

But it is only rather later that we find the name being used

as a pseudonym with a more general import, as a way of iden-
tifying a particular modern poet with some kind of archaic
and prophetic authority. The American poet Richard Hovey
in 1900 published *Taliesin: A Masque*, which was a highly
charged meditation on the nature of poetry, foreshadowing the
way in which the Taliesin persona was to be used by a suc-
cession of twentieth-century writers; more immediately, it was
this work which attracted the attention and enthusiasm of the
great architect Frank Lloyd Wright, prompting him to give the
name 'Taliesin' to his estate and studio in Iowa, built in 1911,
and also to a later structure in Arizona ('Taliesin West'). The
Irish poet Paul Muldoon used the English version of Taliesin's
name, 'Shining Brow', as the title of his 1993 libretto about
Wright. There is also a link with American poetic modernism
through the work of Robert Duncan: in his book on the poet
H. D. (Hilda Doolittle), who was familiar with J. E. Caerwyn
Williams's translation of some of the Taliesin material, he im-
agines the poet as a kindred spirit of theosophists like Madame
Blavatsky, representing 'the cooperation of fantasy and reality,
[. . .] the interchange of being, [. . .] very like the affinity that
Celtic art has for interweaving forms, shape-changings, letters
that are alive with animals and flowerings, reincarnations, in
an art where figure and ground may be exchanged as the artist
works.'[35]

Back in Britain, the twentieth century was to see three sig-
nificant and idiosyncratic poets using the persona of Taliesin in
very diverse ways. Perhaps the best-known is the magnificently
eccentric use of the Taliesin material by Robert Graves in his
1948 work, *The White Goddess: A Historical Grammar of Poet-
ic Myth*.[36] He offers a comprehensive interpretation – and re-
writing – of the long 'The Battle of the Trees' poem (here p. 54),
arguing that, when various extraneous elements have been sift-
ed out and the order of the material rationalized, it is to be read
as the coded account of a mediaeval revival of ancient bard-
ic tradition, in which the names of the trees were understood
as names of the letters of the alphabet; bringing this together
with a vastly complex exegesis of one of the poems preserved

in the *Ystoria*, he proposes that the riddles of the latter poem can be solved as coded references to the letters of this archaic alphabet, whose details coincide in part with a bardic alphabet preserved in Irish antiquarian sources.

In the deep hinterland of the poems under discussion, Graves believes, lies the recollection of an event in British prehistory when a major Bronze Age shrine (possibly Stonehenge) was captured from its original devotees and priests by an alliance of newcomers from continental Europe, worshipping a different deity; this displacement was made possible by local allies of the new ethnic/religious group conveying to the newcomers the secret name of the god worshipped in the ancient shrine, so that the incoming group would be able to deploy magical resources against the aboriginals. Knowledge of the hidden name of the god was concealed in a set of riddles whose solution would deliver the holy name to anyone who had the requisite – and, it ought to be said, enormous – range of traditional and legendary knowledge.

Any reader of *The White Goddess* is likely to be staggered by the sheer quantity of esoteric learning brought to bear on its source texts, as also by the exuberant confidence of Graves in his restoration of 'original' forms and idioms and his reconstruction of the abstruse riddles allegedly used both in remote antiquity and in the Middle Ages to encode the sacred alphabet and its ultimate mystery, the name of the divinity. But such a reader may also take warning from the cavalier indifference to historical and textual detail that Graves displays from the very beginning. Not only does he wrongly state that the Taliesin corpus is contained in the 'Red Book of Hergest' (the main manuscript source for the *Mabinogion* stories); his reordering of the text of 'The Battle of the Trees' takes as its starting point what was then the only remotely reliable translation of the text (that by D. W. Nash, published in 1858[37]), a version which makes a number of outright errors because of the undeveloped state of Welsh philology in the mid-nineteenth century. Some of the points which attract Graves's attention and are used to bolster his argument are in fact simple mistakes in translation.

In addition to this, the entire 'tree alphabet' thesis breaks down badly – as Marged Haycock points out[38] – when it is recognized that several of the trees named begin with the same letter; and, despite the Irish evidence, there is nothing to suggest that tree-names were ever consistently used in Wales to designate letters of the alphabet. The bold thesis of the capture of Stonehenge as a result of some kind of ritual contest over divine names is, of its nature, incapable of being falsified or verified, and the detail of Graves's reconstruction depends on his more global theories about ancient religion, which have not exactly found universal scholarly approval.

Yet, when all this is said, Graves's immensely long and intricate discussion conveys, as little else does, something of the sense of a lost world of esoteric bardic learning, the kind of thing that some mediaeval Irish texts embody – etymologies, folklore, legendary elaborations of biblical stories, classical and sub-classical mythologies and much more besides. Though his argument as it stands is simply not credible, and some of his theories are completely unsustainable and founded on plain mistakes, Graves's book still haunts and challenges by inviting us to read with an eye or ear for deeply buried folkloric connections that we shall never fully decode. Like the imagined rivals of the Taliesin figure in many of the poems, we are mercilessly reminded of our uneducated state.

Graves does not mention this, but Taliesin had already been deployed by another eccentric polymath, the Anglican poet, novelist and essayist Charles Williams, who had published in 1938 a sequence of poems under the title of *Taliessin through Logres* (notice the preservation of Tennyson's spelling of the name).[39] In this sequence, Taliesin is the poet and indeed the philosophical theorist of the Arthurian court, the sage who articulates the vision of human society that Arthur's rule seeks to foster. The connection with the Welsh Taliesin material is slight in these poems, though the second of them, 'Taliessin's Return to Logres', seems to reflect, in its economical rhythms and vivid metaphor, something of the force of the original texts.

> The beast ran in the wood
> that had lost the man's mind;
> on a path harder than death
> spectral shapes stood
> propped against trees;
> they gazed as I rode by;
> fast after me poured
> the light of flooding seas.[40]

But the main function of this Taliesin voice is to explore and explain Charles Williams's thesis about the necessity of radical and unconditional mutuality in the social organism and the role of poetry in bringing to visibility the 'precision' of the interwoven relationships that make up the redeemed society – the 'diagram' or 'geometry' of mutual love. Two interesting poems imagine Taliesin meditating on Virgil,[41] a classically authoritative exemplar in founding social vision on poetic narrative: think of Virgil disillusioned by the huge dark bulk of Augustus's Rome, dying in the painful awareness of the failure of his poetry to shape a just social order – yet now 'redeemed' by his admirers and followers who take up his vocation afresh and try once again to imagine human community as a 'net of obedient loves'.[42]

In a second set of poems by Williams, published in 1944 as *The Region of the Summer Stars*[43] (a phrase borrowed from one of the poems from the *Ystoria* as translated by Lady Guest), there is more direct allusion to the legend of Gwion and Ceridwen, but also a wholly new narrative about Taliesin travelling to Byzantium to gain the full theological perspective that will inform his witness at Arthur's court; he is shown as engaged in dialogue with Merlin, just as in the mediaeval tradition – but a Merlin firmly located in the Arthurian narrative heartland (in a way that he is not in the early mediaeval Welsh and Latin material, where 'Myrddin' or 'Merlinus' has no connection with Arthur). One of the poems in this second sequence contains one of Williams's most lapidary and haunting summaries of the logic of the poetic task: 'Flesh tells what spirit tells / (but spirit

knows it tells).'[44] The body is as much a medium of commu-
nication as the spirit, but it is only through language that the
body knows what it communicates; and poetry – insofar as it is
linked with the literal pulse of the body by its patterns of stress
and slack in the placing of words – is uniquely placed to 'tell'
what the body knows.

We are, by this point, some way from the Welsh material,
despite the familiarity with the *Ystoria* narrative as it appears
in Lady Guest's *Mabinogion*: this is a Taliesin very much mod-
elled on the sage who appears in Geoffrey of Monmouth's
twelfth-century verses. Williams's Taliesin is a philosopher and
contemplative, whose observation of and gentle intervention in
the creation of Camelot suggests one way in which theologic-
al vision might transfigure human relations, once we see how
patterns of mutual self-giving and the sharing of experience, es-
pecially suffering, can be traced and imaged in the tight verbal
interweaving of poetry, and offered in turn for contemplation.
Somewhat uncomfortably in the background also is Williams's
painful wrestling with his own confused sexuality: his Taliesin
is – in another phrase taken from a poem in the *Ystoria* – one
of whom it cannot be known 'if [his] body is flesh or fish';[45]
his poetic voice is a necessary form of erotic expression, yet
he himself is never going to be needed by or desired by any
woman. In life, Williams's obsessive identification with his own
mythology meant that he attempted to place himself beyond
ordinary human sexual exchange, but at the cost of involving
many who were close to him in complex and sometimes de-
structive fantasies, never fully or physically consummated.[46]

More clearly connected with the actual songs in the *Ystor-
ia* are the handful of poems by Vernon Watkins to which the
name of Taliesin is attached. Watkins, a poet very much in the
contemplative and metaphysical tradition, returned several
times to the figure of Taliesin to explore the ways in which a
poet identifies with what the poetic eye sees. So, in 'Taliesin in
Gower', Watkins explores how the poet's voice arises from an
identification with the life at the heart of what they contem-
plate in the world around them:

I am nearer the rising peewit's call than the shiver of her own wing.
I ascend in the loud waves' thunder, I am under the last of the nine.
In a hundred dramatic shapes I perish, in the last I live and sing. [47]

Two poems published in a 1962 collection ('Taliesin's Voyage' and 'Taliesin and the Mockers') use the familiar 'I was . . . ' phraseology of the Welsh legendary material, reworking the Ceridwen and Gwion story and echoing Taliesin's claim to have witnessed the very birth of spirit at the beginning of all things. The poet is cast adrift in a coracle, like Gwion:

> Past day and night,
> Past night and day,
> Under the flight
> Of the stars I lay.
>
> At last emerging
> With dawn I woke
> Where rough seas surging
> On shingle broke. [48]

In the second poem, the poet contemplates the world's creation and the events of scriptural history:

> I saw black night
> Flung wide like a curtain.
> I looked up
> At the making of stars.

And again:

> Ancient music
> Of silence born:
> All things born
> At the touch of God.

He built for him
His eternal garden,
Timeless, moving,
And yet in time . . .

Ask my age:
You shall have no answer.
I saw the building
Of Babel's Tower.

I was a lamp
In Solomon's temple;
I, the reed
Of an auguring wind.[49]

The poem 'Taliesin at Pwlldu' (taking us back to the Gower landscape) rehearses the same theme of witness to the moment of creation ('I looked; creation rose, upheld by Three') and the poet's recognition of a coming home to this creative source in his absorbed attention to the running water of the stream falling to the beach:

Pure stream, by pebbles masked and changing skies,
I touch you; then I know my native land.[50]

Watkins uses the Taliesin voice to underline his conviction that poets genuinely 'inhabit' whatever they write about ('I am nearer the rising peewit's call than the shiver of her own wing'); the poet's 'native land' is the interior dimension of the landscape he depicts. There is a real continuity here with some aspects of what the legendary Taliesin poems understand by *awen*. A routine or prosaic sensibility is pushed aside, displaced by a profound sympathetic drawing into the interior life of the world that is seen and experienced.

Less obviously continuous is R. S. Thomas's deployment of the Taliesin trope in an earlyish poem, 'Taliesin 1952'.[51] 'I have been all men known to history', it begins, going on to identify the poet with Merlin, with the mediaeval rebel Owain Glyndwr, and with Goronwy Owen, the eighteenth-century cleric-poet who emigrated to America. The poem is an evocation of different sorts of apparent failure in Welsh history – the legendary madness of Myrddin/Merlin after the Battle of Arfderydd, Glyndwr's Shakespearean scanning of the stars for portents[52] while the body-count of those killed in his unsuccessful campaigns increases, Owen's exile and struggles – but it ends with the promise that, 'Taliesin still', the poet will show 'a new world, risen, / Stubborn with beauty, out of the heart's need.' It is a tantalizing poem whose conclusion does not feel fully achieved, so that the Taliesin-style convention of identification with the past becomes a more obviously *functional* matter, a way of allowing the poet to ventriloquize an assortment of significant historical figures; but what it seems to aim at is an affirmation of poetry's capacity, arising from the underlying stubbornness of the reality that it sees and celebrates, to recreate itself out of defeat, fragmentation or exile – so that the insight we are left with is that political hope cannot survive without this enacted obstinacy on behalf of beauty.

There are other references in modern poetry in English – notably Basil Bunting's allusion to the early Welsh tradition as bound up with his Northumbrian roots:

> Aneurin and Taliesin, cruel owls
> for whom it is never altogether dark, crying
> before the rules made poetry a pedant's game. [53]

Bunting is referring here to the codification of alliteration into 'correct' and 'incorrect' patterns, and paying tribute to the two great early Welsh poets as masters of the flexible forms of *cynghanedd,* the complex system of classical Welsh prosody, which he himself draws on in his work. And a somewhat more unexpected echo can be heard in the lyrics of the 1960s song 'Vishangro' by Robin Williamson of The Incredible String Band, which uses the idioms of the legendary poems to fine and novel effect:

> I was a wasp on a nettled hill [. . .]
> I was a swineherd at the court of Fionn,
> I wore the coat of patches with Jalal[54] beneath the stars [. . .]

But perhaps the most enduring and powerful reworking of the voice of 'Taliesin' in twentieth-century poetry is a passage which does not directly mention his name – the section of David Jones's *In Parenthesis*, Part 4, known as 'Dai's Boast', in which the Welsh soldier in the trenches of the First World War lays claim to witnessing the history of human conflict and slaughter, from Cain and Abel through the struggles and murders of biblical, classical and Arthurian legend to the present:

> I was with Abel when his brother found him,
> under the green tree.
> I built a shit-house for Artaxerxes.
> I was the spear in Balin's hand
>   that made waste King Pellam's land.
> I took the smooth stones of the brook,
> I was with Saul
> playing before him.[55]

He is there at what Christian tradition sees as the focal point of all human violence, the crucifixion of Jesus:

> I served Longinus that Dux bat-blind and bent;
> the dandy Xth are my regiment;
> who diced
> Crown and Mud-hook
> under the Tree
> whose Five Sufficient Blossoms
> yield for us [. . .]
> I heard Him cry:
>   *Apples ben ripe in my gardayne*
> I saw Him die.[56]

And, pushing further back still: 'I was in Michael's trench when bright Lucifer bulged his primal salient out'.[57]

Jones acknowledges in his footnotes[58] the debt to the *Ystoria* poems, and to other boasting catalogues in Welsh and Anglo-Saxon poetry. What he achieves in this passage is an extraordinary fusion of literary reference, theology and vernacular lore that works as a genuine modern variant of the ecstatic poetic idiom that we find in the long poems of *Llyvyr Taliessin*. Jones is exploring what it means for a poet's deepest integrity as a writer to be worked out as the identity of a speaker who is, like the 'Dai Greatcoat' of *In Parenthesis*, displaced, buried, absorbed and dispersed in what s/he witnesses or remembers; the speaker's exuberant and apparently egotistical boasting is in fact a claim to have successfully *let go* of conventional selfhood in the absorbing journey into the past, into the life of another, even into the elusive and miraculous processes of the surrounding world – 'Why silver glitters / And the brook runs dark,' 'the mist's bones / And the wind's twin waterfalls.'[59]

III. READING TALIESIN

The Poet's Self-Representation

In the 'heroic' age of the sixth century which is depicted in the first group of poems here, the relation of the court bard to his royal master was that of client to patron; but the client's role was decidedly an active, not a passive one. His task was to reinforce his lord's status and reputation, and the scale of the rewards given him was significant, as we see in the opening of the very first poem in the *Llyvyr Taliessin*:

> Cynan bestowed on me
> Shelter in a battle –
> My praise is no lie –
> Gifts and property,
> A hundred horses,

> Saddles with silver,
> A hundred mantles
> All equally full;
> My lap's full of armlets
> And many brooches.
> A sword sheathed in jewels,
> Best gold hilt ever.
>
> (ll. 1–12)

This showing off by the poet is authorized because it reflects favourably on Cynan's wealth and generosity. Such favourable reflection can take more than one form. Thus, on the surface, 'To Pacify Urien' looks like an abject attempt to reconcile with a patron after offending him; but it is better read as a theatrical performance, rather than a serious apology, whose effect is to enhance the patron's standing:

> For a joke I poked fun
> At him, the old man,
> Though I loved no one more
> Before I knew him.
> Now I see fully
> How much he gives me.
>
> (ll. 31–6)

The poet's duty is always to promote his employer's renown. In 'First Artful Command', the first poem in the *Llyvyr* manuscript, the poet declares: 'I'm complete, I am renown'.[60] In return, as well as the luxury goods described above (see p. xv), the poet receives an acknowledgement of his status in the order of precedence at the feast:

> With him as protection
> I will be welcomed,
> Placed in prime position,
> With the best chieftain.
>
> ('To Pacify Urien', ll. 5–8)[61]

The reference is to the place of honour granted to a poet in a lord's or king's hall. In later centuries, this position evolved into an actual silver or wooden chair awarded to the winner of a competition. The word 'chair' (*kadeir* – *cadair* in modern Welsh) has, however, a range of secondary meanings, summarized by Haycock as: 'objects branching out from a centre, such as "the udder of a cow", or the crown of a tree, or items forming a frame of some sort'.[62] This etymology suggests an intriguing fractal relationship between the design of a highly regarded poem and the forms found in natural and human material culture. In the 'legendary' poems, we have translated the word as 'Prize Song'.

Unlike his sixth-century forebear, the Taliesin of these later poems belongs within a developed bardic system in which individual poems are given 'ratings' or points. The *Llyvyr Taliessin* copyist notes the score to be assigned to various pieces: 'Young Taliesin's Works', 'I Make My Plea to God', 'A Song about Mead', and 'A Song about Beer' are each, we are told, worth twenty-four points, while 'Teyrnon's Prize Song', 'Ceridwen's Prize Song', and 'A Song of the Wind' are more valuable, being assigned 300 points each. Scholarly opinion is divided as to whether this points system is fictional or not, and what exactly the scoring refers to (rewards for performance? significance in an educational corpus?). They may relate to the bardic competitions held in Wales since 1176.[63] The mediaeval bardic grammars, such as Einion's, show that there was such a practice, but that – unlike, for instance, the way contemporary audiences score in poetry slams – it was closely related to the various authorized poetic genres.[64]

The poems of the legendary Taliesin are a kind of fiction in two senses. The unknown author assumes the voice of an earlier writer in order to co-opt the reputation of an artistic ancestor; but, at the same time, the later Taliesin becomes the main character in the compositions attributed to him – the poet himself as a creative poetic fiction. The Taliesin of 'The Battle of the Trees' describes himself not in historical but in legendary terms. Like Blodeuwedd, the woman made from flowers in the 'Fourth Branch' of *The Mabinogion*, the birth and life of Taliesin are magical and mythological, not hard fact. The poet's words are spoken by a persona which both exists and cannot be pinned down:

> Neither of mother
> Nor of father was I formed;
> My creation was created
> Out of nine elements:[65]
> From fruit, out of fruits,   155
> From the fruit of God's beginning;
> From Primroses and gossiping flowers,
> From wood and trees' pollen;
> From earth, from the soil
> Was I formed;   160
> From Nettle flowers,
> From the ninth wave's water.
> I was conjured by Math –
> Before I was gifted.
> I was conjured by Gwydion,
> Great magician of Britain [. . .]
>
>   (ll. 151–166)

The sensational origin story given for the Taliesin persona in the prose legend of the Renaissance *Ystoria Taliesin* (see pp. xxxii–xxxiii) can be read as a mythological account of any poet's growth into an ecstatic or shamanic figure. The tale features the cauldron (*pair*) of Ceridwen,[66] which is a symbol in the *Llyvyr Taliessin* for the energy of the imagination and the wellspring of poetic talent. We have already noted that the thirteenth-century court poet Llywarch Prydydd y Moch may well have been responsible for editing and revising the 'legendary' poems before they were gathered in the *Llyvyr*. In a poem written under his own name, he calls on 'the words of Ceridfen the director of poetry'. Elsewhere, Prydydd y Moch invokes Ceridfen's cauldron as providing the power that inspires praise poetry – a metaphor also used by Casnodyn in the thirteenth century.

In 'An Unfriendly Crowd' (p. 45), the Taliesin poet gives his own summary of how he became the poet who is now performing:

> A second time my shape shifted
> And I was a blue salmon,
> A hound and a stag,
> A roebuck on the mountain,
> A clod and a spade
> And an axe in the hand,
> An auger gripped in tongs,
> For a year and a half;
> A speckled white cockerel
> For the hens in Eidyn,[67]
> A stallion at stud,
> A ramping bull –
> A sheaf stacked for milling,
> Meal ground for farmers.
> I was a grain in the sieve,
> Grain that grew on the hill,
> I am harvested, stored,
> Sent off to the kiln,
> And scattered by hand,
> Ready for roasting.
> Then a hen took me in,
> Red-clawed, my crested foe,
> And for nine nights I rested
> At peace in her womb.
> When I had matured
> I was drink for the king.
> I was dead and alive.
> A seizure shot through me,
> I stood on my lees:
> Poured off, I was perfect –
> A cup to encourage,
> Stirred up by the red claws.

(ll. 230–61)

Or, in 'Poets' Corner':

> I'm a seasoned singer · of splendid songs.
> Sharp and hard, a shaman, · a sage, a skilled artisan,
> A serpent, a seduction, · greedy for nourishment.
> I'm not struck dumb, · I'm not going to stammer;
> When singers sing · what they've learned by heart,
> No miracle they work · will leave me beaten.
> Contending with me, · their fate will be
> Like dressing yourself · when you have no hands,
> Like diving in lakes · when you know you can't swim.
> The thundering flood · flows on without fear,
> Its high tumult · a terror for homesteads.
> But above the wave, · by God's plan, stands a rock.
> The enemy's refuge · is dark and fearful –
> But that rock is the High King, · the Judge of all,
> The Lord who will make us · drunk with delight.
> I'm a cell, I'm a splinter, · I'm a shape-shifter,
> A library of song, · a sanctuary for the reader.
>
> (ll. 8–24)

The imaginative world of this legendary Taliesin thus involves a great deal more than the traditional praise poems to a patron. This is a poet who conceives of his words not only as a reflection of his lord's power but as an imaginative entry into and sharing in the vital force of what he writes about. In 'The Battle of the Trees' Taliesin describes his lines as weapons: his writing is part of the battle he is celebrating.

> My two eager spears,
> From Heaven they came,
> From Annwfn's[68] streams,
> They come, battle-ready.
> Four score hundred men
> I pierced, for all their greed [. . .]
> A hundred men's ardour they had;
> But I had nine hundred's.

My speckled sword
Brings me fame for blood.

(ll. 187–92, 195–98)

Not only are his words weapons, the Taliesin figure sees his
actual sword as a form of rhetoric.[69] The implication is that
war-making and poetry come from the same impulse and that,
rather than following war, poetry is a partner in it.

We have read the extravagant boasts of the Taliesin persona
as part of an argument about the nature of the imagination,
and its connections with history, the natural world and medi-
aeval politics. The legendary dimension of the Taliesin persona
gives his poetic character a unique degree of creative freedom:

I was a harp string,
Enchanted nine years
In water, foaming.
I was tinder in fire,
I was a forest ablaze.

('The Battle of the Trees', ll. 19–23)

This temporal blurring of sequence is magnified in the legend-
ary Taliesin's boasts when the poet's utterance becomes, so to
speak, the plot of his own poem as he travels through space and
time under different identities. We should not misunderstand
this: a poet who describes himself as standing at the centre of
time and space is not exhibiting pathological egotism but mak-
ing a claim about the intimate way in which the cosmos and
the poet are united in art. This fluidity gives the poet energy
and, in the context of the poetic culture in which these poems
work, authority:

I know the sword's clamour
Round the blood-streaked hero,
I know all the levels
Between Heaven and earth –
Why the hollow echoes,

> Why death comes suddenly,
> Why silver glitters
> And the brook runs dark,
> Why breath is black
> And the liver's full of blood,
> Why the buck has horns,
> Why a woman's hot with lust,
> Why milk is white
> And holly green,
>
> ('An Unfriendly Crowd', ll. 122–35)

It is also possible for this authority to be more explicitly Christianized, as in 'Teyrnon's Prize Song', where the poet's inspiration is defined as coming 'from the Trinity's *awen*.'[70] The 'legendary' poems oscillate tantalizingly between these orthodox expressions and the language of a spiritual world that is far less conventionally Christian.

The *History of the Britons,* as we have seen, implicitly presents Neirin and Taliesin as contemporaries – the two most celebrated and apparently most clearly remembered poets of the heroic age. Their styles are notably different. Neirin's *Gododdin* is almost entirely elegiac, a lament for the individual heroes massacred in the Battle of Catraeth. Taliesin's heroic poems are mostly – with a couple of notable exceptions – praise poetry, celebrating court life and its pleasures. But there are intriguing echoes. In the *Gododdin*, Neirin, who seems to be a prisoner of some kind, writes:

> Of mead from drinking-horn,
> Of Catraeth's men,
> I, not I, Aneirin,
> (Taliesin knows it,
> Skilled in word-craft),
> Sang the *Gododdin*
> Before next day dawned.[71]

liv   INTRODUCTION

The poet, in other words, is and is not the 'author' of what is sung; and Taliesin is referred to as if he were the great exemplar of this aspect of poetic composition. That 'not I' suddenly reappears in 'The Battle of the Trees' in the middle of the passage on his shape-shifting already quoted:

> I was a harp string,
> Enchanted nine years
> In water, foaming.
> I was tinder in fire,
> I was a forest ablaze.
> *Not I who's not singing,*
> Which I did since my youth,
> Sang when trees went to war;
>
> (ll. 19–26; emphasis ours)

Taliesin reproduces Neirin's paradoxical description of himself as both a self and an absence of self, and the apparent boastfulness of the passage must be read in that light: indeed, there is a glimpse here of the poet's radical poetic humility, which allows the elements of the world to pass through him as though he were an instrument to be played on, not only by his lords both secular and divine, but also by the whole of creation. This is very much an explicitly incarnational poetry with an implicit theological weight. The poet under the sway of *awen* is at once himself and an embodiment of the constantly transformative force that has possessed him:

> I was a speckled snake on a hill
> I was a viper in a lake,
> I was a sickle in Dog-heads' hands.
> I was a hunting lance.
> My vestment and chalice,
> I prepare them well,
> And fourscore clouds of incense
> Waft over all.
>
> (ll. 207–14)

Obscurity in the Poems

The opening line of 'Teyrnon's Prize Song'[72] calls it 'a clear poem'. The irony of this characterization will not be lost on the reader working through what follows. The obscurity of much of the Taliesin material is a challenge in both editing and translating the poems. But this difficulty is not all of one kind. There are the straightforward textual problems, on which Ifor Williams, Marged Haycock and other scholars and editors have taken a view. We have accepted most of the scholarly emendations proposed by these editors to solve various localized problems of meaning. Because the poems' metre is so regular, anomalies in the rhyme provide important clues about passages where the text we now have appears to be irregular; this allows informed guesses about what may originally have stood in a more consistent version of the poem with its rhyme scheme or syllable count intact. We always have to reckon with the entropy that is inevitable in the process of a scribe copying earlier texts, the sedimentation of simple errors, and the casual variations or updating of words and word order or idioms that accrue over time. In addition, the writer or writers of the 'legendary' Taliesin poems often imitate the word order of Old Welsh prose so as to give an archaic feel to the verse, and this effect is strengthened by their use of archaic and therefore obscure vocabulary.[73] Bardic poetry does not rely on a naturalistic word order but on concentrated patterns of consonantal echoing; so where we can discern these patterns we have a better chance of reconstructing meanings. We have aimed to give a translation of the explicit content as fully as possible, while also trying to convey something of the feel of the pulse of the poem's metrical structures.

But this content is often itself very complex; and this is where we encounter a second level of obscurity in the text. Sometimes the obscurity seems to be deliberate, with arcane material used to give an impression that the poet has access to esoteric knowledge unknown to the lesser mortals in the audience – and to poetic rivals. We have provided information in footnotes to elucidate what can be gleaned from such passages, but some allusions are irrecoverably lost to us because of the gaps in our own knowledge of the bardic tradition. While we have some of the poetry ascribed to Neirin and Taliesin, the work of the other poets named in the *History of the Britons*, our first witness to Taliesin (see p. xviii), is entirely lost. A good deal of the swaggering esoterica of the Taliesin persona – the historical, biblical (including apocryphal) and mythological references – is likewise beyond recovery. And how literally we are intended to take references to what might be understood as actual shamanic experience in the legendary poems remains an open question. It could be, as some would still argue, that in these moments the poems presuppose a genuine lost shamanistic, even druidic, traditional lore; but it could equally – and more plausibly – be that the poet is once again simply seeking to give the impression of esoteric knowledge, to baffle and impress the susceptible rather than to impart anything that was ever really comprehensible to him or his contemporaries.

At times, where there is information that would have been not only comprehensible but well known to his audiences, the poet works to cast it in an allusive and supernaturally shaded light.[74] Thus in the 'prophetic' poems, events which by the eleventh or twelfth century had already happened or were thought likely to happen are referred to as though they have not yet taken place, and what was in fact contemporary political commentary is cast in vague futuristic terms. Here, again, our limited knowledge creates a problem: we do not have a complete picture of the current events of seven centuries ago, so we are reduced to guesswork when it comes to tracing many of the allusions in these texts. Making the predictions poetically vague was, of course, a strategy to maximize the situations to which an audience could apply them. Marged Haycock has characterized her line-by-line translation of *Llyvyr Taliessin* prophecies as

a fog-lamp through what Keith Thomas called 'the cloudy language' of prophecy, or as a rough causeway across what Tatlock rightly recognized as 'quivering ground.'[75]

The Taliesin of the legendary poems possesses – or rather has access to – an uncommon knowledge of past and future alike; and this implies that his readers, thirteenth-century as much as twenty-first century, are not meant or expected to grasp all that he says or to recognize all his references. In this light, the frustration felt by the baffled reader would appear to be a reasonable response to a quite deliberate strategy, deployed by poets who were pursuing specific artistic and political goals; it is not simply the result of an inadequate grasp of remote history and mythology.

IV. TEXT AND TRANSLATION

The Manuscript

This is the first time that all the poems in the *Llyvyr Taliessin* have been translated in one volume since J. Gwenogvryn Evans's (wildly eccentric) version, published in 1910 and 1915 along with his excellent facsimile of the manuscript (see Bibliography, p. 197). We have translated only the sixty-one pieces in the *Llyvyr* manuscript: poems from other sources that are ascribed to Taliesin or associated with him in some way (those in the Red Book of Hergest, for example,[76] and those found in the *Ystoria* manuscripts) are not included here. The manuscript was written in the first half of the fourteenth century by a single scribe (of whose work we have several other examples), probably in mid-Wales or the south-east of the country. As we have already noted, it is impossible to say with certainty at what point all the poems had been assembled in a single collection, though it is likely that this was about a hundred years before the copying of this manuscript. There are obvious groups of poems that belong together and share references and idioms – heroic, devotional, riddling or legendary, and so on. If all these were regarded as characteristic of the style and subject matter associated with the figure of Taliesin, they may originally have been brought together as what Haycock calls[77] a 'Taliesin compendium', a collection exemplifying what could be expected of compositions linked with the name of Taliesin. The development and collection of the devotional items as one element in this spectrum is probably due, as we have already suggested (p. xiv), to a desire to establish both the Christian bona fides of the compiler and the claim of the Taliesin figure to represent a Christian imagination that might be anti-clerical but was unquestionably orthodox. The inclusion of the fine poem about Tenby and the enigmatic 'Disaster for the Island' is hard to explain, but the scribe may have simply added pieces that would neatly fill up his allotted space and which had a few features in common with the other items. Ifor Williams, writing on the 'heroic' poems, assumes that the scribe was frequently copying from a faulty older text and did not always understand what he was reproducing;[78] the same is probably true to some extent even of the later works.

The original *Llyvyr Taliessin* is housed in the National Library of Wales and is catalogued as Peniarth 2. It is missing its first leaf and a number of quires (that is, groups of four sheets of paper folded to create eight leaves). A digital facsimile of the book and its sixty-one poems can be seen on the National Library of Wales website.[79] In this period, poems were written out continuously, like prose, so as to fill the whole line, with breaks noted with a full stop. The text is laid out in a visually simple fashion, written in black ink, with red and blue capitals used in turn to mark the start of each *awdl* or stanza. Each *awdl* is composed with the same rhyme at the end of the line, so the start of a new one is often indicated by a change in the monorhyme.

The Translation

We have followed the groupings by genre established by Ifor Williams and Marged Haycock: the early heroic poems apparently connected with an 'historical' Taliesin; the 'legendary' poems which fill out the picture of the poet as a sage and riddler; the 'prophetic' poems announcing future victories for the Welsh; and the various devotional pieces in the collection –

although this is not the order in which the poems appear in the *Llyvyr Taliessin* manuscript.

In his edition of the heroic poems, Ifor Williams marks the regular metrical breaks in a single line by separating the two halves and justifying them in parallel columns so as to show clearly how the second half of each line answers the first. We have preferred in these cases to print the halves as separate lines. We have taken Marged Haycock's transcription of the 'legendary' poems in her edition as the overall basis for our versions of these pieces. Some of the text as we have it is not intelligible – either because it has been miscopied or because we do not have clear evidence for the meaning of some of the vocabulary; Haycock offers a considerable number of emendations, clearly noted in her edition, in order to make sense of the poems. We have gratefully accepted many of these, but have occasionally reverted to the original text or accepted another conjecture where there was a reading that made better sense to us. In 'The Battle of the Trees', for example, when Taliesin is describing how he is conjured into being from flowers, Haycock alters the text so as to preserve a more formally satisfying rhyme, so that Taliesin declares himself made o *vriallu a blodeu* ('from primroses and flowers') rather than o *vriallu a blodeu bre*. But it seems odd to use the general 'flowers' after the specific 'primroses'; and the word *bre* introduces the idea of language into the moment when this primordial poet is first created – we have reinstated the, o *vriallu a blodeu bre* ('From Primroses and gossiping flowers'). This interpretation is supported by the fact that, although *bre* and *dechreu* appear to end with different sounds, they rhyme fully if *dechreu* is pronounced in a South Walian accent.

> Nyt o vam a that
> pan y'm digonat
> a'm creu a'm creat
> o naw rith llafanat:
> o ffrwyth, o ffrwytheu,
> o ffrwyth Duw dechreu;

> o vriallu a blodeu bre,
> o vlawt gwyd a godeu,
> o prid o pridret.[80]
>
> Neither of mother
> Nor of father was I formed;
> My creation was created
> Out of nine elements:[64]
> From fruit, out of fruits,
> From the fruit of God's beginning;
> From Primroses and gossiping flowers,
> From wood and trees' pollen,
> From earth, from the soil

The text is sometimes so corrupt that it is incomprehensible, and we have had to guess at meanings. This must in some cases be the result of errors by a scribe, but sometimes seems to be because the manuscript has been mutilated or otherwise left incomplete for some reason (for example in the piece known as 'The Wild Horse is Broken'[81]). We have marked such instances with square brackets. We have also marked with square brackets those places where a text is so corrupt that it is generally agreed that it is impossible to decipher.

Some of the poems in the *Llyvyr Taliessin* have headings in the manuscript, and some do not. We have translated headings where they occur, but have not invented our own titles for the others, as some translators have done;[82] where a poem has no title in the manuscript, we refer to it by its first line. Stanza breaks have been introduced where there is a notable change of subject or mood in a poem. We have silently capitalized the first word of each line and added our own punctuation. The writing contains instances of mediaeval Latin, and of Greek or Hebrew names, often used inaccurately or copied incorrectly. John Koch and others refer to the patchily accurate Latin in texts like these as 'Cambro-Latin',[83] designed to reinforce the scholarly credibility of the writer; but it is only fair to add that the copyist rather than the author should be blamed for many of

the incomprehensible words and phrases; some can be restored
to sense with a little judicious emendation, and where this is
possible such passages are translated in the footnotes; but we
have generally kept the original in the text, to give a sense of
the multilingual flavour of the poem. Macaronic rhymes, e.g.
linking the Latin *terra* with the name *Beda,* give an internation
al texture to the fabric of the poetry. In 'Saints and Martyrs of
the Faith' (p. 169) the poet refers to *Ieithoed Gröc ac Efrei, / A
Lladin, gwyr llacharte* ('speakers of Greek and Hebrew / And
of Latin, fervent men'). Place names and proper nouns have
been silently capitalized. We have aimed to balance the need
to keep these names as close to the Welsh-language original –
this is important, as they play a significant part in the sound of
the lines – with the need to make them easily identifiable to a
contemporary audience. The contemporary location of places,
where known, is specified in footnotes. Where there is no note,
scholars have not been able to identify the relevant place or
person. Contemporary Welsh does not use the letter 'k', so we
have silently emended names beginning with 'k' in the original
(so that 'Kynan' becomes 'Cynan'). Proper nouns, such as *Sais*
for the English, *Cymry* for the Welsh and *Prydain* for Britain,
have generally been modernized, but we have noted this the
first time they are used.

We have retained the Welsh word for some key concepts in
the Taliesin world, the most important of these being *awen* for
'inspiration'[84] (for a discussion of this term, see p. xxv–xxvi).
Another key term is *Annwfn* (pronounced 'An-oovn'), which
refers to the Otherworld of early Welsh myth. It can be liter-
ally rendered as the 'undeep';[85] it is different from the classical
Underworld in that its uncanniness exists alongside or even
within ordinary life, rather than being a separate territory. *The
Mabinogion* contains a number of instances of mortals stray-
ing into *Annwfn* almost by mistake. For example, in the 'First
Branch' of the Mabinogi, the first of the four great prose nar-
ratives about archaic rulers and heroes, Pwyll Prince of Dyfed
meets the King of *Annwfn* out hunting and they decide to swap
places for a while.[86] In the 'Second Branch', Bendigeidfran,

the Welsh hero who has been decapitated but whose head is still talking spends eighty years feasting with his company on Gwales, or Grassholm Island, off the coast of Pembrokeshire, holding them in an enchanted state that is still located within the geographical world we know but suspending them in time.

The Texture of the Poetry

The most cursory look at the Taliesin poems in Welsh shows that rhyme is a dominant part of the poets' technique. Many of the poems are divided not into what we now called *awdlau* ('stanzas'), but instead into passages of irregular length, each one held together by a single repeated rhyme. In 'A Song of the Wind', for example, extended monorhymes are used for lines depicting one aspect of a phenomenon:

> Ny byd hyn, ny byd i*eu*
> noget ydechr*eu.*
> Ny daw o'e od*eu*
> yr ofyn nac agh*eu.*
> Ny dioes eiss*eu*
> gan greadur*yeu.*
> Mawr Duw, mor wynn*eu*
> ban daw odechr*eu;*
> mawr y verthid*eu*
> y Gwr a'e gor*eu.*
> Ef ymaes, ef yg ko*et,*
> heb law a heb tro*et.*
>
>   (ll. 7–18)

Most of this passage is an evocation of the wind's general activities; but the final two lines, with their change of rhyme, turn in another direction to focus on the wind's movements in specific features of the landscape, and we have signalled this shift in our own unrhymed translation:

No older, no younger
Than he was before.
He's not turned aside
By fear, nor by death.
He doesn't experience
The needs of creatures.
Great God, he's so lively
When first he comes by;
Surely his creator
Is full of glories.
He's in fields, in woods,
With no hand, no foot;

Thus, when the rhyme changes, a different aspect of the subject is usually introduced. Overall, these verses show the poet considering his or her subject from all points of view, slowly turning the wind around for close attention, so to speak. In the Welsh, the rhyme is so insistent as almost to give the impression that the poet has been hijacked by his or her chosen rhyme and will not be released until that particular consonance is exhausted. The monorhyme is made easier in Middle Welsh by the use of generic or so-called 'Irish' rhymes. These are near-rhymes in which the rhyming syllables contain identical vowels followed by consonants that are not identical but belong generically to the same phonetic class.[87] For example, groups like p-t-c, ph/f-th-ch, b-d-g/bh-dh gh, mh-l-n-r, m-ll-nn-rr, ng and s are considered interchangeable. These rhymes are still very familiar from modern pop and rap lyrics, where exact consonantal repetitions are not required, so that 'stone' can perfectly well rhyme with 'home'. The subtlety of these rhyming patterns means that the poet has a much larger choice of words to range against and with each other, so that the chime of sounds suggests almost subliminally an echo of meaning. In our translations, we have not tried to reproduce the monorhyme in full – though a more ambitious translator might try their hand at a 'rap' version! But we have where possible suggested something of the sound of monorhyme in significant passages. We have not marked every change of rhyme with a new stanza; we have, however, allowed ourselves the liberty of a stanza break to mark major alterations of subject and tone.

The monorhyme, as we have noted, has the effect of subliminally linking words of very diverse meaning; and something of the same effect can be seen in the use of vowel rhymes, which are also regularly deployed – as in the lines *Duw etuynt,* yn of / *yt wyd* yn y vod from 'A Song about Beer' ('Please God, it tastes sharp, / That is His nature'). By rhyming the 'o' in *yn of* (pronounced *un-ov,* meaning 'sharp') with the same vowel in *y vod* (pronounced *uv-odd,* 'nature'), the poet suggests a relationship between ale's bitterness and the nature of God – as if God can taste bitter.

In such patterns we can see the origins of the system of *cynghanedd* ('chiming' or 'harmony'). These intricate patterns of sound were first codified in the bardic schools of the fourteenth century and became an effect unique to Welsh-language poetry. Eventually, four kinds of *cynghanedd* were recognized and a metrical line could be judged correct or incorrect according to the rules governing the mirroring of consonants, accents and rhyme. Neither the early 'heroic' poems nor the mediaeval compositions in the *Llyvyr Taliessin* apply these later rules in their full strictness, but we can rightly say that there is a sort of proto-*cynghanedd* at work in their repertoire of techniques.

Wherever possible, we have tried to reproduce some elements of this 'chiming', because it is as much part of how the lines work as is their grammatical sense. Aesthetic choices in the Taliesin poetry are never decorative, but are central to the social and theological meaning. In 'First Artful Command', a poem in which God Himself is seen as an artist, the verse gathers momentum through a list of questions which place very different entities – such as linnets and night – in relation to each other.

> Pan yw tywyll n*o*s?
> pan yw gwyrd llin*o*s?
> Mor pan dyuerw*y*d?

cwd a nys gwelyd.
Yssit teir ffynnawn
YMynyd S'yawn;
Yssit gaer garthlawn
a dan donn eigyawn.
Gor-ith gyuarchawr·
pwy enw y parthawr?

(ll. 14–23)

Why's it dark at night?
How are finches green?
Whence the sea's seething?
It rises, nobody sees.
There are three springs
That rise on Mount Zion;
And a fort's ruins
Lie under the ocean.
You're asked, when you come,
What's the gatekeeper's name?

Here, rhyme becomes a way of enacting the unity and inter-connectedness of the Christian creation, in which previously disconnected entities, such as ruins and oceans, are seen as intimately related in virtue of their common status as part of God's creation. Rhyme is thus far more than a sonic ornament; it is a roadmap for the hidden connections that hold the world together. In the legendary Taliesin's imagination, even the most outlandish or remote relationships are re-ordered by sound in the poem to show the integrity of the poet and God's creation. In 'I Am the Vigour', the poet asks a series of questions about how things are connected. By being listed in a passage sharing one rhyme, a whole sequence of objects acquires a mutual relationship not directly asserted in the surface 'sense' of the line:

a rudem a grawn
ac ewyn eigyawn?

(ll. 32–33)

>   And ruby and berries?
>   And the waves' foam?

Ruby and berries are connected not only by standing together in the same line but by the colour they share. In the Welsh, however, the end-word *grawn* ('berries') is then also connected musically with its rhyme at the end of the following line, *eigyawn* ('waves'). Aside from the sonic connection, the shape of a cluster of berries is thus – in an ingenious piece of poetic noticing – made to 'rhyme' visually with the foam of a breaking wave.

Much of the effect of rhyme relies on repetition with variation. This can be achieved on a larger scale, in the echoes constructed between stanzas. The first stanza of 'Elegy for Cú Roi mac Dáir' (p. 105), an elegy for a sailor, opens with words describing the movement of the tide. The second half of l. 2 in Welsh employs two words spelt differently but almost identical in pronunciation, as if to suggest that the water advances and retreats an equal distance, as it would at high or low water:

>   Dy ffynhawn lydan · dylleinw aches,
>   dydaw, dyhebcyr, · dybris, dybrys.

>   (ll. 1–2)

>   From sea's wide spring · out flows the tide:
>   It advances, retreats, · it smashes, crushes.

In the opening two lines of the second stanza, the poet uses a version of the same trick to convey the tide turning:

>   Dy ffynhawn lydan · delleinw nanneu,
>   dydaw, dyhebcyr, · dybrys, dybreu.

>   (ll. 8–9)

Slightly different spellings of the Welsh verb for 'to flow' – *dylleinw* in the first couplet and *delleinw* in the second – convey the rhythm of a repeated action with a minuscule difference in sound, even before the symmetry of the ebb or flood can be perceived in terms of duration:

> From sea's wide spring · out flow the currents:
> It advances, retreats, · it crushes, rushes.

Three-quarters of the second lines of both stanzas are identical, so that the ear experiences the new word, *dybreu*, as a manifest novelty, a variation both in the tidal flow and the poem's refrain. This subtle variation suggests that the poem itself is an extension of the wild that it describes. Appropriately enough, in 'I Am the Vigour', poetry is called 'Gwion's river' (l. 66): it is itself a natural movement, a force of nature.

Welsh verse is further structured by a series of tropes called *cymeriadau*, or correspondences.[88] A *cymeriad* tends to occur at the beginning of a line and links a series in various ways; these include 'beginning each line with the same letter or word, alliterating or rhyming the first word in each consecutive line and by allowing sense to extend from one line to another'.[89] For example, the poem 'Taliesin's Sweetnesses' (p. 42) consists of a list of objects and qualities that delight the poet. Every single line except the final one begins with the letter A. In addition, the para-rhyme of *–wyn* with *–ein* and *–in* links the objects described in a chain of echoes (we have taken *arall atwyn* as a first word because it is part of the formula of the poem):

> At*wyn* idryf ewiç aç el*ein*;
> Arall at*wyn* ewynawc archu*ein*.
>
> At*wyn* lluarth pan llwyd y genh*in*;
> At*wyn* arall katawarth yn eg*in*.
>
> At*wyn* edystyr yg kebystyr lletr*in*;
> Arall at*wyn* kyweithas a brenh*in*.

(ll. 39–44)

Sweet in the wild is a doe or fawn;
Sweet too is a slim steed lathered with foam.

Sweet is the garden when leeks are thriving;
Sweet, also, is field mustard sprouting.

Sweet is a horse in its leather halter;
Sweet, too, it is, to be with a king.

The multiple internal and end-word rhymes (along with the repetition of the 'a' sound, which opens the mouth in praise) gives the sense that diverse objects do not only exist in the world 'out there' but are artfully woven into a musical unity when they are spoken of. The poem seems to say not only that the individual elements are delightful to Taliesin, but that part of their delight and delightfulness consists in their chiming with each other.

Metre

Early Welsh poetry is structured firstly by stress, along with alliteration – consonants repeated so as to create an aural and semantic link between two parts of a line or poem. Secondly, the poet can provide further structure for a poem by using a fixed number of syllables for the lines – 'syllabic' verse. Other early poetries, Irish and Anglo-Saxon, for example, use alliteration as Welsh poetry does, in order to weave patterns of sound and sense uniting different parts of a line or stanza. But the unique feature of the Welsh is *cynghanedd*, 'chiming' (see p. lxiv), the careful patterning of alliteration, assonance and rhyme within and between lines. The poems of the *Llyvyr Taliessin* show the first beginnings of this system before it becomes more strictly codified in the late Middle Ages (when a similar process leads to greater precision and regularity in syllable counting as well). The complexity of Welsh diphthongs (combinations of vowels; see the 'Guide to Welsh Pronunciation', p. lxxxi) adds a third element to the structure of the verse. In Classical Greek and Roman poetry, certain accents were counted as heavy and others as light, depending on the 'value' or duration of the vowels used. This was known as 'quantitative verse'. Early Welsh-language poetry is remarkable in that it combines all three types of metrical unit – stress, syllables and quantity or weight. Whereas poetry of the late mediaeval period in Welsh moved in the direction of ever-greater metrical, especially alliterative, complexity, the development of English poetry in the same period shows alliteration becoming more subtle and less dominant as it turns into just one of a number of devices alongside rhyme, assonance and consonance.[90]

The contents of the *Llyvyr Taliessin* display quite a variety of metrical forms and this survey will not attempt to do more than outline some of the more common ones, to give some notion of how the poetry moves and works in its original language. Most of the early 'heroic' poems are written in one of two metres. The first of these has a pair of rhyming half-lines, each with four or five syllables (as in poems 1, 3, 4 and 5 in this group). The rhyme is then repeated in one or both members of the next pair of half-lines. 'Here at My Rest' (poem 4 in the heroic sequence) also regularly carries over the last word of one line as the first of the next or picks up a word or phrase to repeat in the following line:

> Parch a chynnwys, · a med meuedwys,
> Meuedwys med · y oruoled
> a chein tired · imi yn ryfed.
> A ryfed mawr · ac eur ac awr,
> ac awr a chet · a chyfriuet
> a chyfriuyant.

And as this example illustrates, there are also minor internal alliterations within the lines and couplets. The second common form, found in poems 2, 7 and 8 of this early group, uses a longer line, normally of nine syllables (hence the technical name, *cyhydedd naw ban*, 'nine-syllable metre'), but sometimes varying to eight or ten syllables, with a less regular rhyme pattern; this form is also marked out by a feature of the opening couplet which was to become a distinctive element in some later Welsh verse forms: the first two lines rhyme, but the rhyming syllable is stressed in the first line and unstressed in the second. There is none of the elaboration of later *cynghanedd*, but, as Ifor Williams remarked, it is 'on the way'. [91]

There are four common forms in use in the later poems, especially in the 'legendary' group, distinguished from one another by length of line and patterns of stress. First, there is what the later bardic grammars, codifying the craft of the mediaeval poet, call the 'Taliesin metre', found in a great many of the riddling and 'shamanic' poems ascribed to Taliesin. This is characterized by short lines (between four and seven syllables) yoked together in a rhyming couplet.[92] A clear example is 'The Battle of the Trees':

> Bum yn lliaws rith
> kyn bum disgyfrith:
> bum cledyf culurith,
> or adaf pan writh.
>
> (ll. 1–4)

The second pattern is a line between seven and twelve syllables with four clear stresses and a caesura in the middle. The second part of the line is shorter than the first, and there is a marked use of alliteration and assonance between the two parts of the line. The beginning of 'The Spoils of Annwfn' shows all these features:

> Golychaf Wledic, · Pendeuic gwlat ri,
> ry ledas y pennaeth · dros traeth *Mundi*.
> Bu kyweir karchar Gweir · yg Kare Sidi,
> trwy ebostol Pwyll · a Phryderi.
>
> (ll. 1–4)

A third variety of line in the 'legendary' poems is the *cyhydedd fer* ('short metre') – similar to the *cyhydedd naw ban*, but usually with eight rather than nine syllables. There may be one caesura or two, with a strong stress in each part of the line (sometimes one stress in each of the first two parts and two in the last, often trisyllabic, section). The line is sometimes shortened or lengthened by a couple of syllables. Sometimes a section of a poem in this metre will close with the *toddaid byr* ('a short *toddaid*', *toddaid* being one of the technical terms of mediaeval prosody) – two lines broken into units of 5, 5 and 6 syllables. 'Poets' Corner' uses the *cyhydedd fer*, employing both single and double caesura:

> Creic am wanec · wrth vawr trefnat –
> anclyt yscryt · escar nodyat –
> creic pen perchen · pennaf ygnat,
> y'n gwna medut · med-dawt meidat.
>
> Wyf kell, wyf dellt, · wyf datweirllet;
> wyf llogell kerd, · wyf lle ynnyet.

> (ll. 19–24)

Finally, there is a more complex threefold metre, used once in the 'legendary' poems, in the 'Elegy for Dylan, Son of the Sea' – the *rhupunt*, which consists of a series of three four-syllable units per line; the first three units rhyme with each other, and the last is answered by a rhyme at the beginning of the subsequent line. It is also used in the prophetic poems and some of the devotional pieces, as well as (with some variants) in 'Disaster for the Island'. This example, from the 'prophetic' group, is the opening of 'Fine Feasting' (bold, underlining and italics mark the different rhymes):

> Kein gyfed*wch* · y am deul*wch*, · ll*wch* am pleit,
> Pleit am g*aer*, · k*aer* yn eh*aer* · ryyscrif*yat*.
> Vir*ein* ffo racd*aw* · arlleg *kaw* · mwyedic u*ein*.
> Dr*eic* amgyffr*eu* · oduch lle*eu* · llestr*eu* llat. [93]

> (ll. 1–4)

Fine feasting · around two lakes, · one lake round our host,
A host in a fort, · an unfallen fort, · famed far and wide –
A wondrous retreat, · a well-made refuge, · of reinforced stones.

The writer or writers of the 'legendary' poems clearly believed that it was entirely permissible to vary the syllable-count of a so-called regular line (like the five-, eight- or nine-syllable lines), and so were free to create very subtle transitions of feeling and focus. For example, the original Welsh of 'First Artful Command', 'Prif Gyuarch Geluyd', is based on the nine-syllable line but sometimes drops to eight or stretches to ten. In our translations, we have tried, as much as possible, to reflect this variety (though it seemed to us that looking for an exact correspondence of syllables would be the kiss of death in translating poetry):

First artful command: who pronounced it?
What comes first, darkness or light?
Adam, where was he? Which day created?
As for the earth, on what was it set?
Those in orders don't like to think
Est qui peccator[94] in their midst;
To parish priests, Heaven is lost.

(ll. 1–7)

But with the mention of clerics, the poem switches to a shorter line, a different rhythm echoing the changes in the peal of church bells that call the young. This measure is based on the five-syllable line but, as usual, with variations of the number:

A youth would rise early [. . .]
On three bells' peal [. . .]

This subtle technique of variation reminds us of the importance of recognizing that poetry can derive its power as much from the ways in which it breaks its own rules as from its adherence to them. But the rules still matter. It was with patterns like this in mind that W. H. Auden used to recommend that poets early in their craft should practise by writing in the Welsh measures; he reasoned that, if you could master using so many poetic effects together (alliteration, rhyme and strict syllable counting) in such density, then even the most complex forms in modern English – like the sestina, the villanelle, or even the sonnet – would present no technical difficulty. It is perhaps appropriate to end a discussion of the various metres of the Taliesin poems with this tribute from one of the most metrically skilful and nimble of modern English poets.

GL/RW

NOTES

1   Ifor Williams, *Canu Taliesin: gyda Rhagymadrodd a Nodiadau* (Cardiff, University of Wales Press, 1960, henceforth *CT*); *The Poems of Taliesin*, tr. J. E. Caerwyn Williams (Dublin, DIAS, 1968, henceforth *PT*).

2   *Legendary Poems from the Book of Taliesin* (Aberystwyth, CMCS, 2007, henceforth *LPBT*).

3   *Prophecies from the Book of Taliesin* (Aberystwyth, CMCS, 2013, henceforth *PBT*).

4   See *LPBT*, p. 94.

5   *Exodus* 34:29.

6   *Historia Brittonum*, 62 (there are several editions available of J. A. Giles's translation of the *historia*, including one from the Dodo Press, Gloucester, published in 2007).

7   Catterick had been a quite significant Roman military township (Cataractonium), which somewhat increases the likelihood of its being the site of both settlement and conflict in the post-Roman period. But some recent scholars have pointed out the problems in envisaging a military force originating in Edinburgh travelling through a region already settled by the Angles for a battle in Yorkshire. See the discussion in Tim Clarkson's excellent study of the Northern British kingdoms, *The Men of the North: The Britons of Southern Scotland* (Edinburgh, Birlinn, 2010), especially chapter 5; and John T. Koch, 'Waiting for Gododdin: Thoughts on Taliesin and Iudic-hael, Catraeth, and Unripe Time in Celtic

Studies', in Alex Woolf, ed., *Beyond the* Gododdin: *Dark Age Scotland in Mediaeval Wales* (St Andrews, Committee for Dark Age Studies, 2013), pp. 177–204.

8   *De sancto Iudicaelo rege historia*, attributed to the eleventh-century monk Ingomar; the reference is to *Taliosinus bardus filius Donis*.

9   Urien's name appears fleetingly in Geoffrey of Monmouth's *History of the Kings of Britain* (IX.12) as 'Urbgennius' – a garbled form of the original Latin name 'Urbigenus'. Like his son Owain (originally 'Eugenius'; re-christened 'Yvain' or 'Ywaine' in mediaeval romances), and indeed many other roughly sixth-century figures, including Merlin and Taliesin himself, Urien is sucked into the orbit of the Arthurian cycle of the later Middle Ages, appearing in Malory's *Morte d'Arthur* as King 'Uriens' or 'Urience' of Gore.

10 The Yorkshire Aire may be a Scandinavian rather than a British name, and if so it would be later than the setting of these poems, and therefore a less likely candidate than Ayrshire; but the question is not settled.

11 *PT*, pp. xlii–xliii.

12 Andrew Breeze, 'Yrechwydd and the River Ribble', *Northern History* 47.2, 2010, pp. 319–28.

13 *LPBT*, p.36

14 The Breton designation of Taliesin as 'son of Don' (above, n. 6) is interesting in this respect, and may indicate that some connection between Taliesin and the narrative cycles about the children of Don goes back to a period earlier than the 'legendary' poems. It is also possible that 'son of Don' might have been a traditional designation for shamans or magicians, like the Gwydion of the *Mabinogion* story.

15 In the edition already cited; above, n. 2.

16 Famously translated by Augusta, Lady Gregory in her *Gods and Fighting Men* (London, John Murray, 1904), Part I, Book III.

17 Estuaries.

18 See, for example, John Matthews (with additional material by Caitlin Matthews), *Taliesin: The Last Celtic Shaman* (2nd edn, Rochester, Vermont, Inner Traditions, 2002).

19 *Descriptio Kambriae* I.16 (Lewis Thorpe, *Gerald of Wales: The Journey through Wales/ The Description of Wales* (Harmondsworth, Penguin Books, 1978)), pp. 246–7.

20 For a twentieth-century example of classical praise-song com-

position, see Jeff Opland and Peter T. Mtuze, eds., *John Solilo: Umoya Wembongi. Collected Poems (1922–1935)* (Pietermaritz-burg, University of KwaZulu-Natal Press, 2016).

21   See p. xx.

22   Active between around 1175 and 1220; see *LPBT*, pp. 27–36.

23   Andrew Breeze's studies have been particularly useful here; see especially 'Cruxes in "The Saints and Martyrs of Christendom"', *Studia Celtica* 42.1, 2008, pp. 149–53.

24   *PT*, pp. lix–lxiii.

25   Here, of course, the story's relevance depends on the assumption that the list of Arthur's men in that text goes back to its eleventh-century core, and was not a later addition.

26   See 'An Unfriendly Crowd', ll. 159–160 (p. 50) and 'I Make My Plea to God', ll. 31–39 (p. 70).

27   For an authoritative modern edition of this text (written by Elis Gruffydd in the 1520s or 1530s), see Patrick K. Ford, *Ystoria Taliesin*, ed. with an introduction and notes (Cardiff, University of Wales Press, 1992). Gruffydd claims that the story was already well known in his day and refers to earlier written versions.

28   Among many folkloric parallels, one of the most interesting is that with the legends of Finn MacCumhaill, who acquires wisdom either from burning his thumb on a magical salmon cooking at the fire, or from being splashed by water from a sacred well. Patrick Ford's introduction contains a wealth of information about both legendary parallels and accounts – especially Irish – of bardic initiation rituals or disciplines and their bearing on the Taliesin story.

29   The mediaeval genealogies mention a son of Urien of Rheged named Elffin; there may have been 'Taliesin' poems associated with this figure, making a later confusion with a West Welsh Elffin more understandable.

30   See the notes on the translation (p. 45); the fact that the story of a shape-shifting hunt is a widespread folkloric theme makes it unlikely that this narrative development is simply a mistake. Shape-shifting hunts or combats are used by a number of modern fantasy writers, including T. H. White in *The Once and Future King*, Alan Garner in *The Moon of Gomrath* and Terry Pratchett in *Equal Rites*.

31   London, Black Raven Press, 1983; 2nd edn, Bridgend, Seren Books, 2000.

32   Marilyn Butler, 'Romanticism in England', in Roy Porter and Mi-

kulas Teich, ed, *Romanticism in National Context* (Cambridge, Cambridge University Press, 1988), p. 50.

33 For more on Iolo Morganwg, see Geraint H. Jenkins, ed., *A Rattleskull Genius: The Many Faces of Iolo Morganwg* (Cardiff, University of Wales Press, 2005).

34 'Taliessin' appears in John Cowper Powys's celebrated Arthurian novel *Porius* (London, Macdonald, 1951) as a sage and seer; and he is the central figure in the first volume of Stephen Lawhead's 'Pendragon Cycle', *Taliesin* (New York, HarperCollins, 1987), which deals with the 'Arthurian Age'.

35 Robert Duncan, *The H. D. Book*, ed. with an introduction by Michael Boughn and Victor Coleman (Berkeley, University of California Press, 2011), p. 74.

36 London, Faber and Faber, 1948.

37 *Taliesin, or, Bards and Druids of Britain* (London, Pickton, 1858). Despite all sorts of problems in its treatment of the text and the inadequate philological equipment of mid-nineteenth-century scholarship, this book represents an important advance in the study of the text on a responsible historical basis.

38 *LP*, pp. 172–3.

39 Charles Williams, *Taliessin through Logres* (Oxford, Oxford University Press, 1938). The 'Logres' of the title corresponds to the *Lloegyr* of early Welsh poetry, but this form of the word derives from late-mediaeval English Arthurian literature.

40 *Taliessin through Logres*, p. 4.

41 Ibid., pp. 27–32.

42 Ibid., p. 32.

43 London, Editions Poetry, 1944; the two 'Taliessin' sequences are published together as *The Arthurian Poems of Charles Williams* (Cambridge, D. S. Brewer, 1982).

44 *The Region of the Summer Stars*, p. 27.

45 Ibid., p. 7.

46 On this see Grevel Lindop's sympathetic biography, *Charles Williams: The Third Inkling* (Oxford, Oxford University Press, 2015).

47 *The Collected Poems of Vernon Watkins* (Ipswich: Golgonooza Press, 2000), p. 184.

48 Ibid., p. 317.

49 Ibid., p. 320.

50 Ibid., p. 353.

51 Published in *Song at the Year's Turning: Poems 1942–1954* (London, Rupert Hart-Davis, 1955).

52 Thomas's 'the vast night' here surely echoes Shakespeare's Glendower in *Henry IV Part 1*, claiming to 'call spirits from the vasty deep'.

53 Basil Bunting, *Briggflatts* (Hexham, Bloodaxe, 2009), p. 27.

54 The Sufi mystic, Jalal ud-Din Rumi.

55 David Jones, *In Parenthesis* (London, Faber and Faber, 1937), p. 80.

56 Ibid., p. 83.

57 Ibid., p. 84.

58 Ibid., p. 207.

59 See pp. 49, 52.

60 'First Artful Command', l. 85, see p. 38.

61 'To Pacify Urien', see p. 22.

62 *LP*, p. 263.

63 Ibid., pp. 257–8.

64 See Ceri W. Lewis, 'Einion Offeiriad and the Bardic Grammar', in A. O. H. Jarman and Gwilym Rees Hughes, eds, rev. Dafydd Johnston, *A Guide to Welsh Literature 1282 c.1550* (Cardiff, University of Wales Press, 1997), p. 44.

65 For an account of the elements or constituents of the universe in Taliesin's cosmology see *LP*, pp. 223–5.

66 Ifor Williams speculates that Ceridwen's name derives from *cwr(r)*, which can mean 'crooked', or may refer, more generally, to something angular. Marged Haycock follows this up with the suggestion that we could break her name down to the elements *cwrr+rhit+ben*, which would give us something like 'woman with angular embrace' (*LP*, pp. 319–20), perhaps a metaphor for the stakes propping up a cauldron.

67 Edinburgh.

68 'Annwfn' is the traditional name for the magical and often menacing Otherworld of Welsh legend.

69 'In the King of Heaven's Name, They Remember', l. 16 (see p. 28).

70 L. 36, see p. 73.

71 Thomas Owen Clancy, ed., *The Triumph Tree: Scotland's Earliest Poetry AD 550–1350* (Edinburgh, Canongate, 1998), p. 58.

72 See p. 72.

73 John T. Koch, 'Obscurity and the Figure of Taliesin', *Mediaevalia* 19, 1993, pp. 41–73; referring to pp. 53–4.

74 Ibid., p. 51.

75 *PBT*, p. 4.

76 See *LP*, p. 15.

77   Ibid, p. 9.

78   *PT*, p. xxvi.

79   https://www.llgc.org.uk/index.php?id=254. (May 2018).

80   *LPBT*, p. 182, ll. 151–9.

81   See p. 90.

82   See Joseph Clancy, *The Earliest Welsh Poetry* (London Macmillan, 1970); *The Triumph Tree*; Tony Conran, *Welsh Verse: Translations* (Bridgend, Seren Books, 1992).

83   John T. Koch, art. cit., p. 52.

84   See 'Guide to Welsh Pronunciation', pp. lxxxi.

85   Matthew Francis in his splendid poetic reworking of the first four *Mabinogion* stories, *The Mabinogi* (London, Faber, 2017), uses 'Unland' to translate *Annwfn*.

86   *The Mabinogion*, ed. and tr. Sioned Davies (Oxford, Oxford University Press, 2007), p. 4f.. The 'Four Branches of the Mabinogi' are the most archaic elements in *The Mabinogion*, relating the deeds of heroic figures who may originally have been gods of pre-Christian British mythology. For a note on *Annwfn* see Davies, pp. 228–9.

87   *Princeton Encylopedia of Poetry and Poetics*, ed. Roland Greene et al (4th edn, Princeton, Princeton University Press, 2012), p. 548.

88   See Jarman and Rees Hughes, *A Guide to Welsh Literature: 1282–c.1550*.

89   See *Geiriadur Prifysgol Cymru*.

90   See *The Princeton Encyclopedia of Poetry and Poetics*, pp. 40–41.

91   *CT*, p. lxiv.

92   G. J. Williams, and E. J. Jones, *Gramadegau'r Penceirddiaid* (*The Grammars of the Chief Bards*) (Caerdydd, Gwasg Prifysgol Cymru, 1934). See, in English, Lewis Turco, *The Book of Forms: A Handbook of Poetics* (3rd rev. edn, Lebanon, NH, University Press of New England, 2000). For a brief account of modern *cynghanedd*, see Mererid Hopwood, *Singing in Chains: Listening to Welsh Verse* (2nd edn, Llandysul, Gomer Press, 2015).

93   See p. 139.

94   'There is someone who is a sinner'.

Guide to Welsh Pronunciation

Welsh is a phonetic language, in that every letter is pronounced. Unless otherwise indicated, words are stressed on the last but one syllable, as in Taliésin, Carádog, Gwállawg. Letters are pronounced as in English, with the following exceptions.

Consonants in Welsh that differ from English

dd	A soft 'th', as in 'there'.
ch	As in 'loch' or the German 'Bach'.
f	As in 'v', for example, 'love'.
ff	Identical to the 'f' in 'ford'.
ng	Letter following 'g', not 'n' in the Welsh alphabet. Pronounced as in 'thing'.
ll	Unique to Welsh. Tongue is placed on palate behind teeth, breath blown both sides of it. Closest approximation: 'hl'.
r	Trilled.
rh	Trilled, followed by aspiration.
th	Always hard, 'death', rather than 'this'.

Ordinary consonants and vowels

In addition to the English letters, Welsh counts 'w' and 'y' as vowels. 'J', 'k' and 'z' don't exist in Welsh, though they may be used in proper nouns.

c   As in 'cat'; never changes to an 's', as in 'nice'.

g   As in 'God'; never a 'j' sound, as in 'Nigel'.

s   As in 'noose'; never a 'z' sound, as in 'nose'.

The following letters may be short or long, producing two distinct sounds:

a   As in 'cat'; or in 'father'.

e   As in 'egg'; or in 'fête'.

i   As in 'knit'; or in 'machine'.

o   As in 'cop'; or in 'comb'.

u   Sounds like 'i'. As in 'kiss'; or in the French 'pointu'.

w   As in 'quick'; or in 'cool'.

y   As in 'sick'; or in 'machine'.

Diphthongs (combinations of vowels)

ae, ai, au   As in 'kind'.

aw   As in 'ouch'.

ei eu   As in 'weight'.

ew   As in 'phew', said quickly.

iw, uw, yw   As in 'pew'.

oe   As in 'spoil'.

ow   As in 'crow', not 'crowd'.

yw   As in 'clue'.

wy   Pronounced as one vowel, as in 'we'; or 'oo-ee'.

HEROIC POEMS

I

In Praise of Cynan Garwyn, Son of Brochfael

This is a eulogy for Cynan of the White Chariot, King of Powys in the North-East and East of Wales, who fought the Anglo-Saxons with his Irish allies in the second half of the sixth century. The poem praises him by means of his genealogy. The title refers to his father, Brochfael Ysgithrawg (Brochfael of the Huge Eye Teeth, or Fangs). Cadell was one of Cynan's fore-fathers, a King of Powys, which at one time extended to the east of Shrewsbury and to the north and east of Chester. Although considered a hero in Powys, especially by Taliesin, to whom he was a patron, Cynan's raids against fellow Britons in Gwent, Anglesey, Dyfed and Cornwall made him so hated that nobody gave his son Selyf help in the crucial Battle of Chester in 615, when he was defeated by Aethelfrith of Northumbria. T. M. Charles-Edwards dates this poem at the turn of the seventh century CE[1] but it is more likely that in its present form it belongs – like the poems addressed to the royal house of Rheged in this collection – to a later period.

Cynan bestowed on me
Shelter in a battle –
My praise is no lie –
Gifts and property,
A hundred horses,
Saddles with silver,
A hundred mantles
All equally full;
My lap's full of armlets
And many brooches.
A sword sheathed in jewels,
The best gold hilt ever.

I had these from Cynan,
Who's hated by no one.
Descended from Cadell,
Steadfast in battle,
Attacking the Wye
With numberless spears;
Gwentmen are killed
By his blood-drenched blades.
War waged in fair Môn:*
Shout loud his renown!
Once across Menai†
The rest was easy.
Down to Crug Dyfed:‡
Aergol§ resurrected
To see his realm raided,
Foes leading his herds.
Broad-landed Cynan
With lust for possession,
Craving for Cornwall.
Bad luck is their fate;
He gives them distress
Till they sue for peace.
Cynan's my patron –
Soldier supreme.
In the light of wide flames
He makes battle blaze!
Takes war to Brecon,
Heights molehills to him.
Pitiful tyrants,
Tremble at Cynan!

20

30

40

*   *Môn*: Mona, or Anglesey, the island off the north-west coast of Wales.
†   *Menai*: The Menai Strait.
‡   *Crug Dyfed*: Location unknown, but obviously somewhere in South-
    West Wales (the modern county of Dyfed).
§   *Aergol*: Originally Aircol ('Agricola') Lawhir, or 'Aergol of the Long
    Hand'. He appears in royal genealogies from Dyfed and seems to have
    lived in the early sixth century.

He's a shield in attack,
He's like a dragon.
A second Cyngen,*
He commands wide lands.
He's the talk of all men,
So says everyone;
And without exception
They're captive to Cynan.   50

---

*   *Cyngen*: Cynan's grandfather.

2

The Men of Catraeth*

This is the first of the poems celebrating Urien, King of Rheged, his military exploits and his generosity to his followers. He is sometimes described as 'Lord of Catraeth' in these poems; this may mean either that Catraeth was a major fortress or residence of his, or that he was remembered for having conquered and held it. It is not clear who his enemies are here, but the reference to 'Prydyn' in line 6 might indicate forces from further north, possibly fighting alongside other groups.

The men of Catraeth are up with the sun
Around their commander, the triumphant cattle-thief.
It's Urien himself, the far-famed chieftain,
Who holds kings in check and cuts them down.
His passion's for war, true lord of the faithful.
Misfortune for the men of Prydyn's†1 armies!
Gwen Ystrad's‡2 a fort fit for warriors' struggle –
There's no shelter found in forest or field
When they come to battle – defender of your folk –
Like waves roaring savagely over the land.
I saw valiant men assembled in armies –
After a morning's fighting, mangled flesh!
I saw crowds slaughtered from over the border.
A cry of triumph, a fierce shout, is heard.

10

---

*   *Catraeth*: Long identified with Catterick in North Yorkshire. This is philologically quite possible, but harder evidence is lacking. Some scholars favour a location in southern Scotland.

†   *Prydyn*: In the early Middle Ages, the areas north of the Antonine Wall, i.e. 'Pictland'.

‡   *Gwen Ystrad*: Often identified with Wensleydale. Others have suggested Winsterdale, a site in the Lake District.

In the struggle for Gwen Ystrad, a man might see
Trouble closing in, champions tired out with killing.
Going down to the ford, I saw bloodstained men
Laying their swords at the grey-haired king's feet.
They sue for peace, finding no way out,
Pale-faced, hands crossed, on the ford's gravel,   20
Drunk and dazed on the Idon's* red wine,[3]
Its waves washing through their dead horses' hair.
I saw those who'd ruined the land cast down,
Blood spattered over their garments.
And he, keen for battle, swift in mustering for war,
Protector in conflict, never thinking of flight,
The lord of Rheged, I marvel at his daring.
I saw great heroes gather round Urien
When he slaughtered his enemies at Llech Wen,[4]
Scattering foes to the birds of prey, he rejoiced.   30
Men, brace your shields ready for battle!
No shortage of fights for Urien's followers.

> When I'm old, out of breath,
> Commanded by death,
> I will feel delight
> Praising Urien aright.[5]

---

*   *the Idon*: The River Eden in Cumbria – which makes a Lake District
setting for the battle a bit more likely.

3

Urien of Erechwydd

A further paean to Urien, emphasizing his savagery in war, his generosity to his followers and his Christian credentials. The identification of 'Erechwydd' or 'Yrechwydd' is uncertain (see Introduction, p. xxi), but it may refer to north-eastern Yorkshire.

Urien of Erechwydd,
Most generous Christian.
With a free hand he gives
To men of this land.
As you shall gather,
So shall you share.
Christian poets thrive,
Happy, while you live;
They rejoice even more
At the hero's rich store,
Give greater renown
To children of Urien.
Leader supreme,
Most glorious king.
Far-famed shelter,
The strongest of fighters.
The English know him
When his name's mentioned –
Had death at his hands,
And many afflictions:
Their houses burning,
Their chattels stolen,
With frequent losses
And bitter distress.

No way to avoid it
From Urien of Rheged.
Rheged's defender,
Fame's lord, your land's anchor,
You're my delight.
All gossips relate   30
That your spearplay is savage
When war is waged.
When in battle you rage
There follows carnage.
Homes burnt at dawn
By Erechwydd's chieftain.
Lovely Erechwydd –
Most generous men!
The bravest of chiefs
Left Angles bereft.   40
Your bravest offspring,
The most valiant king
That was or will be:
There's no competition.
Watch him in battle,
It's nothing but terror;
Seen as a leader,
He's full of good humour.
Surrounded by joy
And abundant treasures: 50
Gold king of the north,
Supreme among kings.

   When I'm old, out of breath,
   Commanded by death
   I will feel delight
   Praising Urien aright.

4

Here at My Rest

*In this poem, Taliesin describes the abundance that characterizes
Urien's court and the generosity with which he is rewarded for
his service as court poet.*

Here at my rest
With the men of Rheged,
Respect and welcome
And mead for me!
Mead for me
To mark his triumph,
Gifts of fine land
To win me wealth,
Wealth in plenty
Of glittering gold,
Golden good times
And glowing esteem,
High esteem
And gifts to satisfy,
Gifts from one satisfied
When he gives me joy.
Slaughtering, cooking,
Feeding, preparing,
Preparing, feeding,
Beasts slaughtered before us,[1]
And great respect rendered
To the world's great poets!
Be sure that all
Bow down to you,
And bend to your will
(So God has granted).

Great men snort and groan
For fear of your onslaught,
Stirrer of battle,
Buttress of the land!   30
Always surrounded
By trampling horses –
Horses trampling,
And beer for drinking,
Beer to drink
And fine farmsteads,
Fine adornments
Showered upon me!
Llwyfennydd's* people,
Arkle's† fighters,   40
Both great and small,
Join with one voice,
In the song of Taliesin,
Heartening them all.
You are the best,
The highest I've heard of
In your great merits;
I'll sing the praises
Of all you've done.

When I'm old, out of breath,   50
Commanded by death,
I will feel delight
Praising Urien aright.

---

*   *Llwyfennydd*: Almost certainly the region around the River Lyvennet in
    Cumbria.
†   *Arkle*: 'Eirch' in the original. Assuming that this is a place name, it may
    refer to the river Arkle Beck, which runs through Arkengarthdale in
    North Yorkshire, and flows into the Swale, on which Catterick is located.

5

All through One Year

In a variation on the praise poem format, Taliesin here follows his portrayal of a year of celebrating military successes in the banqueting hall with a fantasy of the death of Urien. The poet has not gone out on the military campaign, but is waiting at home and having a daymare about his patron being killed. With sorrow, and in a notably percussive passage, the poet sees Urien's white hair covered in blood. Taliesin then sends a boy to the door as he imagines hearing the rallying cry of Urien's troops, leading to an even more glorious victory. In the original Welsh, the poem is written in a combination of cyhydedd naw ban *('nine-syllable measure'), rounded off by a stock quatrain of the basic metrical unit of variations on five syllables (see Introduction, p. lxx).*

All through one year
He poured out freely
Wine, bragget,* mead
As bravery's fee.
Parties of poets:
A swarm around spits,
Each with his torque,
Sitting in order.[1]
Each went on campaign,
Riding out keenly,
Intent on rich spoils
From battle in Manaw,†

10

---

*   *bragget*: Sweet beer made with honey.
†   *Manaw*: *Manaw Gododdin*, the coastal region on the south side of the
     Firth of Forth in Scotland (rather than *Ynys Manaw*, the Isle of Man).

Lusting for profit
And plentiful plunder:
Of cattle eight score,
Cows, calves the same colour,
Oxen and milk cows,
And all other riches.
I couldn't feel joy
If Urien died: 20
He was dear before leaving
For battle's uproar;
His blood-soaked white hair,
Him, borne on a bier,
His cheek all red
And stained with his blood.
A proud man always –
His wife made a widow.
He's my leader for life,
He's my hope for life,   30
My fate, my help and head.

Son, go to the door –
Listen to the noise.
What's the commotion?
Is the earth shaking?
The sea rushing in?
Approaching, a tide
Of foot soldiers cry:
'Foe on the hill,
Urien kills.   40
Foe in the vale,
Urien impales.
Foe on the mountain,
Urien smites him.
Foe on the slope,
Urien will slice him.
Foe on the ditch,
Urien will fright him.'

Foe on paths, foe above,
Foe round all river bends –
Not a sneeze nor three
Will stop him advancing.
No one goes hungry
Who's near to his booty.
His loud men roaring,
Their armour shining.
Like death is his spear,
Slaying the foe.

When I'm old, out of breath,
Commanded by death
I will feel delight
Praising Urien aright.

6

The Battle of Argoed Llwyfain

*In contrast to 'The Men of Catraeth', this poem probably al-
ludes to conflict with the Angles settling in Bernicia (what
is now northern Northumberland); their leader, here called
'Fflamddwyn', is associated elsewhere in these poems with
'Lloegr', usually a name for the lands occupied by the Germanic
incomers.*

Saturday morning there was great conflict
From the sun's rising to when it went down.
Fflamddwyn* marched forward in four battalions
To lay waste the lands of Goddeu[†] and Rheged.
From Argoed to Arfynydd[‡] the muster was summoned;
Not one delaying so much as a day.
Fflamddwyn bellowed, blustering away,
'Are the hostages here? Are they ready for taking?'
And Owain answered – scourge of the Eastlands –
'No, they are not! They're not here for the taking!   10
And the hounds of Coel's[§][1] litter would be hard-pressed
    indeed
Before they'd hand over one man as a hostage!'
Urien too answered, Lord of Erechwydd,
'If this meeting has only been called to talk treaties,

---

*   *Fflamddywn*: A nickname for the leader of the Anglian army, meaning
'Flamebearer', or perhaps (metaphorically) 'The Flamboyant One'. He is
sometimes identified with one of the early Northumbrian kings, possibly
Theodric of Bernicia (who ruled *c.*584–*c.*91); the *historia Brittonum*
describes conflicts between him and Urien.

†   *Goddeu*: Here a name for an area of southern Scotland.

‡   *Argoed to Arfynydd*: If not specific place names, these might be translated
as 'the forest areas' and 'the mountain areas', respectively.

§   *Coel*: Thought to be an ancestor of the kings of Rheged, and therefore of
Urien and his kinsmen Llywarch and Gwallawg.

We shall raise up our ramparts higher than
    mountains,
And lift our faces above their ridge,
And raise our weapons above our men's heads,
And march on Fflamddwyn with his battalions,
And cut him down and his company with him!'
20   There, before Argoed Llwyfain,
An abundance of corpses,
Crows red with warriors' blood,
As the people marched with their lord.
I shall plan a whole year for my victory song.

    When I'm old, out of breath,
    Commanded by death
    I will feel delight
    Praising Urien aright.

7

Rheged, Arise, its Lords Are its Glory

The text of this piece is very corrupt in the Llyvyr Taliessin
manuscript; Ifor Williams *argues in* Canu Taliesin *that the
scribe may have combined a number of pre-existing poems to
fashion a paean of praise for Urien, King of Rheged.*[1] *The poem
is notable both for its emphasis, in line 2, on the poet as a non-
native of Rheged and for his criticism of Urien's war against the
Angles of Northumbria.*

Rheged, arise, its lords are its glory.
I've watched you, though I'm not of you:
They groan facing sword-blades and battle,
Men groan underneath their round shields,
Wailing like greedy white gulls in Mathry.*
This fight against kings was unwise, I won't lie.
Still, a true sovereign fights other kings,
Not driven by those asking favours.
He enjoys his repute, a swift rider.
As Gwydion's† skills came from Dôn, his father,[2]   10
When Ulph[3] comes shall he not have an answer?
Till Urien in his day took Aeron,‡
There was no fight, it wasn't welcome;
Till Urien opened a front with Powys,
No ferocity drove the tribe of Gyrrwys

---

*   *Mathry*: Location uncertain; it can hardly be the modern Mathry in Pem-
brokeshire. The name suggests a settlement on a plain, which might have
been almost anywhere in the Old North.
†   *Gwydion*: The skilful and resourceful wizard and story-telling magician
in the 'Fourth Branch' of *The Mabinogion*.
‡   *Aeron*: Either the Scottish Ayrshire or (less probably) Airedale in York-
shire.

Nor Hyfeidd*nor Gododdin.[14]
Brave men enduring torture from spears –
I saw Gwydden‡ carried off in his blood
In Llwyfenydd.§ My lord was shaken
20   In defence of a fort.

A fight for the crown at Alclud¶ ford:
Battle for Brewyn's** cells, a battle long famed,
Battle in a wood, battle in an estuary,
There was fighting with clamorous steel:
Battle at Clutuein, fighting at Pencoed,
Drawing wolves to gorge on cascading blood.
Fierce men are brought to their knees;
The Angles' plans are defeated,
Made bloody by steadfast Ulph at the ford.

30   It is better to praise the king who's been praised.
The lord of Britain's leaders loves rhymes;
He does not delight in clothes, blue or gold
Or red or heather, nor superlative heroes.
He's not sailed over the noble backs
He has not mounted the lordly flanks
Of brindled horses, fierce in spirit.
From summer to winter, weapons in hand,
He's kept his watch at ford and rampart,
Sleeping stretched out in trenches.
40   Till the end of the world, all accounts will agree:
He sweeps aside enemies; he deserves the image,

*   *Ulph, Gyrrwys, Hyfeidd*: Identities unknown.
†   *Gododdin*: The kingdom of Gododdin was located south of the Firth of
       Forth.
‡   *Gwydden*: Unknown, but probably an ally of the royal house of Rheged.
§   *Llwyfenydd*: See note on p. 11.
¶   *Alclud*, otherwise Alt Clud or Alt Clut: Dumbarton.
**   *Brewyn*: Possibly Bremenium, a Roman fort in Northumbria, near High
       Rochester. It may be identical with 'Breguoin', which appears in some
       manuscripts of the *historia Brittonum* as the site of one of Arthur's battles.

'Lightning-destroyer.'
I roared, my breast full of tumult,
Lance on my shoulder, shield in my hand
When Goddeu and Rheged were ranged for war.
I saw a man who was raiding cattle –
Famous dragon, unique trampler.
I foresee war, and what will be lost,
How much I shall lose when that is lost.
It is I who'll be raging, drunk with mead.   50
Following Hyfeidd's bold, suffering men –
It is I who declared him my shelter in battle.
With joy my lord distributed gifts.
No leader can compare with Urien.

When I'm old, out of breath,
Commanded by death
I will feel delight
Praising Urien aright.

8

Taliesin's Plunder

This is a difficult text, but its overall sense is clear: the poet's songs are his contribution to Urien's war effort, corresponding to the military service done by the king's warriors ('My spear shaft of ash is my holy awen*') and is rewarded with the same generosity. The reference to the Easter ceremonies underlines (as in 'Urien of Erechwydd', p. 8) Urien's status as* ud *or* ri bedyd *and* haelaf dyn bedyd *– 'Lord of the baptized', 'most open-handed of Christians'.*

My courage stirred, I take heart and ask,
Shall I announce in truth what I see?
I saw in the king's presence – though he did not see me –
Every man that he loves speaking out boldly.
I saw a paschal blaze of candles and foliage,[1]
I saw leaves on the trees breaking forth in season,
I saw branches all alike laden with blossom;
I saw the lord of Catraeth beyond the plains.[2]
May my lord have no love for what's sorrowful![3]
10 To repay my song, may the gifts be great
From the chief of men who rewards me richly!
My spear shaft of ash is my holy *awen*,
The joy of my face is my master's shieldwall.
A generous prince, most valiant, is Urien –
The thunderous cattle-raider never denies me,
The warlord, the ironclad, the shining one,
The far-feared, the exalted. Everyone
Despises the coward, the fool, in the court
Of the lord who is swift wherever he travels.
20 The splendour of yellow gold shines in his hall,

The wealthy protector of Aeron.*
His delight is great in his poets and his deer,
His anger is great against his enemies.
His power is great over the clans of the Britons.
Like a wheel of fire across the earth,
Like a river in spate is Llwyfennydd's true lord;
Like a hymn or a battle-song known to all,
Like the great-souled sea is Urien.

Dear[4] is the spreading of light at daybreak,
Dear is the warrior chief, the king.   30
Dear are the warhorses that make soldiers swift,
And the first days of May for warriors resting.[5]
Dear is the Defwy[†6] for the folk who go there,
And the eagle traversing the land and the long ridge.
I should gladly have joined, on a spirited horse,
The mighty host that earns plunder for Taliesin.
Dear is the gallop of the hero and his steed,
Dear is the nobleman, a gift to his lord.
Dear are the stags and the hinds in wild places,
Dear is the greedy wolf in the gorse.   40
Dear is the lord of Eginyr's[‡] sons.
And one kind of delight[7] is the clashing of warriors,
The delight of the fierce warcry.
The whelps of Nudd Hael,[§] may their lands spread far!
And if I'm to be blessed,
Let him make the world's poets happy
Before I see Gwydden's[¶] sons laid low!
Chief of the army of this fine land is Urien.

---

*   *Aeron*: See note on p. 17.
†   *the Defwy*: Presumably a river.
‡   *Eginyr*: Otherwise unknown, but on this evidence either an ancestor of
    Urien's family or an ally against the Angles.
§   *Nudd Hael*: Identified by the genealogies and other sources as a sixth-
    century king in southern Scotland; presumably another ally of Urien's.
¶   *Gwydden*: See note on p. 18.

9

To Pacify Urien

As we have seen, for all that his name is most often associated with the court of Urien of Rheged, Taliesin is also credited with writing praise poems to other rulers, including Gwallawg, a king of the Old North somewhere around Elmet in West Yorkshire (see Introduction, p. xxi, and p. 31) and Cynan of Powys (see p. xxvii); Gwallawg, for instance, appears as an enemy of Urien in 'In the King of Heaven's Name, They Remember'. Poets were not exclusively attached to one royal master, and shifting allegiances and power relations between warlords would have given wide scope for offence in high places. This has led some who are optimistic about reconstructing a historical career for Taliesin to conclude that his praise of Gwallawg was the occasion of a breach with Urien. But the present poem suggests that Taliesin needs to make amends to Urien simply because 'for a joke I poked fun / At him, the old man'. Perhaps the gaffe was made in 'Rheged, Arise'; in any case, if the offence had been a serious one, Taliesin would hardly have drawn attention to it by mentioning it in this apology. The poet portrays himself as eager to bask in a patron's reflected glory. Urien is described as teyrned pop ieith: 'king of all nations', or, taking another meaning of iaith, 'king of all languages'. If Urien was indeed a master of many tongues, this would have made him a particularly attractive lord for a poet.

> The bravest leader
> I'll not throw over.
> I will seek Urien,
> To him will I sing.
> With him as protection
> I will be welcomed,

Placed in prime position,
With the best chieftain.

I couldn't care less
For paltry princes.   10
I won't go northwards
To be with those cowards.
I'm willing to pay –
I'd bet all my money;
I don't need to boast;
Urien won't cut me.

Llwyfenydd's rich lands
Are here in my hand.
Mine is their joy,
Mine is their bounty,   20
Mine the fine threads,
Mine, luxury goods,
The horns full of mead
And things I don't need.
King of all nations
I've heard mentioned:
Head of all kings
You turn into slaves.
They rail against you,
And have to evade you.   30

For a joke I poked fun
At him, the old man,
Though I loved no one more
Before I knew him.
Now I see fully
How much he gives me.
To God in Heaven
Alone will I yield him.
Your regal sons,
Most generous men,   40

The spears that they fling
At enemies sing.

When I'm old, out of breath,
Commanded by death
I will feel delight
Praising Urien aright.

Lament for Owain, Son of Urien

Recognized as one of the great works of early Welsh literature, this poem depicts the heroic Owain as a champion against the Angles, 'Lloegr's hosts'. There is no historical evidence to clarify whether Owain succeeded his father as king of Rheged or died before him; the latter is more likely, as the poem does not use any of the usual royal titles for him.

The soul of Owain, Urien's son –
May the Lord note its needs.
Rheged's prince hidden deep under heavy turf –
No shallow matter to sing his praise.
An underground cell for this glorious hero –
His spear in flight like the wings of dawn.
You'll find none to compare with him,
Prince of joy,[1] prince of brilliance,
His grip hard, harvesting enemies,
His spirit that of his father and forebears.   10
When Owain slaughtered Fflamddwyn,*
He might have done it in his sleep.
Sleep holds the wide horde of Lloegr's hosts,
Their dead eyes stare into the light.
And those who didn't flee far enough
Displayed more nerve than they needed.
Owain punished them, he showed no pity,
Like wolves laying waste to the flock.
A fine figure in bright-coloured battledress,
He gave horses freely to those who asked.   20
Though he stored up wealth like a miser,

---

*   *Fflamddwyn*: See note on p. 15.

He shared it freely for his soul's sake.
[The soul of Owain, Urien's son –
May the Lord note its needs.][2]

In the King of Heaven's Name, They Remember[1]

According to the later genealogies, Gwallawg – like Urien – was a fifth-generation descendant of the semi-mythical Coel Hen. In this poem his activities seem to be largely based in the Scottish Borders. He seems to have been an enemy, or at any rate not an ally, of the Rheged dynasty. As we have noted, if the 'reconciliation' poem for Urien ('To Pacify Urien', p. 22) does represent any narrative tradition – and even then we should remain cautious about speculative reconstructions of history from these texts – this poem and the one that follows it could be associated with a period when Taliesin is at the court of a rival monarch, an episode that would require some fence-mending. The poem lists Gwallawg's battles and portrays him as the ideal soldier. After line 31 the metre and subject of the poem change, with fighters other than Gwallawg being praised.

In the King of Heaven's name, they remember
To stand for him who sustains them.
His lordly lances are daunting
And bitter to kings against him.
He defended delightful Llan Lleenawg, *
He breaks the defence of Unhwch. †
They tell me lengthy memorial tales
Of events from Maw Hedge[2] and Eiddin. ‡
They'll offer opposition,

*   *Llan Lleenawg*: This may refer to a church or monastery dedicated to the memory of Gwallawg's father, who is named in the genealogies as 'Lleen-nawg'.
†   *Unhwch*: Unknown; probably the name of a person.
‡   *Eiddin*: Edinburgh ('Caeredin' in Welsh; also spelled elsewhere in the manuscript as 'Eidyn').

10   Clytwyn's* close-knit men.
            You could build a good-enough fleet,
            Bending spear shafts in the fighting's heat.
            The fire of his rage made wood of us all.
            Enemies were wiped out by Gwallawg.
            You're a better stockade than a pack of bears.
            War by the sea from the pulse of song,
            His fight was more than York's men could endure.
            War in Bretrwyn,† by conflagration,
            Royal is his great searing fire.
20   War, with the Cymry seizing forts.
            War's armies shaking Aeron.‡
            War, out of wanting the highlands and Aeron,
            Bringing sorrow to sons.
            War in Boar Woods, spears all day,
            You disdained the enemy.
            War near Gwyddawl against Mabon,§
            No survivors to tell what went on.
            War in Gwensteri, the Angles subdued
            By spearmen among the army;
30   War on Snow Moor at dawn.
            Skilful in battle was Gwrangawn.¶

            Since the first lines of my song
            In battle kings are blotted out.
            Men with plenty of cattle in stables –
            Haerarddur and Hyfeidd** and Gwallawg,
            Owain of Môn, in Maelgwn's line
            Make the rustlers lie flat down.

---

*   *Clytwyn*: Possibly a son of Brychan; he won a famous victory against the
       Picts. (See *PT*, p. 212.)
†   *Bretrwyn*: The Troon peninsula in Ayrshire.
‡   *Aeron*: See note on p. 17.
§   *Gwyddawl*: Location unknown. *Mabon*: A personal name, associated
       with one of the great mythical figures in early Welsh tales, but presum-
       ably referring here to a historical ruler.
¶   *Gwrangawn*: Another unknown figure.
**   *Haerarddur*: Unknown. *Hyfeidd*: Unknown; see also p.18.

In Pencoed are many daggers,
A massacre of corpses
And a scattering of crows.   40
In Britain and Eiddin he's known.
In Gafran and all around Brechin.*
If you missed Gwallawg, swift in his weapons,
Then you never saw a man.

---

*   *Gafran ... Brechin*: Gowrie and Brechin in Scotland.

12

In the King of Heaven's Name, the Hosts Are Keening

This is a further catalogue of Gwallawg's military successes,
but whereas 'In the King of Heaven's Name, They Remember'
(p. 27) places his activity around the Scottish Border, certain
place-names in this poem point to a location further south
and west than the Urien poems, between West Yorkshire and
the West Midlands. The mention of Dumbarton and of the
Northern kings with whom Gwallawg is fighting does, how-
ever, recall the more obviously Lowland Scottish references of
the preceding poem.

In the King of Heaven's name, the hosts are keening,
They sing laments, grieve for their dragon-lord
He who fought back the great crowd of foes,
The armies of Rhun, of Nudd and of Nwython.*1
For him I shall sing the bard's songs of the British.
A chief's troop of sage druids, with one voice,
May celebrate their king in trivial verses –
But I'll weave an intricate music for my master,
The lord, the one whom the whole land dreads:
10   I do him no disservice, he does me none.
Losing you's hard, lord; wealth is not lacking
For the king who never holds back his bounty –
But to the beholder, all kings are ill-fated
In life, for their wealth does not go to the grave.
Never sated with boasting of prowess in raids,

*   *Rhun . . . Nudd . . . Nwython*: Probably three members of the ruling
house of the kingdom of Nudd Hael (identified by some as Selkirkshire
or thereabouts). For Nudd Hael, see note on p. 21.

A harsher destiny faces them now.
The boastful crowds who are strangers to Britain,
Who vex beyond measure, are shamed – shame on them!
They are routed for good, they are doomed to disaster,
All condemned by a man of sound judgement,   20
His name known in Elmet* as giver of laws.
It's no unskilful man to whom tribute's paid,
No slave to his rage, stumbling reckless in pride.
Gwallawg is swift in battle's advance;
Gwallawg is slow to retreat from the battle.
No-one asks what the king will do next;
No-one denies him, refuses his will.

May he sell his fat cattle at summer's end.
He never prospers except by fair dealing.
Still fairer for you is this triumph's telling   30
By a licensed singer, skilled in rhetoric.
The king's battle-vigour is nourished by mead;
His splendour shines like the summer sun.
His glory is sung with most expert skill
By the wise man, the army's leader.
May the army's soothsayer be the face of summer,
The lively face of Lleenawg's son.
Round the rampart I sense its light,
I sense the heat, the heat's haze, the haze of heat.
While it shone, none escaped the stroke without shame   40
Of the fatal blade that the slaughterer wielded.[2]
Our force breaking through – no thief in the night!
Opponents like slaves – they're not slow to flee!
Ahead of the horses, shield bosses break through,
And from the cavalry, the cry for a kill!
Your warband loves you, their masterful lord:
Hostages are offered you of highest degree.

---

*   *Elmet*: A kingdom in West Yorkshire.

And from Caer Glud to Caer Caradawg,[*]
The border of Penprys,[†] O lord Gwallawg,
50   All the princes are at peace.

---

*   *Caer Glud*: Probably the same as 'Alt Clud', Dumbarton.
        Caer Caradawg: Possibly Caer Caradoc in Shropshire.
†   *Penprys*: Unknown; it could literally mean 'the edge of the forest'.

LEGENDARY POEMS

13

First Artful Command: Who Pronounced It?

*Each of the poems in this section would have been performed
by a poet pretending to be the Taliesin of Urien's time; they are,
therefore, inherently dramatic texts. The first seventy-nine lines
of this poem are supplied from* The Red Book of Hergest, *the
fourteenth-century manuscript, now housed in Jesus College,
Oxford, which contains the* Mabinogion *tales. The text then
returns to the* Llyvyr Taliessin. *The poem firmly links the cre-
ation narrative of Genesis with the creativity of the poet who
describes it and moves into passages of prophecy. The poet cul-
tivates an appearance of learning by incorporating bits of Latin
into the text, but it is often hard to make sense of them. Their
function is primarily to mystify.*

First artful command: who pronounced it?
What comes first, darkness or light?
Adam, where was he? Which day created?
As for the earth, on what was it set?
Those in orders don't like to think
*Est qui peccator** in their midst;
To parish priests, Heaven is lost.
A youth would rise early [. . .]
On three bells' peal [. . .]¹
Bastard Irish and Angles   10
Will begin battle.

Whence come night and day?
Why's an eagle grey?²
Why's it dark at night?

---

*   *Est qui peccator*: 'There is someone who is a sinner.'

How are finches green?
Whence the sea's seething?
It rises, nobody sees.
There are three springs
That rise on Mount Zion;[3]
20   And a fort's ruins
Lie under the ocean.*
You're asked, when you come,
What's the gatekeeper's name?[4]

Who heard the confession
Of Mary's openhanded son?
By what loving measure
Was Adam created?
What's the measure of hell?
How thick is the veil?[5]
30   How wide are Hell's jaws?
How many lost souls?
What forces over
Tree-tops, when bare?
Or how many evils
Hide in their boles?
And Lleu and Gwydion,†
Were they magicians?
Do librarians know
Whence night and floods flow?
40   How they are laid low?
Where does night flee from dawn
So it can't be seen?

---

*   *a fort . . . under the ocean*: Cantre'r Gwaelod, in Cardigan Bay, which was
      flooded due to the negligence of its gatekeeper.
†   *Lleu and Gwydion*: In the 'Fourth Branch' of *The Mabinogion*, the wiz-
      ard Gwydion (see also the note on p. 17) is the uncle of Lleu, whose
      mother curses him. Gwydion later collaborates with his uncle, Math, to
      conjure into existence Blodeuwedd, a woman made of flowers, as a wife
      for Lleu.

Pater noster ambulo
Gentis tonans in adiuuando
Sibilem signum
Rogantes fortium.[*][6]

To put matters right
Two artful ones[†] fought.
Of Hell's punishing fire
Speaks God's *rector*.   50
Those Welsh, now rejoicing,
Will meet Hell's fierce fire.
How then they will roar!
Souls put to the test
Among the accursed.
The Welsh will be first
Of the utterly lost.
There will be long moans,
Much blood will be shed.
And, to our sea of shame,   60
Wooden horses[‡] will come:
Angles invading.
Signs will be seen.
Revenge on the Saxon!
Our rumours will falter.
From [among] the leaders
Will emerge a master.
Against fierce Vikings
Fight the British *marini*.[§]
Our men shall divine,   70
Mow scattered men down
Round the river Severn.

---

[*]   *Pater noster ambulo* . . . : Garbled Latin. A best guess would be, 'Our
        Father, I am walking – you from whom the thunder comes for the help of
        a people praying for the whispered sign of the strong ones.'
[†]   *Two artful ones*: Probably Lleu and Gwydion.
[‡]   *Wooden horses*: Ships.
[§]   *marini*: Latin for 'sailors'.

Loot from monks in loose habits
[. . .]
While I live, I will pray,
Creator, Adonai:*
May the heathens be sent far away,[7]
Condigni cota† from the wall guard, *cornu
      amandur*‡.[8]
And I have been with artful men,
With old Math, with Gofannon,§

80   With Eufydd,¶ with Elestron,
Mighty men my companions.
A year in fort Gofannon,
I'm old, I'm new, I'm Gwion;**
I'm complete, I am renown.
In future, armed Irishmen
Will pillage ancient Britons,
[. . .] the revels of the drunken.
I'm a poet, don't rate lesser men.
I lead, I win the *ymryson.*††

90   He would scatter his seed widely,
But never be able to store it away,
A mumbling monk in refectory.
Poets obscure and haughty
Will lord it over mead crockery,
Singing untruthful poetry
But fail to secure a salary,

---

*   *Adonai*: One of the Hebrew names of God in the Old Testament.
†   *Condigni cota*: Probably *condigni quota*, 'as many as deserve it'.
‡   *cornu amandur*: Probably 'are driven away at horn's point'.
§   *Math . . . Gofannon*: Math, son of Mathonwy, is a powerful magician in
    The Mabinogion; see also the note on p. 59. Gofannon is his nephew.
¶   *Eufydd*: Perhaps the 'Iewydd' who appears elsewhere as a magician asso-
    ciated with Math.
** *Gwion*: In the *Ystoria Taliesin*, the servant who receives poetic inspir-
    ation from Ceridwen's cauldron and is later reborn as Taliesin; some-
    times spelled 'Gwiawn'. See Introduction, p. xxxii.
†† *ymryson*: A poetic competition, like that held by Lord Rhys ap Gruffudd
    in Cardigan in 1176. The prize was a chair.

No laws, no generosity,
And after that you'll see
Turmoil, the world topsy-turvy.
Don't ask for peace, it's gone away!   100

14

Poets' Corner

Typical of the Taliesin persona as it appears in many of these poems, this lively and witty piece sets the real poet apart from second-hand practitioners and builds up a series of vivid metaphors for the futility of their efforts. It fits within a tradition, much elaborated in later mediaeval Wales, of satirical contests between poets – classically described in the Ystoria Taliesin *(see Introduction, pp. xxxii–xxxiii). There is extensive but flexible use of rhyme in the original.*

A time of sifting · and of pondering
For British poets · with pointless verses.
My own great strength, · my own great standing
Give dismay · to the chorus of poets.
I'm a rod for the back · of the poet's efforts –
The poets' corner · where the amateurs sit,
Fifteen thousand of them, · struggling to get it straight!
I'm a seasoned singer · of splendid songs.
Sharp and hard, a shaman, · a sage, a skilled artisan,
A serpent, a seduction, · greedy for nourishment.
I'm not struck dumb, · I'm not going to stammer;
When singers sing · what they've learned by heart,
No miracle they work · will leave me beaten.
Contending with me, · their fate will be
Like dressing yourself · when you have no hands,
Like diving in lakes · when you know you can't swim.
The thundering flood · flows on without fear,
Its high tumult · a terror for homesteads.
But above the wave, · by God's plan, stands a rock.
The enemy's refuge · is dark and fearful –
But that rock is the High King, · the Judge of all,

The Lord who will make us · drunk with delight.
I'm a cell, I'm a splinter, · I'm a shape-shifter,
A library of song, · a sanctuary for the reader.
I love wooded slopes, · I love warm shelters,
I love real poets · who don't buy reputations.
I don't love those · who live by argument,
And mockers of poetry · will merit no wealth.
But now it's time · to take up arms –
Along with those skilled · in the arts of verse –   30
Against the cack-handed · fiddling of my foes
(O Shepherd of all pastures, · be my refuge and help!),
That sounds like marching · without feet to war,
Like planning to travel · without any feet,
Like gathering nuts · where there aren't any trees,
Like hunting for boars · in upland heather,
Like ordering a raid · without uttering a sound,
Like an army of soldiers · with no one in command,
Like feeding the needy · with scrapings of skin,
Like a badger rootling · in the ruins of houses,   40
Like catching the air · with a farmyard hook,
Like thistles that can't · be bothered to draw blood,
Like a light that you show · to a man who's blind,
Like a naked man · giving clothes away,
Like pouring out foam · along the seashore,
Like feeding fish · on a diet of milk,
Like covering a hall · with a roof of leaves,
Like using twigs · to trim your cudgel,
Like dissolving Dyfed · with a single word.[1]
I'm the bard of the hall, · I'm the lad in the chair,   50
I make poets · stutter when they speak.
And before I'm laid · in a comfortless grave,
May we all find room · in your house, Mary's Son.

15

Taliesin's Sweetnesses

This charming catalogue of Taliesin's favourite aspects of cre-
ation is one of the few poems that directly introduces the poet's
name in its title. Its linguistic characteristics suggest that the
text in its present form comes from the twelfth or thirteenth
century.[1] The couplets range from descriptions of the blessings
of repentance to observations on the appeal of jewellery to
young girls and the joys of gardening.

Sweet is my virtue when I repent sin;
Sweet, too, is God, who is my salvation.

Sweet is a feast not spoiled by concerns;
Sweet, too, a feast round the drinking horns.

Sweet is Nudd,*[2] lord fierce as a wolf;
Sweet, too, is a generous, prominent man.

Sweet are the berries at harvest time;
Sweet, also, is wheat on the stem.

Sweet is the sun on clouds in the sky;
Sweet, too, is light on the evening's brow.

Sweet is a thick-maned stallion in a herd;
Sweet, too, is the warp of a spider's web.

Sweet is desire and a silver chain;
Sweet, also, to a maid is a ring.

*   *Nudd*: See note on p. 21.

Sweet are ospreys on shore at high tide;
Sweet, too, is watching the seagulls play.

Sweet is a stallion and a gold-painted shield;
Sweet, too, is a fine man holding a breach.*

Sweet is Doctor Einion to many;†3
Sweet, too, a skilful, generous musician.   20

Sweet for the cuckoo and nightingale's May;
Sweet, too, is when the weather grows finer.

Sweet are witnesses to a proper wedding;
Sweet is the tip for a poet's singing.

Sweet the intention to do a priest's penance;
Sweet, too, are bread and wine at the altar.

Sweet is the upper-hall mead for the singer;
Sweet, too, a crowd gathered round a soldier.

Sweet is a cleric in church if he's faithful;
Sweet, too, is a chieftain installed in his hall.   30

Sweet are God's followers when they lead;
Sweet, too, was the time of Paradise.

Sweet is the moon that shines on the world;
Sweet, too, is to encounter the good.

Sweet is the summer, the livelong day;
Sweet, too, is visiting the one I love.

---

*   *holding a breach*: Filling the gap in a defence – whether the result of a
broken rampart or a fallen comrade in the line.
†   *Doctor Einion*: Either a reference to the way a smith's anvil (*eynawn*)
'heals' weapons, or an unknown person's name.

Sweet are fruit blossoms high in a tree;
Sweet, too, is to reconcile with the Creator.

Sweet in the wild is a doe or fawn;
40   Sweet too is a slim steed lathered with foam.

Sweet is the garden when leeks are thriving;
Sweet, also, is field mustard sprouting.

Sweet is a horse in its leather halter;
Sweet, too, it is to be with a king.

Sweet is the man who doesn't shirk harm;
Sweet, too, is Welsh, whenever well-spoken.

Sweet is heather when it blossoms purple;
Sweet, too, is a sea marsh for cattle.

Sweet is a calf at suckling time;
50   Sweet, too, is riding a horse frothing foam.

And I have a sweet thing that's far from the worst:
Sweet mead, a reward from the horn at a feast.

Sweet are the fish in the shining lake;
Sweet, too, is water's play of light and dark.

Sweet is the word that the Trinity speaks;
Sweet, too, is heart-felt penance for sin.

Sweetest of all sweet things I can say:
Reconciling with God on Judgement Day.

16

An Unfriendly Crowd

Like 'Poets' Corner' (p. 40), this is an exercise in the mode of satirical contest, but on a very much extended scale, laying claim to all kinds of esoteric knowledge. There are elements here of what we could call, not very accurately, the 'transmigration' theme – the poet having lived many lives and experienced other worlds. Reference to Prince Elffin shows that the Taliesin tradition has already been transferred to the Welsh context from that of the Old North. The final sequence of images, describing the journey of grain from the field to the malthouse, is widely paralleled in folklore (as in the English folksong, 'John Barley corn'). The swallowing of the grain by the 'red-clawed hen' must refer to grain being malted in the fiery kiln; but it also echoes the episode in the Ystoria Taliesin *in which the young Gwion is swallowed by the witch Ceridwen and subsequently reborn from her. Did the story originate in a literal reading of this metaphor? Or was there already a folktale which gave an added piquancy to the metaphor in this context?*

A poet? Here's one to hand,[1]
But he'll sing only what I've sung already.
Let him start singing when the wise man
Finishes, falls silent in his place.
The generous patron who says no to me
Gets nothing from me he can give in turn.
But through the speaking of Taliesin
Comes nourishment like heavenly manna.
When Cian's* words were ended,

---

* *Cian*: Mentioned in the *historia Brittonum* as a poetic contemporary of Talhaearn, Taliesin, Aneirin and Blwchfardd (see Introduction, p. xix).

10 Came peace, protection on all sides.
    Till death arrives, mystery attends
    On what Afagddu* announces:
    With skill he marshalled
    His sayings in good order.
    And Gwion† ups and says:
    'There is one coming from the depths,
    To bring the dead to life –
    For all that he's not rich.'2
    They all would craft their cauldrons
20 To boil when no fire was lit;
    They would weave their word-knots
    World without end.
    Passion it is that brings forth
    Song from the deep-meditating sage.
    And as for this unfriendly crowd,
    What lore is it *they* know?
    So great a hoard of the people's poetry
    Has been laid upon your tongues,
    Why not declaim your declamations,
30 Pouring benediction over sparkling liquor?
    When you've done with your doggerel,
    I shall come with a real song –
    About one from the depths who took on [our]
        flesh:
    A conqueror has come,
    One of creation's three judges‡
    [. . .]
    For sixty full years
    I lived in solitude,3
    In the waters that girdle the earth,
    In all the lands of this world;

*   *Afagddu*: Either Ceridwen's son or Taliesin's; see the introduction to
    'Ceridwen's Prize Song' on p. 76.
†   *Gwion*: See note on p. 38.
‡   *creation's three judges*: Probably the three Persons of the Trinity (one of
    whom has taken on flesh).

A hundred servants were there   40
To wait on me in splendour –
They were born with the yew-tree,
They will go when it falls,[4]
With the army's song,
The song of prophecy.
Lladon ferch Liant*
Had little desire
For gold or for silver.
What being let flow
The innocent lad's blood?[5]   50
They speak of one only,
They praise a great one.
And I am Taliesin:
I sing of one true-born,
My praise of Prince Elffin†[6]
Will endure till the Last Day –
It drew for reward
A due sum of gold.
When that payment was welcomed
There was no love for treason,   60
But now there's no thirst
For our song – a grave failing!
Those who hail me as brother –
Beside me they know nothing.
I'm the sage, the chief poet.
The wise man instructs
About battle and hunting,
And the poet's deep tangles
And the men skilled in song.

---

*   *Lladon ferch Liant*: Literally, 'Liquid, daughter of Ocean/Flood'; no other references are known.

†   *Prince Elffin*: In the *Ystoria*, the son of Gwyddno Garanhir, ruler of Cantre'r Gwaelod, the Cardigan Bay area supposedly inundated in a great flood.

70 So to God let us go,
Who is (says Talhaearn*)
The judge of the world's worth,
Who judged all the excellencies
Of poetry's passion.
In miracles he granted
Awen past measure:
There are seven score metres
That are given by *awen*,
Eight score [. . .]
80 [. . .] also in one.
In the underworld he ordered them,
In the underworld shaped them,
Deep underground,
In the air far above.
There is someone who knows –
Which sorrow it is
That is better than joy.
I know all the metres
Of *awen* in full flood,
90 Know what's owed to a poet,
Know of well-omened days,
Of joyful desire,
And the castle's customs,
Of men like kings
And how long their dwellings stand.
[. . .] they become like [. . .]
Through the saving grace
Of the exalted wise bard.

The high vault's wind –
100 How does it spread abroad?
Why's the mind full of life,
Why so full of beauty?

* *Talhaearn*: One of the poets mentioned in the *historia Brittonum*; see
Introduction, p. xix and the note on p. 45.

Why are men so courageous?
How was Heaven's arc made
And the sun set in place?
How was earth roofed over?
Earth's roof, what's its size?
From where are streams drawn,
The streams, where drawn from?
Why is the earth green,   110
The earth, why green?
Who made poems spring up,
Poems, who called them up?
And who's set out the tale?
It is told in books –
How many the winds, the waters,
How many the waters, the winds,
How many rivers run by,
How many the rivers,
The earth, how wide,   120
How thick its measure.
I know the sword's clamour
Round the blood-streaked hero,
I know all the levels
Between Heaven and earth –
Why the hollow echoes,
Why death comes suddenly,
Why silver glitters
And the brook runs dark,
Why breath is black   130
And the liver's full of blood,
Why the buck has horns,
Why a woman's hot with lust,
Why milk is white
And holly green,
Why the young goat's always bearded,
No matter where you are;
[. . .]⁷
Why cow-parsley's hollow-stemmed,

140   Why the puppy staggers like a drunk,
       Why the mallet strikes flat,
       Why the roebuck is dappled,
       Why salt is salty
       And beer is bitter;
       Why the alder's streaked blood-red
       And the linnet is green
       And rosehips are crimson –
       And the woman who gathered them;
       Where the night falls from,
150   What changes are shaped
       In the golden sea.
       No one knows why
       The sun's breast blushes,
       The colour so dazzling;
       Nor the fall of the famous,
       What the harpstring mourns for,
       What the cuckoo's song laments,
       How its sound is sustained;
       What brings the siege-tents
160   Of Geraint to Garmon;*
       What makes a jewel
       From the hardness of stones;
       Why meadowsweet smells fragrant,
       Why the raven's wing shimmers.
       [It is Talhaearn who
       Is greatest of sages][8]
       What tempest shakes trees
       In the Last Day's Deluge?
       I know good and evil
170   Where [. . .][9]
       When the smoke is scattered
       In a great drift;
       Who shaped the world's vessel,

---

*   *Geraint*: Possibly Geraint, son of Erbin, a heroic figure of the sixth
       century, but the name is not uncommon. *Garmon*: Possibly Wexford in
       Ireland.

Brought dawn to perfection;
What they used to preach –
Elijah and Enoch.[10]
The cuckoos of summer –
I know them in winter.
The *awen* of my song
I draw up from the depths.   180
The world-circling river –
I know its great power:
I know how it ebbs,
I know how it flows,
I know how it runs on
And how it falls back.
I know all the life
That lives under the sea,
I know the true nature
Of each in its kind,   190
How many instants a day has,
How many days in the year,
How many shafts fall in battle
And drops fall in rain.
The untroubled singer
Shares a radiant song.
I know what's to be known
Of Gwydion's trees on the march,[11]
Why the waters flooded,
Overwhelming Pharaoh's people;   200
Who sweeps away foes
In the thunder of their powers;
What's the structure of the stair
By which we're raised to Heaven;
Who was the roofbeam in the vault
That stretched from earth to sky;
How many the fingers to form me,
The hand, the hollow to hold me;
What the two great words are
That overflow the cauldron,[12]   210

Why the sea rages drunkenly,
Why fishes are black,
Their flesh fed by sea-life;
Why the stag is wise,
Why the fish is scaly,
Why white swans have black feet,
Why no potent sharp spear
Can make Heaven's host yield;
What the four points of earth are
Whose limits are unknown,
What swine or wandering stag [. . .]
So, most learned bard, tell me –
A man so pre-eminent! –
Where are the mist's bones
And the wind's twin waterfalls?

What I sing is declaimed
In Hebrew, in Greek,
In Greek and in Hebrew,[13]
Lauda tu, laudate Jesum.*

A second time my shape shifted
And I was a blue salmon,
A hound and a stag,
A roebuck on the mountain,
A clod and a spade
And an axe in the hand,
An auger gripped in tongs,
For a year and a half;
A speckled white cockerel
For the hens in Eidyn,†
A stallion at stud,
A ramping bull –
A sheaf stacked for milling,

---

*   *Lauda tu, laudate Jesum*: 'One and all, praise Jesus.'
†   *Eidyn*: Edinburgh.

Meal ground for farmers.
I was a grain in the sieve,
Grain that grew on the hill,
I am harvested, stored,
Sent off to the kiln,
And scattered by hand,
Ready for roasting.
Then a hen took me in,   250
Red-clawed, my crested foe,*
And for nine nights I rested
At peace in her womb.
When I had matured
I was drink for the king.
I was dead and alive.
A seizure shot through me,
I stood on my lees:
Poured off, I was perfect –
A cup to encourage,   260
Stirred up by the red claws.

They speak of one only,
They praise one great one.
And I am Taliesin,
I sing of one true-born.
My praise of Prince Elffin
Will endure till the Last Day.

---

*   *Red-clawed . . . foe*: If this section is a metaphorical description of brew-
ing beer, the flames of the brewing kiln.

The Battle of the Trees[1]

*This poem is among the longest and most complex of the
Taliesin corpus. Its 'action' consists of a number of different
passages. It describes how Taliesin has moved through different
forms in the created world; it narrates the mysterious 'Battle of
the Trees'; it gives Taliesin's own account of his creation at the
hands of wizards, and his boasting about his prowess in war; it
describes the Harrowing of Hell; and it concludes with some-
thing like a prayer for prophetic inspiration. What unites them
is the drama of Taliesin as a poet. The 'spears' of his lines are
weapons and the actions of his persona are inseparable from
his ability to make poetic metaphors. The central sequence in
the poem, the war fought between various trees and shrubs,
has attracted widely diverse interpretations. They may be
images for individual soldiers in battle, or the whole section
may depend on long-lost legendary conventions or techniques
for memorizing lists of names. The idea that the trees represent
letters of the ancient Irish or British alphabet was floated by
Iolo Morganwg and elaborately developed by Robert Graves,[2]
but is now generally agreed to be fanciful.*

> I was in many forms
> Before my release:
> I was a slim enchanted sword,
> I believe in its play.
> I was a drop in air,
> The sparkling of stars,
> A word inscribed,
> A book in priest's hands,
> A lantern shining
> For a year and a half.

A bridge for crossing
Over threescore *abers*.*
I was path, I was eagle,
I was a coracle at sea.
I was bubbles in beer,
I was a raindrop in a shower.
I was a sword in the hand;
I was a shield in battle.
I was a harp string,
Enchanted nine years   20
In water, foaming.
I was tinder in fire,
I was a forest ablaze.
Not I who's not singing,[3]
Which I did since my youth,
Sang when trees went to war;
Before Britain's ruler.
I lashed white horses faster
In the rich fleet's wake;
Stabbed the many-scaled monster   30
With its hundred heads
And a crowd of souls captive
At the root of its tongue;
And another battalion
At the back of each neck.[4]
That black forked toad
Of a hundred claws;
That snake, speckled, crested,
In whose flesh are tortured
A hundred souls for their sins.   40

I was in Caer Nefenhir†
When grass and wood went to war.
Poets were singing,

*   *abers*: Estuaries.
†   *Caer Nefenhir*: Thought to be in Galloway, Scotland.

Soldiers attacking.
A new dawn for the Britons
Conjured by Gwydion.*
He called upon Heaven,
On the Christ of all powers,
That he might deliver them,
Their Lord who had made them.
And God gave him answer:
'Through language, skilled man,
Make majestic trees seem
Like a hundred-strong army,
Resisting the vigorous,
Spendthrift warlord.'

When the trees were enchanted –
So our hopes were raised[5] –
They mowed soldiers down
With their mighty boughs.
They fell upon armies
For thirty days' battle.
A woman lamenting:
Mourning is budding.
At the head, first mother;[6]
There was sleepless spoil-hunger.
But it caused us no harm –
Blood up to our thighs.
Worst of three Commotions
That came on the world –
The one that unfolded
Because of the Deluge:
Then Christ's crucifixion,
Then Judgement to come.
First came the Alder,[7]
Which struck the first blow.

*   *Gwydion*: See the note on p. 36.

Willow and Rowan
Came late to the muster.
The spiny Blackthorn
Was hungry for bloodshed.   80
Skillful, the Medlar
Made ready for battle.
Rosewood advanced
On a raging army.
The Bramble came forth,
Raising no rampart
To save his own life.
Privet, Honeysuckle,
Ivy – despite seeming soft –
Were fierce in the fight.   90
The Cherry was wary.
Birch, although noble,
Was slow to get dressed,
Not from being spineless
But due to its greatness.
Golden Rod was resolved –
Foreigners by sea.[8]
The Pine was the best,
Won the chair[9] in the contest.
Ash wrought great deeds   100
In the presence of princes.
Despite its great wealth
Elm budged not an inch –
Raining down blows
On centre, flank, rear.
Hazel gauged weapons
For the tumult of war.
Dogwood, be blessed,
Battle's bull, lord of all.
Morawc and Moryt[*][10] [. . .]   110

---

*   *Morawc and Moryt*: Obscure; possibly personal names, possibly mis-
copied. See endnote.

Beech grew prolific;
Though Holly turned pale
It was brave in battle.
Infamous Hawthorn
Gave festering wounds.
Though slashed at, the Vine
Was cut down in the fray.
Bracken grew rampant;
But broom, at the head,
120   Was trampled in mud.
Though unlucky, Gorse
Still joined in the force.
A spell brought Heather
To join, famous fighter.
[. . .] in pursuit.
Oak's passionate shout
Made earth and sky shake.
Brave pillager, Woad,
Was named in the record.
130   Even the splintered tree[11]
Created panic.
Repulsing, it repelled,
And stabbed others.
At force Pear excelled
On the battlefield –
A terrifying wave
Of sweet-scented Clover.[12]
Though shy, the Chestnut[13]
Fought alongside bold trees.

140   Just as jet is black,
And a mountain's round,
And the stag is armed,
And the great seas are swift;[14]
So, since the battle-cry,
The Birch put out leaves for us,
Its vigour transformed us;

The Oak's buds snared us
With Maelderw's poem.[*][15]
As sea breaks on rocks, laughing,
So is a lord who ignores the throng.   150

Neither of mother
Nor of father was I formed;[16]
My creation was created
Out of nine elements:[17]
From fruit, out of fruits,
From the fruit of God's beginning;
From Primroses and gossiping flowers;
From wood and trees' pollen;
From earth, from the soil
Was I formed;   160
From Nettle flowers,
From the ninth wave's water.
I was conjured by Math[†][18] –
Before I was gifted.
I was conjured by Gwydion,
Great magician of Britain;
By Eurwys, by Euron,
By Euron, by Modron,[‡][19]
By five enchanters –
The foster parents –   170
When I was brought up.
I was conjured by a king[§]
From the burning wastes.

*   *Maelderw's poem*: An elegy which appears in other thirteenth-century sources, dating perhaps from the tenth or eleventh century. It refers to its hero as a 'blameless oak-tree'.
†   *Math*: The magician who gives his name to the tale 'Math, son of Mathonwy', the 'Fourth Branch' of the Mabinogi; where, along with his nephew Gwydion, he creates a woman out of flowers as a wife for Gwydion's nephew, Lleu Llaw Gyffes.
‡   *Eurwys ... Euron ... Modron*: All unknown, though for Euron; see also the note on p. 77.
§   *a king*: God.

I was conjured by the wisdom
Of sages before the world,
Before I had being,
Before the world began.
Fair poet of rare talents,
In praise, I possess
180   That which the tongue utters.
I played in the light,
Slept wrapped in purple.
I was in the citadel
With Dylan, Son of the Sea,*
My bed deep within,
Between kings' knees.
My two eager spears,
From Heaven they came,
From Annwfn's streams,
190   They come, battle-ready.
Four score hundred men
I pierced, for all their greed.
They're no older, no younger
Than me in their passions.
A hundred men's ardour they had;[20]
But I had nine hundred's.
My speckled sword
Brings me fame for blood.
[. . .] from God, from the grave he lay in.[21]
200   The gentle one, killed by the boar.
He made, he remade,
He made the nations.
Shining his name, strong of hand,
He commanded a crowd;
They scattered, in showers
Of sparks from above.
I was a speckled snake on a hill,
I was a viper in a lake,

*   Dylan, Son of the Sea: See p. 107.

I was a sickle in Dog-heads'*[22] hands.
I was a hunting lance.   210
My vestment and chalice,
I prepare them well,
And fourscore clouds of incense
Waft over all,
Worth fifty haunches
And my knife to cut them,
Six yellow horses;[23]
And, a hundred times better,
My horse, Melyngan,†
Swift as a seagull.   220
And me, I'm not feeble
Between sea and shore –
I myself massacre
Nine hundred prime soldiers.
My round shield is ruby,
My shield-ring is gold.
Not born in the breach [. . .]
And now no-one visits,
Except for Goronwy
From the meadows of Edrywy.   230
Long and thin are my fingers:
Long the time since I herded.
I took shape as a hero,
Before I was a scholar.
I transformed, I circled,
Slept on a hundred islands,
Stayed in a hundred forts.
Sages, learned men,
Prophesy Arthur's coming!
There is that which was before,   240
They perceived things that had been:
And One who came to be,

*   *Dog-heads*: The mythical Cynocephali sometimes depicted in medieval
     maps.
†   *Melyngan*: 'Pale yellow'.

Because of the Deluge story,
And Christ's crucifixion,
The Day of Judgement to come.
Thus, like a jewel in gold,
I myself am resplendent;
And my spirits leap up
At what Virgil foretold.[24]

18

Young Taliesin's Works

This poem is a milder example of the convention of challenging and obscure questions which we have already seen in 'Poets' Corner' (p. 40); here the purpose seems to be to inculcate humility in both the poet and his hearers (including the clergy) rather than to stress his superior wisdom. The reference to Ceridwen again connects with the Ystoria *tradition; and the mention of Dylan (see 'Elegy for Dylan, Son of the Sea', p. 107) shows knowledge of something like the* Mabinogion *narratives.*

I beg my Lord,
Let me trace *awen*'s tale –
What birthed the thirst for it
Before Ceridwen's day,
The first moment in the world
When the lack of it was felt.
Monks with your book-learning,
Why will you not tell me?
Why do you not truss me up
Now your hunt for me is over?   10
What draws smoke skyward?
What brought evil to birth?
What well pours out radiance
Above darkness's canopy?
Whence came the bright grain-stalks,
Whence the moonlit night,
While another one's too dark to see
(Out in the open) so much as your shield?
Why the great clamour
As waves pound the shore   20
In vengeance for Dylan,

Reaching out towards us?
Why's a stone so heavy,
A thorn so sharp?
Do you know which is better –
Its trunk or its tip?[1]
What can [best] put barriers
Between a man and the cold?
Whose death is better –
A young man or an old?
Do you know what you are
When you're fast asleep –
Body or soul,
Or shining angel?
Now, skilful singer,
Why do you not tell me?
Do you know where
Night waits out the daytime?
Do you know the tally
Of leaves on the trees?
What will lift up the mountains
Before the world ends?
What shores up the wall
Of the earth, day by day?
And the soul that we weep for –
Who's seen it, who knows it?
When I read books, I'm amazed
That they have no clear knowledge
Of where the soul shelters,
Or the shape of its members,
Of which region gives rise
To the great wind and torrent
That wrestle so wondrously
Threatening the sinner.
I wonder as I sing
Whence came the sweet lees,
What makes the derangement
Of mead and of bragget.

What could fix [all] their fates
Except God in Trinity?   60
Why should I extol
Any other but You?
Who made the penny
From a circle of silver?
Whence comes the quick sea,
As loud as a chariot?
Death lies under all,
Dealt out in every land;
Death stands over our heads,
A shroud spread wide –   70
But above its canopy stands Heaven.
[There] a man is old at his birth
And grows younger each day.
A matter for anxiety –
This world's prosperity:
One day, great riches –
Then our lives cut short: why?
It will make for great sorrow,
That long stay in the grave.
May the One who created us   80
(From the land above all),
Our God, be the one
Who at last brings us home to Himself.

19

I Am the Vigour

This is a set-piece poem which, according to the Llyvyr Taliessin *scribe, was worth twenty-four points to the apprentice poet. The reckoning of poems by points in this way is mentioned in connection with a number of other poems in the manuscript (we have noted these in the introductions to the relevant pieces). They occur in only one section of the manuscript. Although there are similar statements of the 'points' value of poems in other early Welsh poetic texts, we do not know exactly what this meant; it may have been a way of reckoning how an apprentice was rated on his learning by heart of certain pieces, or a scale for assessing actual performance. At the foot of this page in the manuscript the title 'Taliesin's Prize Song' has been added by the scribe, but that title would fit the following poem (in both the manuscript sequence and our own) far better. In the first section, Taliesin boasts that his eloquence originates in the energy of praising God. He outlines his particular kind of sagacity by asking questions which link various parts of creation. He draws his examples from, among others, the worlds of medicine, brewing and trade.*

I am the vigour
Of the Lord God's praise.
In a contest of poems
Made of wise poets' words.
Splendid the sage's breast
When he responds.
To where does *awen* flow
Each day at midnight?
Prattling, brash poets –
Their poems displease me.

In battle at Ystrad,*
Great guile arises.
I'm not mute of song:
I challenge the locals,
I quicken the dull,
I slow down the fool,
I waken the dumb,
Fierce, powerful lord.
My song isn't null.
I address battling bards,   20
Who, like Judas, take coins,
Deserve the deep sea.[1]

Who embraced the despised,
Made the crooked straight?
From where does dew spring?
And liquor from wheat?
And liquid from bees?
And gum and resin?
And balm from abroad?
Colour from orpine?[2]   30
A veil's fine silver?
And ruby and berries?
And the waves' foam?
What strengthens a spring?
Watercress boiling.[3]
What connects moisture,
The starter of beer,†
And the moon's drawing power,
With stagnant water?
The sense of wise men   40
With the many-mooned sage?
Or tipsy trees leaning

---

*   *Ystrad*: A very common component in place names, meaning 'strand' or
    'valley floor'. There is no indication of a more precise location.
†   *The starter of beer*: The mixing of water and yeast which starts the fer-
    mentation process.

Into sky's wind, blowing,
With ale, a sea-inlet,
And overseas goods,[4]
A glass vessel,
In a pilgrim's hand,
With pepper and pitch?
The honoured Eucharist
With a doctor's herbs,
His lore and his healing spoon?
Poets with flowers
And plaited hedges,
With primroses, crushed leaves,
And the tops of trees?
And malt and riches
With frequent pledges?
And wine in glasses,
Come from Rome to Rossett,*
And deep, sweet water,
With God's blessed design?

It is the Redeemer's Tree.
Fruitful, it will flourish.
But some He will boil,
Hung on five beams.[5]
By Gwion's river,[6]
With fine fair weather,
And honey and clover,
And mead horns for drinkers –
Sweet to the leader
Are his sages' gifts.

---

* *Rossett*: Perhaps the village near Wrexham in the Welsh county of Clwyd.

20

I Make My Plea to God

As already noted, the manuscript refers to a poem under the title of Kadeir Taliesin *('Taliesin's Prize Song') and appears to identify it as 'I Am the Vigour' (p. 66). The present poem introduces a series of poems with* kadeir *in the titles, which we have translated as 'Prize Song', and the present poem may well in fact be 'Taliesin's Prize Song'. It refers clearly to the stories about Taliesin's adventures at the North Welsh court of Maelgwn Gwynedd which developed in the late Middle Ages (Introduction, pp. xxxii–xxxiii), though it also mentions Urien, as if in a polite nod to the origins of the Taliesin tradition in the Old North. Several of the* Mabinogion *stories are alluded to, as well as 'The Battle of the Trees' (p. 54); and the evocation of the Otherworld fortress is close to the language of* Preideu Annwfn, *'The Spoils of Annwfn' (p. 98), later in the collection.*

I make my plea to God, Lord of all peoples,
Ruler of Heaven's armies – an open plea for what I wish.
I sang at a feast over joyless liquor,
I sang before Llyr's sons in Aber Henfelen.*
I saw battle's brutality, the grief, the mourning;
There were blades shining on the fine spearheads.
I sang for a glorious master on Severnside meadows,
For Brochfael of Powys,† beloved of my *awen*.
I sang in the shield-wall at dawn before Urien –
Till the grass at our feet was running with blood –   10

---

*   *Llyr's sons*: In *The Mabinogion*, Manawydan and Brân or Bendigeidfran. *Aber Henfelen*: Normally the Bristol Channel.

†   *Brochfael*: The father of Cynan Garwyn; see p. 3. Brochfael is a shadowy figure of the mid-sixth century, but one whose name is familiar in mediaeval poetry.

My poetry's patron – songs from Ceridwen's cauldron.
My tongue ran freely, a store of inspiration –
And that inspired voice, my God formed it
Just as he made milk, dew and hazelnuts.
Let us hold in our minds, before confession in the corner,
That death, without doubt, draws nearer and nearer.
And dark days will fall on the fields of Enlli*
When ships are sent forth on the sea's flood.
So let us cry out to the Lord who made us
20   To guard us from the wrath of swarming armies.
While Môn has the name of a place of fair fields,
Good fortune will fall on the Saxon lords' rampage.[1]
I came to Deganwy to fight my corner
With Maelgwn, supreme in royal might.
Before all the courtiers I won my lord's freedom –
Elffin, prince of the finest of subjects.[2]
I have three songs of consistent harmony –
Poets will be singing them till Judgement Day.
In the Battle of the Trees, I was with Lleu and Gwydion,†
30   When they conjured with lichen and irises.
I was there with Brân [when he fought] in Ireland,[3]
And I saw the slaughter of strong-thighed men.[4]
I heard when furious warriors locked arms
In combat with the cunning devils of Ireland.
From Penwith Head[5] as far as Loch Ryan,
The Cymry are of one mind, men of great mettle.
The hope of the Cymry labouring in battle
Is that three warlike races of truest worth –
Goidels‡ and Britons, and Romans too –
40   Will make war and turn things upside down.
And at Prydein's frontier,[6] with its fine dwellings,
I sang before princes over the mead-cups.
The nobles would give me the first draught of liquor,
Since I'm a great sage, overflowing with gifts.

*   *Enlli*: Bardsey Island.
†   *Lleu and Gwydion*: See the note on p. 36.
‡   *Goidels*: Irish.

In Caer Siddi* my song echoes tunefully,
Whose dwellers are untouched by age or sickness
(As Manawydan and Pryderi know well[7]).
In their presence three organs play,
And the springs of the sea wash round its towers;[8]
And the fruitful fountain that rises above it,   50
Whose waters are sweeter than white wine.
And now that my prayer is over, highest of Kings,
Before I lie in the earth, let us make a covenant.

---

* *Caer Siddi*: Perhaps a borrowing from the Irish, meaning 'the dwelling of
the gods / supernatural beings'; see also 'The Spoils of Annwfn' (p. 98).

21

Teyrnon's Prize Song[1]

The name 'Teyrnon' is a combination of teyrn *('lord') and the suffix* -on, *which acts as an intensifier, giving 'great king'. It could refer to Arthur as the model of good leaders, but it may also refer to another individual bearing the name 'Teyrnon' (there is a character with this name in* The Mabinogion*). This poem may have originally been part of some version of the Taliesin legend of the* Ystoria Taliesin. *In that tale, having been flung into the sea by Ceridwen, Gwion, originally Ceridwen's servant, is saved by Elffin, son of King Gwyddno, and renamed Taliesin. In turn, this legendary Taliesin grows into a uniquely skilful poet, who eventually rescues Elffin from imprisonment at the hands of Maelgwn Gwynedd by means of his dramatic victory in a bardic contest. 'Teyrnon's Prize Song' might be an example of a poem that the fictional Taliesin could have written for such a poetic joust. The opening line announces that this is a 'clear' song, but the references in it are largely obscure to scholars. The poem begins by recounting the theft of horses from Cawrnur (the name suggests a giant,* cawr *in Welsh) by Aladur, whose name goes back to that of a Roman Britsh deity, Mars Alator.[2] It then moves on to political prophecy, to a list of admirable qualities in a ruler and poet and, finally, to praise of Arthur as an ideal ruler, couched in prophetic terms. The manuscript assigns* 300 *'points' for the poem (see p. 66).*

Here's a clear poem,
Overspilling with *awen*,
About a brave, strong man
From the line of Aladur.
Is he famous, a wise one?

Or the ruler of Rheon,[*3]
Or a royal leader,
Who honours Scripture,
With his red armour,
His attack on a rampart;   10
The subject of skilful song
Among his royal war band.
He took from Cawrnur[†]
Pale saddled horses;
From the elder, Teyrnon,
The fattener, Heilyn.[‡4]
The sage's third deep song
Was sung to bless Arthur.
So, Arthur is blessed –
In harmonious song –   20
A rampart in battle,
Trampling nine men at once.
Who were the three men
Who guarded the country?
The three knowing men
Who guarded the sign,
Who come, when wanted,
Before their Lord?

Fine is the rampart's strength,
Fine is the presence of a great man,   30
Fine's a drink horn passing round.
Noble are cattle at noon,
Noble is truth when it shines,
More noble when it speaks.
Nobly it came from the cauldron,
From the Trinity's *awen*.
I have been a torqued lord,

---

[*] *Rheon*: Probably the Loch Ryan of 'I Make My Plea to God' (p. 70).
[†] *Cawrnur*: Identity unknown; see also p. 112.
[‡] *Heilyn*: Literally 'provider', but here perhaps a person's name.

Drinking horn in hand.
No poet deserves a prize
40   Who doesn't preserve my words,
My brilliant, prize-winning song –
My fluent, bold *awen*.

What are the three forts' names
Between high and low water?[5]
Only the passionate know
Their master's nature.
There are four fortresses
In the haven of Britain –
Its lords are active.
50   What may not be will never be,
Will never be, since it may not be.[6]
But fleets there will be:
Waves will break over stones,
Land conquered by the sea.
[There will be] no slope nor valley,
No hill nor hollow,
Nor shelter when it freezes
And the wind grows angry.
The prize-song for Teyrnon –
60   The skilful poet will remember.
Ygno* will be sought,
Cedic[†] will be sought –
The missing protectors.
I become angry
At the death of a leader
With a fiery nature,

* *Ygno*: Unknown.
† *Cedic*: This name appears in a couple of Welsh royal genealogies: in one he is a descendant of Cunedda (see p. 108), and in the other, the grand-father of Nudd Hael (see p. 21), but there is no evidence for a more exact identification.

And breastplate of Lleon.*
A ruler shall rise
For the many brave soldiers.
Ale's foam dies down –
Fleeting by nature –
Fighting lasts a short time
On the wild border.
The foreign peoples
Are an untamed flood,
Voyaging by sea.
Saracens' offspring,
Those pagans from Hell,
Let us free Elffin!

---

*   *Lleon*: A proper name obviously connected with *leon*, 'lion', and conventionally used to evoke bravery.

22

Ceridwen's Prize Song

This is a puzzling poem: it is not clear who the speaker is supposed to be. The title suggests it should be Ceridwen herself, as does the line about 'My song, my cauldron, my metres', since Ceridwen appears in some twelfth- and thirteenth-century texts either as the source of inspiration or as the guardian of a cauldron of inspiration (the obscure word ogyrfen, *used here and in poems* 16, 20 *and* 21, *appears to refer to some aspect of* awen, *poetic inspiration). But the voice is recognizably the voice we associate with the persona of 'Taliesin' himself in other poems. Possibly the reference to the cauldron led the scribe to think that Ceridwen was the speaker, and to substitute the name of Afagddu, Ceridwen's son, for that of Afaon, son of Taliesin. The poet makes it plain that he is familiar with the* Mabinogion *narratives of Math, Gwydion and Lleu, but also, less predictably, mentions the scholarly work of the Venerable Bede. The metrical patterns are diverse and irregular in the original, with noticeably longer lines in the second section of the poem (lines* 28–42). *Like the preceding poem, the manuscript assigns it a value of* 300 *points.*

Master, grant mercy to me
For my misdoings.
At midnight and at matins,
My candles burn bright.

Miniawg, son of Lleu,* led a noble life[1] –
It's no time at all since I witnessed it:

---

*   *Lleu*: See note on p. 36.

His end was to lie in Dinlleu's*[2] stony grave,
His thrust was fierce in battle.
And then Afagddu,† my son,
Of God's own gracious making –
In the contests of poetry
His wit left mine well behind.
But the most skilled man I've heard of
Was Gwydion ap Dôn, man of marvels,
Who conjured a woman from flowers,
Who stole the swine of the South;
For he was foremost in learning,
Bold in battle, twisting chains of skill.
He conjured up horses
To soothe discontent,
And magical saddles too.[3]
When prize songs are judged
Mine will stand out from all –
My song, my cauldron, my metres,
My careful delivery, fit for a prize song.
I'm known as an expert at the court of Dôn,
I and Euronwy and Euron.‡

I saw dreadful slaughter in Nant Ffrangcon,[4]
Sunday morning, between Gwydion and birds of prey.
On Thursday, determined, they took ship for Môn
In search of the trickster and the [other] enchanters.
Aranrhod,§[5] in beauty surpassing the light of bright
     weather,
Her greatest shame when she stepped over the magic
     staff[6] –
Around her court a great torrent rages,

10

20

30

---

*   *Dinlleu*: Probably Dinas Dinlle, a hillfort in Gwynedd.
†   *Afagddu*: See p. 46.
‡   *Euronwy, Euron*: On the analogy of 'Math, son of Mathonwy', Euron
    may be the daughter of Euronwy; see also p. 59.
§   *Aranrhod*: In *The Mabinogion*, Gwydion's sister and Lleu's mother.

A river whose fury lashes the dry land.
It brings deadly danger as it whirls round the world
(The books of Bede do not deceive).

Here I stand, then, guardian of the prize song –
It will last in Europe till Doomsday dawns.
40 Now may the Trinity grant us
Forgiveness on Judgement Day,
Kindness from the good Lord.

23

A Song of the Wind

This is 'the earliest surviving example of an extended riddle poem from mediaeval Wales, justly prized for its lively treatment of the wind as a delinquent being'.[1] The poem is a tour de force in the dyfalu *mode.* Dyfalu *('guessing') was a mediaeval poetic technique in which the poet created a sequence of riddles, metaphors and fanciful tropes in order to describe an object; when the 'answer' is given by the title, as in 'A Song of the Wind', the result is a performance of inventive paraphrase, designed to display the poet's virtuosity. In the* Ystoria *the poet's evocation of the wind is part of the story in which Elffin, Taliesin's patron, is imprisoned by Maelgwn Gwynedd in Deganwy Castle: Taliesin's poetry conjures up a gale that demolishes the castle and frees Elffin.[2] However, this is not mentioned in the* Llyvyr *poem translated here. This is one of the few poems in the* Llyvyr Taliessin *for which another, though inferior, version exists in manuscript.[3] It is assigned a value of 300 points, like the two poems which precede it.*

Guess who it is:
Made before the Flood,
A mighty creature,
No flesh, no bone,
No veins, no blood,
No head and no feet.
No older, no younger
Than he was before.
He's not turned aside
By fear, nor by death.   10
He doesn't experience
The needs of creatures.

Great God, he's so lively
When first he comes by;
Surely his creator
Is full of glories.
He's in fields, in woods,
With no hand, no foot;
Feels no age, isn't struck
20   By pain or bad luck.
And he's the same age
As all the Five Ages* –
He's also older,
By many times fifty.
And he's just as wide
As the face of the earth.
And he wasn't born,
So he can't be seen.
He's at sea and on land;
30   He's unseeing, unseen.
He is capricious –
When wanted, won't come.
He's on land, and at sea;
He's necessary.
No one can beat him,
No one can match him.
He comes from all quarters,
Listens to no one.
He drags the anchor
40   Over marble stones.⁴
He's loud, he's mute,
He is uncouth.
He's brave, he's bold
As he crosses the land.
He's mute, he's loud,
He's full of sorrow,

*   *The Five Ages*: In the mediaeval Christian schema, the times of: 1) Adam
      and Eve, 2) Noah, 3) Abraham, 4) Moses and 5) David. The age of Christ
      was the sixth.

He's the noisiest one
On the face of the earth.
He's good, he's evil.
He's hard to see;   50
He can't be perceived,
Our sight can't discern him.
He's evil, he's good,
He's here, he's there,
Creates a mess,
Makes no redress.
He makes no amends,
Because he's blameless.
He's wet, he's dry;
He often comes by   60
Because of sun's heat
And the moon's chill –
The moon brings no good
Because it is cool.[5]
The One God created
All living beings:
To him belongs
The beginning and end.[6]

The poet's no good
Who doesn't praise God;   70
His singing's not proper
Who can't praise the Father.
A plough's not a plough
With no share, no seeds.
No light existed
Before the Creation.
It is a false priest
Who won't bless the host.

A fraud doesn't know
The seven elements.[*]
Ten realms were ordained
In the land of angels.
The tenth one was damned,
By the Father condemned.[7]
A host was rejected,
Completely destroyed.
Lucifer, corrupter
With his cursed nature.
There are seven planets
From God's seven gifts.
I, Seon's[†][8] wise man,
Know well their uses:
Mars, enfeebled,
The Sun, like a wheel,
The moon at its toil,
Jupiter, Venus.
From the Sun, from waters
The moon steals its light.
It's no vain reminder,
No cross to be doubted.
Our Father and Pater,
Our friend who'll receive us.
God, may we not be divided
By Lucifer's hosts.

[*]   *seven elements*: See 'The Great Song of the World' (p. 114) for a list.
[†]   *Seon*: Perhaps the biblical Mount Zion, unless the reference is to 'Caer
Seon', Caernarfon (the Roman Segontium).

24

A Song about Mead

We are back at the court of Maelgwn Gwynedd, with the story
of Elffin in the background (as in 'I Make My Plea to God',
p. 69); but the theme of the poem, like that of the next one in
the collection, is primarily the excellence of the drink being
celebrated. The act of praising the mead is a sort of imitative
share in the frothing overflow of inspiration that will defeat
the power of Maelgwn and set Elffin free. The imagery is of
ferment and overflow as characteristic of creation itself. The
metrical shape is one of longish, rather elegant lines, with a sin-
gle rhyme in the original Welsh for lines 1–14 and another for
lines 15–22. The value assigned to this poem in the manuscript
is twenty-three points.

I will praise the Prince, the Lord of all places,
Who upholds the heavens, Lord of all kinds of life,
Who made the water wholesome for all people,
Who made all kinds of drink and froths them with
    ferment,
To overrule Maelgwn of Môn and make us merry,
The foam from his mead-horn the finest of liquor.
The bees harvest it, but don't enjoy it,
This marvellous clear mead, praised in all places.
Creation's abundance, all that earth nurtures,
Things that God made for man to bestow upon him: 10
Things speaking, things silent, [God] sees with delight;
Things wild, things tame, all are of God's making,
All given freely, for clothing, for goods,
For food and for drink, until Judgement Day.
May it please the Lord, Prince of peace's homeland,
To set free Elffin from his exile –

Who gave me the wine, the ale, the mead,
The princely strong horses, well-shaped to look at –
May he give them again when at length once more
20   God willing, he'll give gifts for his honour's sake,
Five times fifty feasts,[1] all assembled in peace.
Elffin the knightly,[2] be master of the North!

25

A Song about Beer

*This poem is a companion piece to 'A Song about Mead'
(p. 83), and appears on the same page of the manuscript. In
mediaeval Wales, beer was prized much less than mead and
was often drunk in preference to water unfit for human con-
sumption. Although the poem tells us a good deal about how
beer was made in the Middle Ages, the purpose of this poem
is to urge obedience to God. The process of brewing should be
read as a metaphor for what happens to the soul at the Day
of Judgement. The manuscript assigns it the same number of
points (twenty-three) as its predecessor.*

May they admire the nature
Of Him who guards the wind!
When He comes in glory,
With earth full of cries
But bliss in eternity.
It is You who ordains
How night and day flow:
Day's spiritual war,
Night's relaxation –
Praising mirth that comes   10
From the great king.

Great God created
The warm summer sun,
And he created
The trees' and fields' fruit.
The tide will be summoned,
Sea aglitter, unbound:
All ebbs will be summoned.

God, may I be saved!
And before the world comes
To that Judgement Hill,
It can do nothing[1]
Without the Lord's wealth.

He liquefies grain
Until it grows.
He soaks it again
Till it turns into malt:
That which earth rears
Stinks and rots down.
The vat will be washed;
The wort will be pure,
And, when it's matured,
Will be brought from the cell,
Set in front of the King
For his excellent feast.
No couple rejects it;
It's honey that made it.[2]
Please God, it tastes sharp,
That is His nature.
The most generous Trinity
Made drinkers tipsy,
Behaving like fishes,
With as many dwellings
As sand grains in sea;[3]
At neap and spring tides,
As sand grains in sea,
Under the strand.[4]
God justly says: 'I alone
Have ransomed myself.'
Nothing is achieved
Without Trinity's strength.

26

They Praise His Qualities

This poem seems to open in mid-flow, before going on – like many other poems in this collection – to list abstruse matters on which the poet claims superior knowledge. At line 14, it shifts gear to become a lament for a dead ruler, Ynyr, a sixth-century king of Gwent. There are references to other heroic figures of the same period, notably Urien and Maelgwn, and the setting appears to be North Wales. Its composition may be the result of poets at the court of Llywelyn the Great looking back to the heroic age to find precedents for Llywelyn's efforts to create alliances with other Welsh kingdoms further south.

They praise his qualities,
Like true kin of Tryffin,*
The eager fierce fighter:
A pool of sadness
In the harpstring's lament.
Where does night come from?
Where does it hide from day?
Does the artful in verse know
What hearts are concealing?
May he warm me with the sun's blaze   10
From the region where it rises.
Why did winter take our leader?
What sad state now begins?
Our bountiful God,
Wise, famous and fortunate,
He awakens the sleeper,

* *Tryffin*: A name associated with the royal house of Dyfed in the sixth century.

He earns floods of praise
From the Cymry in their castles –
Praise to a loving father.
20   Bitter cries from the armies,
From the prince of Môn;
A great and shameful betrayal
Of the long-haired Gwent men
At Caer Wyragon.[*1]
Who's earned the first cup poured?
Is it Maelgwn of Môn,
Or Dyfydd from Aeron,[†2]
Or Coel and his whelps,[‡3]
Or Gwrfodw[§] and his sons?
30   The enemies' mirth was silenced
When Ynyr[¶] took his hostages.
Poets gather round
The proud seed of Caer Seon.[**]
I have drunk wine
In the hall of Uffin,[††4]
On the seas of Gododdin:
A man skilful, far-famed,
Wise as Brân in the morning.
I'm a seasoned wanderer,
40   Joyful in speech.
On the far side of Dygen[‡‡5]
My task, to praise Urien –

---

*   *Caer Wyragon*: Worcester.
†   *Dyfydd*: Unknown. *Aeron*: Here most likely Aeron in West Wales, though in the heroic poems normally a location in Scotland or Yorkshire (see also the note on p. 17).
‡   *Coel*: Ancestor of the Kings of Rheged; see note on p. 15.
§   *Gwrfodw*: The early seventh-century King of Ergyng in the Hereford area.
¶   *Ynyr*: The ruler of Gwent at the end of the sixth century; mentioned in several saints' lives of the early Middle Ages.
**   *Caer Seon*: See note on p. 82.
††   *Uffin*: Unknown; the form of the name suggests a Germanic ruler.
‡‡   *Dygen*: Perhaps Breiddin Hill in Powys.

Radiant in faith,
An eager commander,
Red harvester from Hell –
Red are all who insult him!
A battle in Harddnenwys*[6] –
Ynyr ran them through.
A hundred feasts welcome him,
A hundred kin eat with him.
I saw mighty men
On their way to battle,
I saw blood on the ground
As the swords rush forward,
The dawn's wings growing blue
As the spears took flight.
For three hundred feasts[7] – a famous number –
Shall Ynyr's borders indeed flow red.

50

*   *Harddnenwys*: Probably Hardenhuish in Wiltshire.

27

The Wild Horse Is Broken[1]

This poem is incomplete in the Llyvyr Taliessin, *due to missing pages. There are several examples of 'list' poems in early Welsh literature, and prose lists are also common, especially in triadic form, as a mnemonic device for the transmission of legendary lore to poets and others.[2] The earliest version of a catalogue pairing legendary warriors with their famous horses appears in the thirteenth-century* Black Book of Carmarthen.[3] *Much of the present poem is very unclear, though it falls into roughly three parts. The first is a general evocation of an exemplary warrior and horse whose qualities are seen against a tumultuous natural world. The second section (lines 25–58) gives an account of heroes and their horses (a number of the 'triad' lists include some of the same names, but with markedly different details). The third part (lines 59–68) lists creatures into which the poet has transformed. Due to its incompleteness and missing text, the final part (from line 69) is particularly obscure.*

The wild horse is broken,
Trotting under the champion.
May God on high be praised,
Lord of blazing fire,
Above the highest wind.
Higher than every cloud,
Or the most distant haze.
It doesn't remain ensnared
After wedding the sea.
[Then] the sea's course flows on
Towards rough estuaries,
To God's resplendent day,
Dawn with an onrush of tide,

Beyond all comparable things.
Because of Nwython's peer,*[4]
Because of the perfect saints,
I praise Him who will judge,
Who judges with fierce wrath:
The roar of his rage is deep.

I'm no cowardly old man,   20
No scum at the gate.
Here are my two friends –
Who heedlessly plod on,[5]
From my hand to yours [. . .].
May the Nine† protect
The old ploughing teams,
And Mayawg's horse,
And Genethog's horse,
And Caradawg's horse[6] –
A strong thoroughbred –   30
And Gwythur's horse,
And Gwawrddur's horse,
And Arthur's horse –
Fearless when bringing pain –
And Taliesin's horse,
And Lleu's‡ horse, hand-reared,
And well-hung Pebyrllei,§
And Cunin's horse Grei,¶
Cornan the steady,
Awydd the eager.   40
Black of the Seas, famous
Brwyn Bron Bradawc's** horse,

---

*   *Nwython's peer*: Unknown; though Nwython (see p. 30) is praised in
    court poetry for his bravery.
†   *the Nine*: The nine heavenly orders.
‡   *Lleu*: The nephew of the wizard Gwydion; see also note on p. 36.
§   *Pebyrllei*: 'Strong Chestnut'.
¶   *Grei*: 'Grey'.
** *Brwyn Bron Bradawc*: 'Brwyn of the Wily Breast'.

And the three geldings
That won't go to stud.
Ceidio's horse Cethin,*
Whose hoof is cloven,
Skittish Yscwydurith,†
A prancing steed,
Generous Rhydderch's horse,
50   Llwyd,‡ the stag-coloured,
And Llamrei§ who jumps like a hart,
And Ffroenfoll,¶ the lively
Sadyrnin's[7] horse,
And Cystenin's**[8] horse
And others in battle
Due to the sad land.
Henwyn,†† who happily
Brought news from Hiraddug.‡‡[9]

I've been a sow, I've been a buck,
60   I've been a sage, I've been a ploughshare,
I've been a piglet, I've been a boar.
I've been the tumult of a storm,
I've been a spreading flood,
I've been a wave in a gale,
I've been the disperser of ruin.[10]
I've been a lynx on three trees,[11]
I've been a godwit on an Elder-tree,
I've been a crane looking to eat its fill.

---

*   *Cethin*: 'Roan'.
†   *Yscwydurith*: 'Dappled Shoulder'.
‡   *Llwyd*: 'Dun'.
§   *Llamrei*: One of King Arthur's two named horses in Welsh tradition.
¶   *Ffroenfoll*: 'Flaring nostrils'.
**   *Cystenin*: Constantine.
††   *Henwyn*: 'Old White'.
‡‡   *Hiraddug*: Moel Hiraddug, an Iron-Age hill fort in Clwyd, North-East
        Wales.

A daring war band is fierce,
Good stock in battle.
All those under the sky,   70
In the wake of foes,
Not alive [. . .]
Equally great as my men.
Sustainer [. . .][12]

28

He Ranged the Whole World

The pages containing the beginning of this poem are missing from the surviving Llyvyr Taliessin *manuscript. 'He Ranged the Whole World' is the first of two poems about Alexander the Great which demonstrate the familiarity of an educated mediaeval Welsh writer with the elaborate legendary and semi-legendary Latin histories of Alexander which had circulated from the fifth century onwards. There is no evidence that a Welsh prose translation of this material existed before the twelfth century. The sonorous list of place names is paralleled in the 'devotional' poems of the* Llyvyr Taliessin. *The text is obscure, but it seems to imply that Alexander's conquest of the Holy Land was what brought down divine judgement on him and his men.*

[. . .] He ranged the whole world,
Conqueror and overlord of twelve far-flung realms,
Most generous, most renowned ever to be born,
A savage slayer – woe to his enemy!
Three times in battle he defeated Darius,
And left in his land not the smallest shrubs standing.
Strong Darius in his plumes[1] fled far away,
But in his fury Alexander tracked him down.
Woe to the prisoner fettered in gold chains!
He did not stay long there; death came for him,
With a mournful cry as the army attacked.
No one before him had broken open
The world's treasury of beauty and splendour.
Open-handed Alexander went on to conquer
Syr's land and Siryoel and the land of Syria,
The land of Dinifdra, the land of Dinitra,

10

Persia and Mersia and the land of Canaan,
The islands of Pleth and Pletheppa too,
The people of Babylon, the people of Asia,
The land of Galldarus, poor in goods.[2]   20
Then at last he arrived in a country – the region
Where they find delight in unnatural hunting,[3]
[Where women] humble hostages taken from Europe,
Laying waste to lands in the earth's wildest places.
Alexander's fierce warriors raped these proud women,
The ones with burned breasts, who know nothing of
    modesty.
As for battles with Porus* – so it is said –
They brought down the ravens, they wrought great havoc.
And – so it is said of Macedon's soldiers –
It was Your servants' land they caused to betray You.[4]   30
For Your enemies there'll be no rest from exhaustion,
From the grip of the fetter and the harsh pain it gives.
A hundred thousand perished of thirst
In their ill-suited helmets – their pack-beasts too.
His servant poisoned him before he found rest;
Had this been done sooner it would have been better.
Now to Him who rules splendidly the realm of glory,
The Lord's lovely land, the best in concord,
May I make my amends, and find refuge with You.
And all those who hear me, may my longings be theirs,   40
May they do God's will before the soil smothers them.

---

*   *Porus*: An Indian king subdued by Alexander in 326 BCE.

29

The Marvels of Alexander

This is the shorter of two poems about Alexander the Great. A fourteenth-century hand (not that of the Llyvyr Taliessin *scribe) has inserted the title for this poem, and has also given the title 'Alexander's Breastplate' to one of the devotional items in the manuscript (see p. 159), although there is no direct allusion there to Alexander. 'The Marvels of Alexander', in contrast to 'He Ranged the Whole World', reads like a conventional elegy. 'He Ranged the Whole World' concentrates on Alexander's conquests, while this piece celebrates his legendary exploits in flight and under the sea – a common theme in mediaeval legends in which Alexander visits realms hidden from ordinary mortals. Line 14 refers to the fact that Alexander is sometimes shown in mediaeval iconography as being carried through the air by griffins (imaginary creatures with the body and tail of a lion and the head and wings of an eagle). In his search for learning and his imaginary travels, the mediaeval Taliesin particularly resembles the Alexander of this poem.*

I wonder at Heaven's abode,
That it doesn't fall down
Due to the leader's death –
Alexander the Great.
Alexander of Macedon
Sowed iron showers.*
He of strong swordplay
Went under the sea;
Under the sea he went
In pursuit of learning.

10

---

*   *Iron showers*: Arrows or spears.

Whoever seeks learning
Must be of bold mind.
He rode on the wind
Between two griffins
To behold what they saw.
He saw a vision:
The world as a whole.
He beheld a wonder:
Fish preying on fish.
That which he desired   20
He won from the world;
And, at his dying,
Mercy from God.

30

The Spoils of Annwfn

This is one of the most tantalizing pieces in the collection, and the only Arthurian item, though Arthur is mentioned briefly in four other poems. There is obviously a massive hinterland of archaic lore about Annwfn, the Otherworld (see Introduction, p. lxii), being taken for granted here; there are connections, though they are none too clear, with material in The Mabinogion *and in some Irish texts about Otherworld voyages. But the poet seems to assume that his allusions to obscure tradition are already going to be problems for the untutored mediaeval reader – specifically the clerical or monastic reader. The scorn poured on the clergy is more savage than in other poems and reflects the tension between two models of learning in mediaeval Wales, bardic and ecclesiastical.*

I will praise the Prince, the Lord of the king's land,
Who has stretched out his power across the wide world.
Gwair's[*][1] cell was locked fast in Caer Siddi[†]
All through the days of Pwyll's deeds and Pryderi's;[‡][2]
None had gone to that place before him,
Where the heavy grey chain held the faithful youth.
Sadly he'd sing before Annwfn's treasures;
We poets pray for him till Judgement Day dawns.

---

[*]   *Gwair*: In the Triads, one of the 'Three Distinguished Prisoners of the Island of Britain'.
[†]   *Caer Siddi*: See note on p. 71.
[‡]   *Pwyll and Pryderi*: Father and son in the 'First Branch' of the Mabinogi, rulers of Dyfed.

Three full loads of Prydwen*³ we sailed there;
And seven men only returned from Caer Siddi.   10

I'm famed for my praise songs; the music is heard
In the four-cornered castle with its four sentry-posts.⁴
The first song I sang was concerning the cauldron
That's warmed at the fire by the breath of nine virgins.⁵
The cauldron of Annwfn's king, what's its nature –
The black-rimmed cauldron with its trim of pearls?
It was never designed to boil food for a coward;⁶
Lleog's† flashing sword was thrust into its depths,
And then it passed into the hands of the Leaper.‡
And before Annwfn's portals, the lamps were burning.   20

When we voyaged with Arthur, famed for his labours,
Seven men only returned from Caer Medwit.§

I'm famed for my praise-songs; the music resounds
In the four-cornered castle, the island's strong bastion.
Fresh water and jet mix together [and kindle],
The wine glows for their drink, set before their ranks.

Three full loads of Prydwen we sailed on that sea,
And seven men only returned from Caer Rigor.¶

I've no praise to give to small men who write piously** –
Not one witnessed Arthur's great deeds round Caer
    Wydr††⁷ –   30

---

*   *Prydwen*: Arthur's warship.
†   *Lleog*: Unidentifiable, but the name may mean 'destroyer'.
‡   *the Leaper*: Usually the name given to the expected national deliverer (see
     Introduction, p. xxvii, and p. 137), but here possibly King Arthur.
§   *Caer Medwit*: 'The castle of feasting/mead-drinking'.
¶   *Caer Rigor*: Probably 'the freezing castle'.
**   *small men . . . piously*: The clergy (especially the monastic clergy), partic-
     ular targets of scorn and mockery in this poem.
††   *Caer Wydr*: 'The glass castle'.

There were six thousand men lined up on its ramparts
(Hard were the words exchanged with their watchman).

Three full loads of Prydwen voyaged with Arthur,
And seven men only returned from Caer Golud.[*]

I've no words of praise for small men trailing girdles,[8]
Who don't know who was brought into being and when,
At what noonday hour God himself came to birth,
Who made the one who fled Doleu Defwy.[†]
They don't know of the Brindled Ox,[‡9] its strong halter,
40   (Seven score links to make up its chain).

When we voyaged with Arthur – that ill-starred journey –
Seven men only returned from Caer Manddwy.[§10]

I've no words of praise for small men's trailing spirits,
Who don't know the day when the Lord came to be,
At what noonday hour the Master was born,
Or what creature they guard, with its silver head.[11]

When we voyaged with Arthur – that ill-starred conflict –
Seven men only returned from Caer Ochren.[¶]

And the monks herd together, a pack of dogs,
50   In the contest with those who have mastered the lore –
Whether wind takes one path, whether sea is one water,
Whether fire's unstoppable force is one spark.

---

*   *Caer Golud*: 'The castle of prevention/obstacles'.
†   *Doleu Defwy*: Perhaps a river between this world and Annwfn (the
        Otherworld: see Introduction, p. lxii).
‡   *the Brindled Ox*: In the Triads, one of the 'Three Principal Oxen of the
        Island of Britain'.
§   *Caer Manddwy*: Possibly 'the castle of the protector'.
¶   *Caer Ochren*: Obscure; perhaps 'the foursquare castle'.

The monks herd together, a pack of wolves,
In the contest with those who have mastered the lore –
They don't know how darkness is severed from light,
They don't know the course of the wind in its rushing,
Where the wind will lay waste, what land it strikes,
How many saints in the sky's vault, and how many
    shrines.[12]

I will praise the Prince, the Lord, the Great One:
Let me not be sad: Christ will repay me.   60

31

Elegy for Hercules

This is the first of seven elegies in Llyvyr Taliessin *referring to historical and mythical figures. In mediaeval typology, Hercules was thought of as a prefiguration of Alexander the Great. It is uncertain which source for details about the labours of Hercules is being followed by the writer, but he may have known the* Epistola Alexandri ad Aristotelem *('Letter from Alexander to Aristotle'), which mentions not the traditional two but, rather, four pillars erected by Hercules. Those in the west marked the end of the known world, at the Straits of Gibraltar. The other two, mentioned in the* Epistola *and in this poem, marked the eastern boundary of the world; they were said to be covered in red gold.*

The earth upturned,
Like night during day,
When Hercules, famed
Lord of Christendom, died.
Hercules, who'd say
That he scorned to die.
In feasting halls shields
Broke over his head –
Hercules, who could hold
A golden moon whole![1]
Four red and gold pillars
All of one height –
The Pillars of Hercules –
No coward could do it.
No coward would dare –
Sun's heat would forbid it.
No man under Heaven

Travelled such distance.
Hercules – rampart,
Now buried in sand.   20
May the Trinity grant him
Mercy on Judgement Day –
God's unity, lacking nothing.

Brave Madog

In this unusually short poem of lament, Madog ('Madawc' in the older spelling used in the manuscript) is presented as the son of Uther, Arthur's father in the mediaeval tradition, but no surviving narratives are attached to his name. He remains a mystery.

Madog, a wall of well-being,
Madog, before he went to his rest,
Was a fortress of splendour,
Of contest and merriment.
Uther's son, before his slaughter,
Pledged himself with his own hand.

Elegy for Cú Roí mac Dáiri

A nautical theme connects the next two items in the group of elegies that begins with the 'Elegy for Hercules'. Cú Roí mac Dáiri was a legendary mariner and, according to Marged Haycock, was 'an Irish Alexander'.[1] *He was said to have plundered cattle from Manaw. In the earlier heroic poem 'All through One Year' (see p. 12), Manaw referred not to Ynys Manaw (The Isle of Man) but the area surrounding the Firth of Forth in Scotland. However, given that the tradition has Cú Roí mac Dáiri sailing with Cú Chulainn for the Isle of Man, this seems the likelier location here. The poem is evidence of the Irish influence on Welsh poetry of this period.*

From sea's wide spring · out flows the tide:
It advances, retreats, · it smashes, crushes.
The lament for Cú Roí · has distressed me;
The cold silencing, of a hard man · full of passion:
I've seldom heard · of greater misfortune.
The son of Dáiri, · he helmed the south sea;
His fame was unsullied · before he died.

From sea's wide spring · out flow the currents:
It advances, retreats, · it crushes, rushes.
The lament for Cú Roí · affects me also: 10
The cold silencing of a hard man · so full of passion:
I've seldom heard · of greater misfortune.

From sea's wide spring · out flows a flooding,
Rushing, attacking the beach, · swiftly surging.
A man who conquers · is of great wealth;
And, after Manaw, · sets out for homesteads.

Do the monks know · of the treasure collector?
While alive, the swift victor · was fierce and early –
I've heard these true stories · from across the world –
Cú Roí had conflict · with Cú Chulainn,
With frequent disorder · around their borders.
Split is the mast[2] · of a suffering people.
God has a fortress · that won't fall, nor tremble:
Blessed be the soul · deserving of Him.

Elegy for Dylan, Son of the Sea

Dylan appears briefly in the 'Fourth Branch' of the Mabinogi, but what was obviously once a fuller story of his death at the hands of his uncle, Gofannon, has been lost. Gofannon (like the Irish Goibniu) is a smith endowed with supernatural powers, which makes some sense of the allusions to metalworking and farriery in these lines. This is one of the more difficult texts in the Llyvyr Taliessin, *with quite complex syntax, long lines and an intricate rhyme scheme impossible to reproduce in translation.*

One highest God, wisest of sages, greatest in might –
Who was it held the metal, who forged its hot blows?
And before him, who held still the force of the tongs?[1]
The horsemaster stares – he has done lethal hurt, a deed of
    outrage,
Striking down Dylan on the fatal strand, violence on the
    shore's waters,
The wave from Ireland, the wave from Manaw, the wave from
    the North,
And fourth, the wave of Britain of the shining armies.[2]
I plead with God, God and Father of the Kingdom that knows
    no refusal,
The maker of Heaven, who will welcome us in his mercy.

I Am Fiery Taliesin

The Cunedda commemorated in this poem appears in early mediaeval royal genealogies as a great-grandfather of the sixth-century king Maelgwn Gwynedd. In the ninth-century historia Brittonum,[1] *Cunedda is credited with expelling the Irish from North Wales, though this is not mentioned in the present poem. Partly because of the difference between how Cunedda is represented in this poem and in the ninth-century material, it has been argued that the song is an authentic early elegy, predating the* Historia, *perhaps even going back in some form to a period close to Cunedda himself. But – although much of it has a strong archaic feel, with what must be a deliberate use of obscure words and old-fashioned phrasing – it is more likely to be a composition designed to show that 'Taliesin' had served as the faithful poet and elegist of Maelgwn Gwynedd's ancestor, and so was linked to the royal house of North Wales and to Llywelyn the Great, the distant successor of Maelgwn.[2] Three different metres are used: the nine-syllable* cyhydedd naw ban *(see Introduction, p. lxxi) with a central caesura; the same line divided into three; and each stanza, or* awdl, *concluded with a* toddaid byr, *thus punctuating the cadence of the poem as a whole (see p. lxxi). The arrangement and division of lines in our translation reflect those in* Haycock's *edition of the text, and are designed to bring out the metrical variations in the original.*

I am fiery Taliesin.
I give Christendom song:
I praise Christendom's bounteous wonders,
Between heights, · sea · and sweet water.
The tremors · of Cunedda's · fall

Are felt · in Caer Wair*[3] · and Carlisle.
A wave of war · will break · on towns:
Many people · will fear · the onslaught,
The wave · of fire, · a surge from the seas;
The brave · will call each other · to war.   10
Since he secured · his lodging · in Heaven,
The wind's · like a sigh · in the Ash trees.
His hounds[†] · are longing · for his presence.
They kept peace · with the descendants · of Coel.[‡][4]
They clothe poets · who know · the rules,
They mourned · Cunedda's death, · as I do:
Mourning is made · for the staunch defender, · the staunch
    comrade,[5]
Invincible, · noble, · now he is bound,
In the deep · grave's wound · he is bound.
The question is: · where's the hard, · bare grave   20
Of one harder · on his foes · than bone?
  Cunedda the surging, · before destruction · and earth,
      His honour was maintained.

Many times · before our defender · was killed,
In battle · he swept · Bernicians[§] away.
They wailed · at the fear · and terror [he caused],
The cold walk · towards earth · and sore death,
Like a swarm · [making for] the woven · wood thicket.[6]
Sheathing arms · is a cowardice · worse than death.
It is death's · sad sleep · that I grieve,
For the court, · and Cunedda's · shroud.   30
  I long for · a sea inlet, · for the sea's flow,
      For the herd · and hearth · I'm longing.

*   *Caer Wair*: Here most likely a location in Northumbria, though see also
    the note on p. 122.
†   *His hounds*: Cunedda's followers.
‡   *Coel*: Ancestor of the Kings of Rheged; cf. note on p. 15.
§   *Bernicians*: Bernicia was the northern part of what became the Anglo-
    Saxon kingdom of Northumbria.

I mock · those poets · who begrudge,
I esteem · those who offer · praise.
   Battle wonders with nine hundred horses,
     Before Cunedda's last Communion.
He gave me milk cows in summer,
He gave me horses in winter;
He gave me bright wine and oil;
He gave me slaves for protection.
He was a fierce, aggressive attacker,
Keen-eyed, a lion-like leader.
   Edern's* son laid enemy land to ashes
     Before the pain of his death.
He was bold, · invincible, · implacable,
A surge, · a cruel wave · of death.
He'd bear · his shield · in the vanguard,
     His nobles were men of valour.
I awake · to lament, · to repay the hero's wine,
     This scion of Coel · is destroyed.

40

50

---

*   *Edern*: The name of both Cunedda's father and his son.

36

Elegy for Uther Pendragon

*There is very little surviving material about Uther, the father
of Arthur, in early Welsh tradition, and the allusions made to
him in this poem do not correspond to any elements in the
non-Welsh literature. Nothing suggests that the writer has
read Geoffrey of Monmouth, the first to give us (in the twelfth
century) a connected narrative about Uther. It does not read
like a death song, being essentially a boast of both military
and poetic achievement, cast in the first person. It seems likely
that the title was attached to a poem in the voice of a now
unknown warrior poet – unless there is meant to be a break
between what would then be a warrior's declamation (lines
1–24) on the one hand and a poet's (lines 25–34) on the other;
but there is no obvious clear break and no metrical grounds
for separating the two. As in the preceding poem, we have kept
an internal division of lines to indicate the strong triple struc-
ture with its double caesura.*

It is I · who command · in battle;
I will not halt · the conflict · till blood's been shed.
It is I · who am named · 'Shining Armour,'[1]
Mine is · the fierceness · that turned on all foes.
It is I · who am the prince · leading on in darkness.
[. . .][2]
It is I · who am a second Sawyl*[3] · as the light fails.
Till blood's been shed, · I will not part · armies fighting.
It is I · who fought · to drive home my advantage

---

* *Sawyl*: A name mentioned in the Triads and elsewhere as an arrogant
tyrant; equivalent to 'Samuel'.

10 In the mortal combat · with the kindred · of Casnur.*
I was no stranger · to bloodletting · with Gwythur,†
The clashing of swords · against the sons · of Cawrnur.‡4
It was I · who shared · the shelter of my stronghold.
Arthur himself · has no more · than a ninth of my valour.5
It was I · who stormed · a hundred castles,
It was I · who slaughtered · a hundred castellans,
It was I · who shared out · a hundred of their cloaks,
It was I · who struck off · a hundred heads,
It was I · who gave · to Henben§
20 Swords · that were mighty · for his protection.
It was I · who set my seal · on the peace treaty,
An iron door, · a wall of fire · on the mountain,
Forsaken, · beleaguered, · I'm still strong of sinew.
The world · wouldn't last · without my descendants.
I'm a poet · worth praising · for my skill –
Let praise arise · among ravens, · eagles, birds of prey!6
Afagddu¶ · has received · no less a reward
For supporting · seasoned warriors · [trapped] between
      ridges.
Ascending · to Heaven · was what I yearned for,
30 Beyond the eagle's flight, · beyond all fear · of injury.
I'm a bard, · and I'm also · a harpist,
I play on the pipe · and also · the crwth.**
As great as that · of seven score poets7
Is the greatness · of skill [that is mine].
I was a shield · for those whose defence was shattered,
A swift flyer, · a winged one.

---

*   *Casnur*: Unknown.
†   *Gwythur*: Unknown.
‡   *Cawrnur*: Unknown; see also p. 73.
§   *Henben*: Perhaps the Henin or Heinin who appears as chief bard at Mael-
       gwn's court in the *Ystoria Taliesin*.
¶   *Afagddu*: See note on p. 46.
**   *crwth*: A simple bowed lyre, widely used in traditional Welsh music.

To the Son, · a song from the bard,
And to Mary, · O Father of all skill,
My tongue turns · to declaim · my elegy.
Rock-founded · is the rampart · of the whole world;   40
And in Britain's day of triumph – · my thoughts · soar on
    high –
King of Heaven, · may you never let go · of my prayers.

37

The Great Song of the World

'The Great Song of the World' and 'The Small Song of the World' are poems in oblique dialogue with each other. They conform generally to mainstream mediaeval cosmology as described in sources such as Isidore of Seville and the Venerable Bede.

I praise my Father,
my God, my sustainer,
who placed in my skull,
to form me, a soul.
Happily, he made for me
My seven elements:[1]
Of earth and fire,
And water and air,
Flowers and cloud,
And wind from the south.

Second, my Father formed
For me the senses' design:
By one, I breathe out,
And two, I breathe in,
And three, I give voice,
And by four, I taste,
And by five I see,
And by six I hear,
And by seven I smell –
To follow a trail.

Seven heavens there are
Above the astronomer;

There are three divisions of sea*2 –
Ever restless they are.
What a great wonder –
The world's always changing.

God on high made
The delightful planets:
He made the *Sola*,†
He made the *Luna*,‡
He made *Marca*,§
And *Marcarucia*;¶
He made Venus,
He made *Venerus*,**3
He made *Severus*,††4
And seventh, *Saturnus*.‡‡

The good God made
the five belts of *Terra*§§5 –
how long will they last?
The first is frozen,
As is the second;
The third has a heat
That makes man feel weak;
Fourth is a Paradise,
Which welcomes all people;
The fifth is cool
And feeds the world.

30

40

---

*   *three divisions of sea*: Hot, cold and temperate.
†   *Sola*: The sun (Latin).
‡   *Luna*: The moon.
§   *Marca*: Mars.
¶   *Marcarucia*: Mercury.
**   *Venerus*: Perhaps *Vesperus*, the evening Venus.
††   *Severus*: Uncertain.
‡‡   *Saturnus*: Saturn.
§§   *Terra*: Earth.

Earth's divided in three
By a different scheme:
One is Asia,
Two is Africa,
Three is Europa,
Where Christendom lies
Until Judgement Day
When He will judge all.
He gave me my *awen*
To praise my king.
I am Taliesin,
Speech flowing with wisdom:
I will praise Elffin
Till the end of time.

38

The Small Song of the World

*Although this has a superficial resemblance to other sets of
'learned' questions, it has a more obvious continuity, pursu-
ing a single line of reflection about what upholds the world.
There is a much later (sixteenth-century) Welsh text which goes
through a similar set of questions about the basis of the world's
existence and gives answers as well. The idea that the four
Gospel writers are the four columns upholding the earth relates
to the notion (found in Latin, Irish and Welsh sources) that
they correspond to the four elements. The title suggests that
this is a brief poem about the world, in contrast to the lon-
ger poem that precedes it in the manuscript. This seems rather
more likely than the idea that it is a composition about the
'microcosm' – the human body and soul sustained by grace and
by the doctrine of the evangelists – but the question is open.*

I have sung with skill, and still I shall sing
Until the greatest day of all shall dawn,
Many matters in my mind,
Over which I worry.
I challenge the wide world's poets –
Why will you not tell me
What holds up the world
Lest it fall into emptiness?[1]
Or if the world fell,
On to what would it drop?
Who holds it in place?
What a vain thing, a world
Falling into the void!
And yet, truth to tell,
What a wonder's a world

10

That never thus falls!
What a singular thing,
And how great its radiance!
St John and St Matthew,
St Luke and St Mark –
They hold up the world
Through the grace of the Spirit.

PROPHETIC POEMS

39

The Great Prophecy of Britain

This prophecy is generally thought to have originated in the tenth century, as it describes the campaign which culminated in 937 CE with the destruction of the allied Norse and Celtic forces at Brunanburh.[1] Thus, Athelstan of Wessex would be the 'Overlord' in the poem, taxing the Welsh on their Wye border after the unification of Wessex and Mercia. A slightly later date has recently been proposed by Andrew Breeze, who has argued that it relates instead to the surrender at Leicester in 940 of an English army to Olaf Guthfrithson, King of Dublin, an event likely to stir Welsh hopes of an anti-English coalition. Whatever the precise setting, however, the poem does not refer to any particular historical figure on the Welsh side. As in the later 'prophetic' poems in this section, the expected leaders are more archetypal than actual; the poet refers to earlier 'saviours' of Britain like Cynan and Cadwaladr. Many of the other 'prophetic' pieces in the Llyvyr Taliessin *which were composed at a later date faithfully reproduce many aspects of this poem's language, vocabulary and mythology, and it can be regarded as one of the most influential and significant poems of mediaeval Wales.*

The *awen* predicts they* will make haste:
We shall have treasures, possessions and peace
And broader lordship and lively leaders;
And after war, dwellings in every area;
Men fierce in fight-clamour, furious warriors,
Swift in attack, slow to leave defence –

---

*   *they*: Cynan and Cadwaladr, the saviours of Britain; see Introduction, p. xxvii.

Fighters that scatter foreigners as far as Caer Wair.*2
They will rejoice after devastation,
Giving peace between the Cymry and the men of Dublin,3
The Irish of Ireland, Man and Britain,
Including the Cornish and the men of Strathclyde.
The Britons will rise and then they shall prevail.4
The time when they shall come has long been prophesied,
Lords whose possession is by descent.
Northmen,†5 in a circle, the place of honour,
Will attack in the centre of the van.

Myrddin6 predicts that they will meet
The Overlord's ‡7 stewards in Aber Peryddon.§8
And though, by one right, they all bewail death,
They will, with one will, stand firm and give battle.
The stewards will collect their taxes,
Though the Cymry's armies refuse to pay –
It is a nobleman who says this,
(Refusing to pay despite threat of prison).
By Mary's Son, great of word, why don't they burst forth
Against the Saxons' lordship and their pride?
Away with those scavengers of Vortigern of Gwynedd!¶9
The foreigners will be driven into exile.
No one will help them, they own no land,
Unknowing, they wander up every *aber*.**
Thanet they bought by cunning deceit.
With Hengist and Horsa their rule was confined.

---

* *Caer Wair*: Here most likely Caithness, though see also the note on p.
   109.
† *Northmen*: Presumably warriors from the surviving British Kingdom of
   Strathclyde in southern Scotland.
‡ *The Overlord*: Aethelstan, or his successor Edmund.
§ *Aber Peryddon*: The upper River Wye.
¶ *Vortigern*: A British ruler remembered in tradition as having welcomed
   the Saxons Hengist and Horsa to the Isle of Thanet, where they first set-
   tled, and then having built a fortress in North Wales to defend himself
   against both the invaders and his vengeful countrymen.
** *aber*: 'Estuary'.

They grew at our cost in an ignoble fashion:
After secret slaughter, churls wear the crown.
Drunkenness goes with drinking much mead;
Want is the result of many deaths;
Women's tears go with affliction;
Savage rule will cause grief to swell,
The roaring world leads to sorrow.
When the looters at Thanet are our lords, 40
May the Trinity fend off the blow intended
To destroy the British, make a home for the English!
Better they should retreat into exile
Than that the Cymry should be homeless.

By Mary's son (great of word), why don't they burst forth –
The Cymry – against the shame of barons and chieftains.
Petitioners and patrons complain all the same:
They are of one voice, one counsel, one nature.
It wasn't pride caused them not to parley
But to spare them from making an inglorious peace. 50
They submit themselves to God and Dewi,*
May he repay and repulse the deceit of foreigners,
Who do shameful deeds for lack of a homeland.

The Cymry and Saxons will meet each other
On the shore, destroying and fighting,
Vast armies will make trial of each other:
And blades on the hill, yelling and clashing.
Shout answering shout over Wye's shining water,
Banners abandoned, ruthless attacking,
And, like food for wild beasts, Saxons falling. 60
The Cymry, as one, will form orderly ranks;
Their van will press the white-faced†10 ones hard.
For their lies, the stewards will cringe,

---

*   *Dewi*: David, the patron saint of Wales.
†   *the white-faced*: The fair-headed and pale-skinned (or frightened?)
     Saxons.

Their army, blood-stained, all around them.
Others will flee on foot through the forest.
Through fortress ramparts, the foxes will flee.
War won't return to the land of Britain
But in sorrowful counsel slip back like the sea.

Caer Geri's* stewards will bitterly complain
70   In valley, on hill, and some will lament
That coming to Aber Peryddon was not wise;
All the tax they will gather is sorrow.
With nine score hundred men they'll attack –
What a joke! – and only four hundred come back.
They'll recount the tumult to their women
Who'll wash out their blood-soaked shirts.
The Cymry's allies will risk their lives,
Men from the South will defend their taxes.
With blades whetted sharp they will slaughter:
80   No healer will profit from what they do.
Cadwaladr's armies will come bravely,
Let the Cymry attack, they will give battle!
[The English] have sought unavoidable death;
The end of their taxes is knowledge of death.
They planted [. . .] in others.
They won't gather their taxes ever again.

Through woods and fields, over hill [and dale],
A candle† walks with us in the dark.
Cynan in the front at every attack,
90   Due to the Britons, Saxons will sing woe.
Cadwaladr's a spear shaft among his chieftains,
Picking each one with wisdom and skill.
As his people fall fighting for their protector,
Lamenting, red's smeared on the foreigners' cheeks,[11]
To end all resistance and lay hold on much spoil.

---

*   *Caer Geri*: Cirencester.
†   *A candle*: An idealized leader, such as Cadwaladr or Cynan.

The Saxon will flee to Winchester, fast as he can.
Blessed be the Welsh when they shall say:
'The Trinity saved us from our former troubles;
No need for Dyfed or Glywyssing* to tremble –
The Overlord's stewards won't gain any praise,   100
Nor shall the Saxon's savage advisors.
They won't find a way to get drunk at our cost,
Without losing from Fate all they may have taken
From orphaned children and others freezing.
By the prayers of Dewi and the British saints,
To the river Arlego†12 the foreigners flee.'

The *awen* predicts the day will come
When Wessex men will be of one mind,
One heart, one purpose with fiery Lloegr,‡13
Hoping to humble our finest forces.   110
Off the foreigner will march, and flee all day long,
Not knowing where he'll move, where to go, where to halt.
Like a bear from the mountain, our men rush to battle
To exact full payment for their comrades' blood.
No pause in the flow of their thrusting spears,
No pity felt for a fallen man's carcase.
Heads will be split and emptied of brains,
Women will be widowed, horses left riderless.
In the face of the warriors' charge, there are fearful groans
Hands will hurt many before the armies part.   120
Death's messengers will meet
When corpses stand, propping up each other.
This will avenge the taxes, the daily tolls,
The constant invasions, the treacherous armies.
The Cymry will win by sustained assault,

---

*   *Glywyssing*: A kingdom in South-East Wales, roughly covering the terri-
     tory between the Swansea and Usk valleys.
†   *the river Arlego*: Possibly near Leicester.
‡   *Lloegr*: In the older poems, this name would refer to Northumbria, but it
     may have a looser reference here, possibly to the Midland kingdom of
     Mercia.

Well-prepared, united in word, speech and faith.
The Cymry will prevail in making war,
And they will bring together a host from many lands.
They will lift high Dewi's holy standard, leading the Irish
    with a linen flag.
130 And the ranks of Dublin will be ranged alongside us –
When they march to battle, they won't refuse us help.
They'll ask the Saxons to list their demands,
How much of a claim they can make on the land,
Where their own lands are, from which they set out,
Where their kindred belong, the country they came from.
Since Vortigern's day they've trodden us down.
It is not by right that they hold our kin's portion –
Why else have they trampled on the privileges of our
    saints?
Why have they robbed Dewi of his holy rights?[14]
140 When they face off, the Cymry will make sure
No foreigners will walk away from that spot
Till they've paid sevenfold for all that they've done.
Thus they'll avenge Garmon's friends with force.[*15]
Four hundred and forty years on,[16]
Long-haired champions, masters in war
Will come from Ireland to drive out the Saxons.
From Lego[†17] a rapacious fleet will arrive,
They'll wreak havoc in battle, tear armies to pieces.
Bold loyal men will come from Alt Clud,[‡]
150 A resplendent army, to drive them from Britain.
A powerful host will come from Llydaw,[§]
Warriors on warhorses, pitiless to enemies.
On all sides shame will be the Saxons' destiny –
Their time is over, they've no land left.

*   *Garmon*: Presumably St Germanus, the Gaulish bishop who visited Brit-
     ain in the first half of the fifth century.
†   *Lego*: Perhaps Leicester.
‡   *Alt Clud*: Dumbarton Rock, the main citadel of the kingdom of Strath-
     clyde.
§   *Llydaw*: Brittany.

Death will arrive for their black army,
Sword and disaster and disgrace.
After all the gold and silver they once owned,
Let them retreat under bushes to pay back their treachery!
Let the sea and the anchor be their counsellors now!
Let blood and death be their brothers-in-arms!   160
Cynan and Cadwaladr, warlords in the armies,
Will be honoured till Doomsday, good fortune will be
    theirs:
Two royal lords, wise in their counsel,
Two generous men, lavish with land and cattle,
Two ready and fearless, one in destiny and faith,
Two protectors of Britain, with their splendid armies,
Two bears never shamed in their daily battles.

The sages predict what will come to pass :
From Manaw* to Llydaw, they'll hold the land,
From Dyfed to Thanet,[18] all will be theirs;   170
From the Wall to the Firth,† as far as the *abers*.‡
Their rule will spread out across Erechwydd.§
There'll be no right of return for the Saxons.
The Irish will come back to join their comrades.
Let the Cymry rise up, a warlike company –
Armies at an ale-feast, a tumult of warriors,
And God's own kings who have kept their faith.
Wessex men fill the ships, the warfare is over,
And Cynan seals a covenant with his neighbour.¶
No foreigners deserve the name of warriors –   180
But Cadwaladr's beggars and pedlars do!
Every Cymro will have joyful words to speak.
As for the Island's tormentors – a passing swarm.

*   *Manaw*: The area south of the Firth of Forth; see note on p. 12.
†   *the Firth*: Uncertain; but the Firth of Forth would make geographical
    sense here.
‡   *abers*: Perhaps the river-mouths on the Firth.
§   *Erechwydd*: Possibly north-eastern Yorkshire; see Introduction, p. xxi.
¶   *his neighbour*: Either Cadwaladr or a neighbouring British kingdom.

[When corpses stand, propping up each other.][19]
As far as Sandwich – may it be blessed! –
The foreigners line up on their way to exile,
One after another, going back to their own kind,
Saxons weighing anchor each day on the sea.
The pious[20] Cymry will triumph till Doomsday.
190   Let them seek out no fortune-teller, no ambitious poet –
There's no prophecy in the world for the Island but this.

Let us pray to the Lord who made Heaven and Earth
That Dewi will be prince over our warriors.
In hard times, the Lord is a fortress, he is my God[21] –
He does not die, or flee, or fall exhausted,
Nor fade nor fail, nor yield, nor waver.

40

Goronwy's Oak

Although there have been elements of prophecy in some of the legendary poems, in 'Goronwy's Oak' and other poems in this section the Taliesin persona is used directly as a vehicle for prophecy relevant to events and situations contemporary with the mediaeval writer. To be acceptable as divination, the events 'foretold' in a prophetic text of this sort – such as women grown bold, free men being bound and victors arriving from Rome – need to be described in indirect and allusive ways, thus making it easy for contemporary readers of Llyvyr Taliessin *to apply a widely varying set of circumstances or political events to any 'prediction'. This is the same principle as a fortune-teller predicting the future of a subject's life in terms so general that, whatever is said, the client is able to match specific details from their own lives to the diviner's words. Thus it is not the primary purpose of these poems to provide anything like exact references to historical realities, whether in a vague 'Heroic Age' past or in the mediaeval present of the anonymous poets. The identity of the Goronwy of this poem is less significant than the metaphorical resonance of the oak, a resonance which, in the course of the poem, is extended to include both the Cross and the wizard's staff in the legendary world of* The Mabinogion.

God saved Noah
From a spreading tide,
He who caught the first bird
That crossed the flood.
What tree is greater
Than the Oak of Goronwy?[1]
My defences are not –
The beams of Noah's Ark.[2]

There's a greater mystery,
Few men know it –
Save Goronwy's bright men.
From the wood where it grew,
Mathonwy's wand's charms
Assure victory in war
On the shore of wild seas.
Cynan*3 will seize them
When he comes to rule.
They shall return,
Over ebbtide and beach –
The four main leaders,
The fifth no weaker,
And many strong men
With Britain in mind.
Women will grow bold
And free men be bound;
A spring tide of longing
For drinking and riding.

From the east there shall come
A widow and slim wife
With iron weapons;
They will roar at men.
There will come victors
From the region of Rome.
The songs will be fitting
And spread far and wide –
As do Oaks and Brambles –
The songs will be fitting.

A dog for scenting, · a stallion for snorting,
A bullock for goring, · a pig for rooting.
The fifth young beast · that Jesus created

*   *Cynan*: An expected heroic deliverer of the Welsh; see Introduction, p.
xxvii.

Of Adam's line · [. . .]
Forest creatures · are fair to see,
As they were before, · and as they will be.
The cowardly Welsh · will be despised
When they go to ground · on foreign soil.

I made a leap · from what you can see –
The lucky person's · not unlucky.
The threat will come · from Rhun's battle-steam
Between Caer Rhian* · and Caer Rhywg,†
Between Dineidyn† · and Dineidwg.§4   50
Those who see clearly · have an end in sight:
There will be smoke · before a great fire.
Our Lord God · will be our defender.

---

*   *Caer Rhian*: Llanrhian in Pembrokeshire.
†   *Caer Rhywg*: Unidentifiable, unless it is the 'Kaerrihoc', which in one
    mediaeval text is the drowned land between Wales and Ireland.
‡   *Dineidyn*: Edinburgh.
§   *Dineidwg*: Unidentifiable, and almost certainly a one-off formation to
    echo 'Dineidyn'. This sort of playing with place names is found in several
    other poems in the collection.

41

Taliesin's Spring Song

The Welsh title for this poem, Glaswawt Taliesin, combines a common word (gwawt) for a praise poem or prophetic utterance with an adjective (glas) which can mean 'green' or 'fresh'. The reference may be to spring as a time for new military campaigning. The probable allusion to the Battle of Brunanburh (937), along with other phrases that may refer to tenth-century persons or events, has led some scholars to date the poem to the mid-tenth century; but literary parallels and language point to a later period, perhaps the twelfth century. The expected military deliverers Cadwaladr and Cynan are semi-legendary figures from the heroic past who quite often appear in texts like this. In the original, there is a single end-rhyme throughout, though the length of the lines varies a good deal. It is described as being worth 'twenty-four points' (see p. 66).

Envoys have come to me – and how noble their rank!
Grief is laid on me – and how full my heart is!
All too familiar, the oars in the sea (Beli's* liquor);[1]
All too familiar, light-armoured men at dead of night;
All too familiar, the fierce attacks after feasts at the castle –
Nine hundred castellans doomed to die!
In May by the Menai – that'll be a place of rough dealings;
By the Conwy still more – a wreaking of vengeance.
Cold is the death dealt out so readily
10   By merciless iron, a massive blow.
Three fine ships, unassailable, heavy with soldiers,
Three fleets in the flood, a foretaste of Doomsday,
Three evenings of battle for the claimants to the land,

---

*   *Beli*: The legendary ancestor of the royal house of Gwynedd.

A plague that will call for many graves,
All three of these threes, all three of these outrages,
A plague to bring judgement on the heights of Eryri.
One army of Saxons, one of Vikings, and a third still
    more cruel:
In Wales what are left are wives made widows.
Before Cynan's roaring, fire will spring forth –
Cadwaladr* in his bitterness   20
Will trample hill and rushes,
The thatch and the rooftops, a house on fire.
A portent will be seen –
A man coupling with his niece.[2]
They will call on a man of steel,
A descendant of Anarawd,†
And from him shall stem
A man battle-red from Brunanburh,‡[3]
Who'll not spare his own kin,
Not his cousin, nor his brother.   30
When the war-horn calls,
Nine hundred will grieve!
It's this cruel man, perfect in power,
Whom the green shoots of this spring song announce –
He's swift to march against all who provoke him!

---

*   *Cynan . . . Cadwaladr*: See Introduction, p. xxvii, and note on p. 130.

†   *Anarawd*: Ruler of Gwynedd around the turn of the tenth century, with a notable record of military triumph against other Welsh rulers and against the English of Mercia.

‡   *Brunanburh*: The Battle of Brunanburh (937 CE, probably somewhere on the Wirral) saw Aethelstan of Wessex defeat an alliance of Danes, Picts and Scots. The ruthless warlord of prophecy who is expected to come to the rescue of the British will be someone who has been 'blooded' at Brunanburh.

42

News Has Reached Me from Calchfynydd

This poem very clearly shows the paradox of the prophetic genre. It uses the fiction of 'news just in from the Limestone Mountain' (possibly Kelso on the Scottish Borders) about a dynastic struggle between two leaders from Welsh heroic history, who share a family connection. The first of the warring lords appears to be Mabon, son of Idno ab Meirchiawn, a cousin of Urien Rheged, patron of the Taliesin of the 'heroic' poems. The second combatant is Owain – presumably Owain, son of Urien (see p. 24), though he is confusingly linked to Dyfed or Deheubarth (that is, South-West Wales). The poem treats both heroes even-handedly, and there is no way of telling who is supposed to be the victor, though the opening seems to give Mabon the edge. Perhaps what is really being celebrated is this poem's evocation of the earlier Taliesin's praise of Urien. Bro ('land, area, region') is a key word in this poem exploring the idea of the ideal ruler's relationship with his native and enemy territories. The same word is used six times from lines 5–18. The poem deploys a variety of metres, including the nine-syllable cyhydedd naw ban, *the* toddaid byr *couplet, and shorter lines based on the five-syllable measure.*

News has reached me · from Calchfynydd[1]
Of shame for Deheubarth* · and one famed for pillage.[2]
He† gives goods to his men, · Christendom's fierce defender,
His valley is full · of joyful plunder,
Generous to the army's people, · generous to other lands;
Tyrant in battle, · a white heat · in the land.

* *Deheubarth*: South-west Wales, here connected to Owain.
† *He*: Here probably Mabon in the North.

What is a Welshman · least likely to say?[3]
'Men of Dyfed, · come for the cattle · of Idno's son.'*
And no one would venture · from where he comes,
Though one calf of his · is worth a hundred cows.   10
Your foes keep away · from around your land:[4]
Like a hot fire · there's smoke where you are.
When we[5] sought safe passage · through Gwyddno's land,†
A slim white body · lay between shingle and strand.
When the waters retreated · from the Cludwys‡ land
No cow would low, · missing her calf[6] –
Mabon was to the fore, · Mabon from far away,
When Owain fought · for his land's stock.
Battle in Altclud,§ · battle in Ygwen,
Battle in Gossulwyt,¶ · with loud wailing;   20
battle against Roda's** men · who look white as snow
with their black spears · flashing in the light.
Battle near a bright place; · leader of a godly line:
The shield in his hand · protects in attack.
Whoever saw Mabon · and his fierce white horse
Riding among Rheged's[7] cattle –
They couldn't flee · unless they could fly
From Mabon, without bloodshed · and dead bodies.
From descent on a fray · to the start of a battle,
Mabon's men spreading out · can't be resisted.   30
When Owain came down · for his father's cattle,
Lime wash and wax · and splinters exploded.[8]
No one considers · hornless cattle as plunder
[. . .] for fear of piling up · stiff, bloodstained bodies,
For fear of a powerful man of fire,††
For fear of a warrior rousing for war,

*   *Idno's son*: Mabon.
†   *Gwyddno*: Ruler of a flooded land in Cardigan Bay (Dyfed) and father of
     Elffin; see note on p. 47.
‡   *Cludwys*: Clydeside.
§   *Altclud*: Dumbarton Rock.
¶   *Ygwen . . . Gossulwyt*: Unknown; presumably locations in the North.
**   *Roda*: No certain identification.
††   *man of fire*: Mabon.

For fear of blood on flesh,
For fear of widespread distress.

News has reached me · from the South's plains
40 Of a famous king, · the best · of the most generous.[9]
No petitioners need · to complain to you.
At many a ford and wood · are his forces:
When battle was caused, · he was lord, king and dragon.
Cattle were wild, · but not panicked · by Mabon.
From a clash with a pack of men,
There was carnage · and plunder in Rhun,[*]
There was joy, · as always, for ravens;
Loud was men's telling · of their wounds – · after battle,
And not undamaged · was the shield of Owain:
50 Shield dented with defending · in battle's confusion.
He didn't steal cattle · without leaving faces bloody:
Blood on the cattle track, · most cruelly spilt.[10]
Gore was washed over · the tops of heads,
And blood over faces · that had turned pale.
Blood stained the leader's · golden saddle.
Gwenhwys's[†] men, seeking spoils, · were scattered.
A herd afraid of hard battle, · stock with stiff manes,
A herd defended by horns – · on their shields are spears:
Great, fearless men, · sword-blades aloft.

60 A fight with Owain the Great, · of great cruelty.
Men fell at noon, · defending their land,
When Owain marched out · for blessed Erechwydd's[‡] sake,
A raid which was toasted · by his father.[§][11]

[*]   *Rhun*: Maelgwn Gwynedd's son; as a place name, perhaps Gwynedd, or
      some district of it.
[†]   *Gwenhwys*: Gwent, in South Wales.
[‡]   *Erechwydd*: Urien's home; see Introduction, p. xxi.
[§]   *his father*: Urien.

43

The *Awen* Predicts

The figure referred to in this poem as 'the Leaper' (Llyminauc or, in Modern Welsh, Lleminog – literally 'the Leaping One') is a frequent character in prophetic texts, a messianic hero arriving from over the sea. It is unlikely that there is a single historical personage who should be identified with this figure in the present poem, though it has been suggested that it might be the twelfth-century King of Gwynedd, Gruffydd ap Cynan. The poem seems to envisage a champion coming from overseas to restore sovereignty to a Gwynedd that has been subdued or corrupted. The opening four lines repeat the opening of 'The Great Prophecy of Britain' (p. 121), the most significant and probably the oldest of the prophetic poems.

The *awen* predicts · they will come without delay –
Wealth and possessions · and peace for us all,
Far-flung dominion · and leaders with mettle,
And, once war is over, · secure dwellings everywhere.
Seven sons had risen · from Beli's lineage[*] –
Caswallon[†] and Lludd[‡] · used to cause much grief;
But the last, worst stroke · was when Prydyn lost Iago.[§]
It will be a land in chaos · as far as Blathaon[¶] –

[*]   *Beli's lineage:* The kingly line of Gwynedd.
[†]   *Caswallon:* A legendary king mentioned in *The Mabinogion*.
[‡]   *Lludd:* Another legendary ruler; see p. 143.
[§]   *Iago:* Probably Iago, son of Beli, ruler of Gwynedd in the late sixth/early seventh century (a different Beli from the legendary ancestor mentioned on p. 132).
[¶]   *Blathaon:* The northernmost point of Britain.

Their champions exhausted,
10   Reins trailing from saddles,
The land ravaged by neighbours.
All of the Cymry · will forsake generous dealing,
Solemnly covenanting · to be governed by slaves.
Then the Leaper will come –
A man who is eager
To subdue Môn,
To lay waste Gwynedd
From frontier to heartland,
From beginning to end,
20   To take hostages from it.
His face is set,
He bows down to none,
Neither Cymry nor Saxons.
There will come a man from his hiding place:
He will shed much blood
And give battle to the Gentiles.[4]
And another will come,
His hosts travelling far,
And give joy to the Britons.

44

Fine Feasting

A victory feast is described – suggesting that a king, named as Beli, son of Manogan, has been successful in repelling five waves of invaders, catalogued by the poet. Beli is described colourfully both as a dragon and as a queen bee, because he presided over Ynys fel Feli ('the Honey-Isle of Beli'), a golden past in which, presumably, his followers drank mead.

Fine feasting · around two lakes,[1] · one lake round our host,
A host in a fort, · an unfallen fort, · famed far and wide –
A wondrous retreat, · a well-made refuge · of reinforced
    stones.
He with a dragon's qualities – · above the seatings · of
    drinking vessels,
Drink in gold horns, · gold horns in hand, · hand covered in
    foam –
Is the lively queen bee. · I now beseech you, · victorious
    King Beli,
King Manogan's son,
To defend your rights.
He's the rightful ruler
Of Honey-Isle of Beli.
Five oppressors will come:
Pirates from Ireland,
War-loving sinners,
A nation of scum.
Five others will come
from Normandy.
The sixth king will reign
from sowing till harvest.
The seventh will be buried

10

20   In an overseas grave.[2]
                        The eighth, a Lynx,[3] will land,
                        Won't protect the old.
                        The people's outcry
                        Will rouse Eryri;*
                        His course[4] won't be easy.
                        Let's beg Elöi†
                        That he'll be our Lord
                        In Heaven, our future home.

*   *Eryri*: Snowdonia.
†   *Elöi*: An Aramaic word for God (as in Mark 15:34).

45

May God Lift up over the British People

Unusually, this poem is found in two different sources. A virtually identical text appears in a seventeenth-century manuscript copied from a mediaeval original. Like others in this group, the poem echoes the language of 'The Great Prophecy of Britain' (p. 121). Looking back to the seventh-century exile and return of King Cadwallon of Gwynedd and his revenge on the Northumbrian invaders (as described by Bede and – more expansively and imaginatively – by Geoffrey of Monmouth), and also to the death of the ninth-century Gwynedd ruler, Idwal Foel, the poem envisages a major campaign of retaliation against the English involving a Welsh alliance led by Gwynedd; this theme recurs in most of the prophetic poems, and points to a date in the early thirteenth century, when Gwynedd persistently sought to create such an alliance against English incursions.

May God lift up over the British people
The joyful ensign of the armies of Môn –
The battle-lines of Gwynedd, swift-moving forces,
Radiant in fame, each fight yields them hostages!
To them Powys men will rally, praised for their mettle,
Proud men who will triumph over unjust laws.
They will go forward in two armies, forward in harmony,
One in spirit, one in command, orderly, united.
Ceredigion men too will take their full part:
When you see fierce men around the Vale of Aeron,   10
When grief shall fall on Tywi and Teifi,*
They will be hastening to war near Llonion's court.†

---

*   *the Vale of Aeron . . . Tywi . . . Teifi*: Places in Ceredigion.
†   *Llonion's court*: Lanion in Pembrokeshire.

Elite troops in their fury, in their great multitudes –
No forts will give refuge from their onward rushing:
Din Clud,* Din Maerud, Din Daryfon,
Even Din Rheiddon,† none will be safe.[1]
When Cadwallon made landfall from across the Irish Sea,
He set up again a royal hall in Ardd Nefon.‡[2]
Soon I shall hear the singers' laments!
20   How fierce the hosts of horsemen at Chester,
And Idwal's§ vengeance on his pale-faced foes,
Playing ball with the heads of Saxons!
May he confound the lynx and her foreign brood
From the ford of the Taradr¶ to Porth Wygr** in Môn –
This modest youth, his people's fortress!
From the day when there's honey and clover to be had,
Their strife and their struggling will vanish away.
It is no sad business to rouse anger against enemies!
May God lift up over the British people
30   The joyful ensign of the armies of Môn.

---

*   *Din Clud*: Dumbarton Rock, centre of the British kingdom of Strathclyde
     (Alt Clud) in the early Middle Ages.
†   *Din Maerud . . . Daryfon . . . Rheiddon*: Unidentifiable.
‡   *Ardd Nefon*: Unidentifiable.
§   *Idwal*: Idwal Foel of Gwynedd. Killed by the English in 942 CE, he was
     an ally of Athelstan, but may also have been involved in anti-English
     campaigning in North-East Wales.
¶   *Taradr*: A stream marking the eastern border of Welsh territory, running
     into the Wye; the exact location is unknown, but it may be related to
     'Tar's Brook' near Aconbury in Herefordshire.
**   *Porth Wygr*: The mouth of the River Gwygyr in Anglesey, depicted as the
     northernmost point of Welsh territory.

46

Long Eulogy for Lludd

Lludd, a legendary king of Britain who saves the island from three magical plagues, is not actually named in this poem, but the Llyvyr Taliessin *scribe evidently wanted to suggest a connection between it and the 'Short Poem on Lludd's Conversation' (p. 152). Lludd and his brother Llefelys appear in* The Mabinogion, *where they have a tale named after them.[1] This poem uses a wide variety of the Welsh metres but in an irregular way – appropriate, perhaps, for an apocalyptic vision. The high-pitched tropes of Welsh-language prophecy are used in the service of an archetypal dread of changes caused by foreigners taking a homeland by force.*

The best song's full of praise
For eight recorded days:[2]
They'll come on Monday;
Shall lay the place waste.
On Tuesday, they'll distribute
Pain to our enemies.
They'll harvest on Wednesday
The full measure of glory.
They'll give birth on Thursday
To eager applause.   10
On Friday, day of domination,
They'll wade through men's blood.
On Saturday [. . .]
On Sunday, it is most certain
That they will have come.
Five ships and five hundred,
So poets will tell,
Of turmoil from races,

Impossible to count.
20   Britons in turmoil,
Thirsting for gold;
Though they fight well,
There will come enemies,
All subject to God,
Who redeemed Eden's fall.

I petition for prophecy,
To protest at oppression –
The well-known prediction
About Cadwaladr and Cynan.*3
30   What use is the world
If the sun's blotted out?

The wise man's predictions
Tell what helps and what hinders.
The poet interprets the cloud
As it crosses the heavens;
It will weep a torrent
On the mountain's slopes.
Loud is the marten, full is the stag,
The Britons wait for counsel.
40   There will come to the Britons
Blood from judicious battle;
Having had gold and jewellery,
Anglesey4 and Lleyn† laid waste,
There's refuge in Eryri.‡5

A perfect one prophesies:
A house is made desolate.
The Cymry who speak perfect Welsh
Will change their language.

*   *Cadwaladr and Cynan*: The legendary saviours of Britain; see Introduc-
      tion, p. xxvii.
†   *Lleyn*: The Lleyn peninsula, just south of Anglesey.
‡   *Eryri*: Snowdonia.

And the Brindled Cow*
Will wreak havoc.   50
At noon it will low,
At midnight cause turmoil;
Farmland will boil,
Our shrines will burn down.
A dirge will be sung
Around Prydain's† border.
Of one mind, we will repel
Shame brought by the sea.⁶
May true joy be found
in a wailing world.   60
[. . .]
He went to Dolaethwy.‡
The leader makes great demands:
Just herding, no foaling,
No breeding from cows –
The world isn't safe.
The world will be laid waste.
Cuckoos will perish⁷ –
Small men with false minds
Won't thrive but will starve.   70
A swift-moving leader of forces –
No knife can defend
Against a coward's sword.
I wouldn't have wished on our men
Such greed for another's home,
Nor the horrors of Creuddyn:§⁸
Cymry will fight Angles, Irish, Picts.
The Cymry will repel the attacks.

---

*   *the Brindled Cow*: Also the Brindled Ox; see note on p. 100.
†   *Prydain*: Britain.
‡   *Dolaethwy*: Possibly Menai Bridge.
§   *Creuddyn*: A common Welsh place name; here possibly Deganwy, where
     several English incursions caused great damage, including a siege by King
     John in 1210–11.

Wooden horses* will arrive by sea:
80   Murdering, Northern outlaws
From a line of savage sea foes,
From the fallen Adam's line.[9]
A starling shall set off to lead
A convoy of ravens and men.[10]
Sluggish Seithennin's† band,
At anchor against Cristin.‡[11]
Hit from at sea, hit from above;
Hit from at sea, tumult in wasteland,
In wood, plain, hollow and hill.
90   Every petition's unheeded – every king,
         No matter where, does nothing.
There will be turmoil; among men – chaos
         And misery spreading:
Revenge mixed in with men's fair vows.

Long before Judgement Day, God the Almighty,
    Creator
         Who is roused to anger, He has fixed
An appointed day
Of reckoning that will be made –
An end to Ireland's temperate lands.
100   In Prydain a revival will come:
A Briton of noble Roman stock.[12]
I shall be judged for these troubled days.

Sages foretell
A land of lost souls;
Druids foresee,
While there are Britons and sea,
That summer will have no sun;
Lords will be fragile,

---

*   Wooden horses: Ships.
†   Seithennin: In The Black Book of Carmarthen, the gate-keeper whose
drunkenness allows the sea to flood Cantre'r Gwaelod.
‡   Cristin: Unknown.

Will lead a weak people astray;
From beyond the sea [. . .]
A thousand Britons will be judged.
Let me be saved from the swamp,
Near where the furnace burns,
From those in the depths of Hell,
Where shivers the blazing Cain,
By the Lord of the world without end.

110

He's on His Way for Sure

*This is a carefully and elaborately crafted poem which – like
'Taliesin's Spring Song' (p. 132), 'Long Eulogy for Lludd' (p.
143) and other poems in this section – once again portrays
the seventh-century figure of Cadwaladr as a deliverer for the
Welsh, fighting against both English and Southern Welsh forces,
restoring legitimate government to Gwynedd and establishing
that kingdom's hegemony throughout the whole country.*

He's on his way for sure, the Roman's kinsman,[1]
A rare one among men, unrivalled in kind.
Before him a great battle cry can be heard,
And a warband, and blood flowing over his foes,
And the sounding of horns and commotion of people.
They stab, they assault in combat with swords –
The ravens and eagles are craving for blood.
His path a wild bear's track, an invincible force –
Cadwaladr the glorious, the shining, the splendid,
10   Defender of warriors in far-flung regions!

It's on its way for sure, from across the waves –
What was promised in prophecy from the beginning:
Years of triumph and plenty, all the rights of royalty.
A winter pact: he will steer his ships by rough passages –
A true hero for captives, generous as the great flood.
At the season of high tides, on the crest of the waves,
He will lead swanlike steeds from the decks of his ship.
Bear and lion, apt for the task, from their bright
    strongholds,
Their fierce followers will strike at him with bloody
    spears.

But suffering will seek them out, a warning against
    treachery,   20
Faced with his fury and all his great forces.
Though these wild boars may fall, they will cut through
    the shieldwalls.
In battle, Cadwaladr's is the glory and bright fame.
May a dragon rise up from the lands of the south,
To join with this young man as day dawns on Thursday.

He's on his way for sure, generous and valiant,
And praise shall be loud for his great renown;
His armies far-ranging, his dominion spread wide,
Till seven nations live under Gwynedd's ruler.
And until he dies, all turmoil is done with,   30
This kindly king of peoples in harmony,
Scourge of the Angles as they hasten from exile –
Through the seas their descendants will slink away home.

He's on his way for sure, the true heir of Môn,
Renowned, a dragon, a deliverer for the British,
Leader of armies, lord of warriors in their cuirasses.
The wise man among the wizards gives this deep
    prophecy –
They will pitch their tents by the Tren* and the
    Tarannon,†2
Holding fast to their longing to capture Môn,
Until the long voyage from Ireland is made   40
By the fair famous saviour of Caesar's people.

The signs foretell the terrors of fighting.
I know what provoked the battle on the Winwaed.‡3
The bear from Deheubarth§ challenges Gwynedd,

---

*   *the Tren*: The Tern in Shropshire is the likeliest identification.
†   *the Tarannon*: The Trannon in Powys, near Caersws.
‡   *Winwaed*: The Battle of Winwaed (Uinued) Field, fought between the
    Northumbrians and the Mercians in 656 CE.
§   *Deheubarth*: South-west Wales.

Battling for glory, for abundance of wealth,
Libations of honour and the free dispersing
Of New-Year gifts in their wide-spreading lands.
May they fix their shield while the swords are clashing
For Cadwaladr's cause, around Gwynedd's lord.

50   It's on its way for sure, the future is certain –
All England in turmoil, their riches ours,
As they see their pale freckled folk[4] run away
Between flying arrows and bright iron weapons.
Ordered on to the sea, spears pushing them out,
They are rocked on the ocean, across the wide flood;
The salt and the far islands will be their refuge.

He's on his way for sure, from across the Severn –
Britain's ordained lord, a mighty monarch,
A generous warlord over many dynasties,
60   Worthy to rule, and unmoved by hostility.
All the world's peoples will surely be glad.
A dynasty of fine men will have the dominion;
Hiriell's[*] flame will blaze out above the Severn.
The Cymry will muster for war without fear –
May joy attend Cadwaladr's fighting,
The loud cries of the poets, a glorious conflict!

It's coming for sure –
His army, his fleet,
His pushing back shields,
70   His clashing of spears.
After savage fighting
His will shall be done.
Round all Britain let him roam!
May his fame blaze in fight,
A dragon, never hiding,

*   *Hiriell*: The name of a North Welsh hero who appears elsewhere in medi-
aeval Welsh poetry.

Whatever befalls him.
No easy goal
Defeating Dyfed!
He'll take tribulation
Beyond Rheged's Firth,[5]   80
And this lord of great bounty
Will be master in Elfed –
Generous, shrewd-planning,
Powerful in conflict.
I shall praise to the skies
Cadwaladr, keen for battle!

48

Short Poem on Lludd's Conversation

This poem forms a companion piece to 'Long Eulogy for Lludd' (p. 143). Unlike the longer poem, however, it directly mentions the events of the Mabinogion *story of Lludd and his brother Llefelys, King of France. In that story, the brothers meet to talk about the curses afflicting Britain. In order to foil the magical powers of the invading aliens, who can hear every word spoken in the land, they speak through a long horn of bronze washed out by wine.*[1] *Rather than simply recounting what the brothers then said to each other, the poem draws a parallel between the* Mabinogion *legend of foreigners bringing turmoil to Britain and its predictions, which must relate to the circumstances of the poet's time; but which time that is, exactly, is never specified, and the language is deliberately vague about historical detail.*

In the Trinity's name: · God's charity's skilful:
A numerous tribe, · bringing violent horror
Shall conquer Prydain, · most renowned of islands.
Men from the land of Asia[2] · and the land of Cafis,
People of godless intent, · from an unknown land.

Famen* of couched lances; · *maris*† raiders,
Wearing long coats – · who else is like them?
Their aims are lawless, · their *ober*‡ hostile:
Europeans, Arabians, · Saracens.
Christ truly saved · the bound and reviled
Before Lludd · and Llefelys's talk.

*   *Famen*: Vulgar Latin for 'people'.
†   *maris*: Latin for 'of the sea'.
‡   *ober*: Presumably 'actions' (Latin *opera*).

10

Albion's ruler · will be shaken
By a Roman leader – · splendid his terror.
He's not a bold, nor a wily · king of fluent speech –
Who'd see those foreigners · as I see them.³
Bonfires of alder⁴ will be set, · at a stout leader's base,
Showing the way – · it will burn with a roar.
May I merit the dear Son, · fluent of speech!
The Cymry, gnashing their teeth, · making war on slaves.
I worry, I wonder · what their course will be: 20
The Briton who, in Wessex, · rose up in triumph [. . .]⁵

49

A Prophecy about Cadwaladr

Here again, we can confidently say that the heroic memory of Cadwaladr is being invoked to encourage hopes for a restoration of Gwynedd's power and integrity; but any attempt at a more detailed interpretation of this text, fragmentary and confused as it is, would be beset by uncertainties. It is the last item in the Llyvyr Taliessin *collection, and its conclusion has been lost along with the final pages of that manuscript.*

A rider swift in the mustering,
Fierce on both flanks,
Doling fear, slaughtering base folk,
He lurks in Eryri.
When Cadwaladr comes, he'll set
His capital in Britain's fields.
[...]¹
As for me, I shall rejoice!
Then the Saxons shall come, demanding to eat
The men's portion belonging to heroes in their
    wealth;
A woman shall be under the yoke of her slave,²
An ancient enemy [...]
The men's portion [...]³
Did you see my kinsman and my brother?
I saw a slender corpse, ravens feeding on flesh,
And another one, bloodsoaked from a false final
    swordstroke,
And on the banks [...]

DEVOTIONAL POEMS

50

Lord of Heaven, Permit My Prayer to You

This is a meditation on imagining one's deathbed and asking for God's grace. The echo between the third line of this poem ('Rex gloriae, ask artfully for me') and the title of the poem immediately preceding it in the Llyvyr Taliessin, *the opener of the whole manuscript ('First Artful Command: Who Pronounced It?', p. 35), suggests that the scribe (or somebody else) may have had the relationship of art to God's justice in mind as a unifying theme for the collection. Here, the Latin syllables don't count towards the total for each line, which becomes infinitely expandable in God's order. The poet's desire to be steadfast for God, like an oak, leads him to think of the wooden boards of his coffin.*

Lord of Heaven, permit my prayer to you;
From wrath, may my praising you save me.
Rex gloriae,* ask artfully for me:
Dominuus fortis† did you see the *Dominus*'s deep prophecies?
He liberated *hic nemo inper p[ro]genio*‡ the spoils of Hell,
He assembled *dominus uirtutum*§ its crowd, that was enslaved
And before I was [. . .]
I'll be like oak for the redeeming God.
And before I come to a bloody end,
And before my mouth becomes a foaming wound,   10
And before I'm made to touch a coffin's boards,

*   *Rex gloriae*: 'King of Glory'.
†   *Dominuus fortis*: 'Strong Lord'.
‡   *hic nemo inper p[ro]genio*: 'This scion [of Adam], inferior to none.' Very
    garbled.
§   *dominus uirtutum*: 'Lord of virtues'.

May my soul receive His wholesome food.
Letters in books say little to me
About the sore grief after the deathbed.
To those who hear my poetic song:
May they gain Heaven's country, the best abode.

51

Alexander's Breastplate

This poem's title (an odd one, in that the actual poem contains no mention of Alexander) may be explained by its proximity in the Llyvyr Taliessin *manuscript to the two 'legendary' poems about Alexander the Great. It is also possible that a composition by a cleric named Alexander has been mistakenly associated with the more famous figure. The designation* llurig *(*lorica *in Latin), meaning 'breastplate', is regularly given to prayers invoking the Holy Trinity for protection. It is a form of prayer particularly associated with mediaeval Welsh and Irish Christianity, the most famous example being the hymn known as 'St Patrick's Breastplate' ('I bind unto myself today / The strong name of the Trinity').*

Since his birth · the earth's face · shows no equal to him:
One gracious Son · in the great Trinity · of divine persons,
Son to the Godhead, · Son of humanity, · miraculous sole
 Son,
God's son, my stronghold, · sweet Mary's little one, · grac-
 ious child revealed,
Great in splendour, · great God the sovereign, · homeland of
 glory.
From Adam's seed · and Abraham's · we have our birth,
But the earth's multitude – · so prophecy's fulfilled – · are
 born of God's own seed.
With a word he delivers · the deaf and the blind · from all
 distress,
The wretched folk · dwelling in darkness · who live in
 disease.
May we ascend · where the Trinity dwells, · salvation's work
 done.

10

Christ's radiant Cross · a shining armour · against all harm:
Against all angry foes – · however fearsome – · a sure
    stronghold.

52

I Make My Prayer to the Trinity

The title of this poem in the manuscript is 'Lament for the Thousand Children', suggesting a reference to the Holy Innocents slaughtered by Herod in his search for the Christ child (Matthew 2:16), but nothing in the text connects with this story. The title must have been incorrectly placed; it likely belongs with a neighbouring poem ('Saints and Martyrs of the Faith', p. 169). Instead, as in 'Lord of Heaven, Permit My Prayer to You' and 'A Prophecy of Judgement Day' (see pp. 157 and 163), the poet is here contemplating the fate of his soul after death, and praying to God for mercy at the Day of Judgement.

I make my prayer to the Trinity:
Lord, let me sing your praise.
The world's roar places us in peril;
Our deeds and law cause grave concern
To the family of saints – that is, the heavenly throng.
Heaven's *Rex*,* make me eloquent in your praise
Before my soul and flesh are sundered;
Give me the *Pater*† for my sin.
May I make my prayer to your glory.
May the Trinity grant me mercy.   10
I ask, I desire, O people of the world,
The nine heavenly orders with their diligent hosts,
And the tenth, with its seven holy saints.[1]
Glorious will be the nations,
A blessed throng that will thrive.
God will see many wretches:

---

*   *Rex*: 'King'.
†   *the Pater*: I.e. the Lord's Prayer, *Pater noster*.

In Heaven, on earth, at the end of all,
Afflicted, lost and in hardship,
Suffering, in body and soul,
20   Far from the presence of God.
I beg You, King of peace,
Grant my soul eternal life.
In Heaven's realm, he won't refuse me.

53

A Prophecy of Judgement Day

There are several versions of parts of this poem in a variety of other mediaeval manuscripts, but the text in the Llyvyr Taliessin *is the most extensive, and probably the earliest. The text uses themes not only from the New Testament but from apocryphal Christian texts like the Apocalypse of Thomas, from a variety of Irish sources, from material ascribed to Bede and from at least one Old English poem on the subject. The tradition of listing a certain number of signs that announce the Last Day lies behind some of the text, but it is difficult to see these signs in the poem as forming a conventional list. We have supplied in square brackets a tentative division of the text according to speakers (following Marged Haycock's edition). Christ's dramatic address to the damned souls finds some parallels in the handling of the Last Judgement in the late-mediaeval English mystery plays. Metrically it is relatively simple, but the sustained double beat of the original Welsh is powerful and insistent.*

> *Deus,** God, Creator,
> King who gives strength to multitudes,
> Christ Jesus, who sees all,
> To whom belongs radiant glory –
> None mightier can be found –
> Do not leave me with no share
> In praising your mercy.
> There never came to this world
> A one like you, Lord –
> There never came, and never will come   10

---

*   *Deus*: 'God'.

An equal to the Godhead.
There never was born among us
An equal to God.
He does not recognize
An equal to himself
Above the skies or under them –
No lord but he
Above the sea or under it.
He it was who created us [. . .]

20   When *Deus* shall come,
He'll bring great turmoil with him.
Wrathful on Judgement Day
Are the messengers of turmoil:
Wind, sea and fire,
Lightning and thunder.
Snow-white, the blessed Son[1] –
The world's hosts will groan,
The sun will be hidden,
Leviathan drawn from the deep;
30   Sea and stars will be hidden
When the *Pater* descends
To speak with his multitudes,
Horns echo to earth's four quarters.
With the sea on fire,
The world's dwellers will burn
Till all have perished.
The desert will burn
Before his great anger.
The flood will overflow
40   Before his fury.
The day of trial in plain sight!
Woe to those who must face it!
The hills will burst,
The sky collapse.
A red wind is stirred up
Out of its chains

Before the world's laid flat
As when it was first made.
St Peter announced it –
The world's last day: 50
One Saturday (he said)
The world will turn furnace;
One Saturday, with no hesitation,
The Lord will do this to us.
The world's weather will be
Wind melting the trees,
Stirring up chaos.
When the mountains are burning
There will be some who sing,
Horns sounding to his glory.   60
The mighty one will set all ablaze –
Sea, land and lake.
There will be shuddering terror
As the earth heaves up,
Lifting high every place,
And the dead in stone shelters,
The hidden multitude.
And the lake will burn
With waves of anger;
Tempestuous thunder –   70
Well may we grieve!
Joy amidst sorrow
Wrath causing burning
Between Heaven and Earth.
When the Trinity comes
In fullness of glory,
Hosts of Heaven around him,
The crowds gather to him –
Songs and hymns,
And the music of angels!   80

They will come from their graves:
From the world's beginning, all will rise.

The wolves will rise,
And all the disfigured,
All destroyed by the sea,
And great will be their cry.

When [God] shall come,
He will separate them out:

GOD

90

'Those who are mine,
Turn to the right;
Those filled with sin,
Let them go to the left.
Have your words not deserved,
Has your mouth's speech not earned,
Being sent to the waters
In darkness, with no light?'

A SINNER

100

'Broad lands were once mine,
And people of many races;
A hundred countries were mine,
A hundred full harvests,
A hundredfold yield in this present world.
I did not live without fighting,
There was much bitter discord
Between me and my kin.
There was plenty of quarrelling
Between me and my neighbours.
There was plenty of violence
Between me and the poor.'

CHRIST

110

'Whoever does this to me
Shall never be mine.
He led me to the Cross
So that I knew pain.[2]
He led me to the tree;
He bent down my head.
Look at my two feet,

How grievous their hurts.
Look: see how painful
Are the bones of my feet.
Look at my two arms
And the burden they carry.   120
Look at my two shoulders,
How distorted they are.
Look at the nails
That pierce through my heart.
Look at the piercing
Between my two eyes.
Look at what's come to pass:
A crown of thorns on my head.
Look – such great sorrow –
At my side that was pierced.   130
All of you, see
How skilful your handiwork.
For you there will be no mercy
For my wounds and spear thrusts.'[3]

SINNERS   'Ah Lord, we did not know
It was you we were crucifying!
Lord of Heaven and of all lands,
We did not know you were Christ!
And if we had known,
We'd have held back from you.'   140

CHRIST   'No denial will be accepted
From the crowd of the accursed.
You have done what is evil
In the face of the Godhead.
A hundred thousand angels
Bear witness to me,
Those who gathered about me
After my hanging,
On the Cross soaked with blood
As I myself wrought healing.   150

In Heaven there was trembling
When I cried out "Eli!"
To the Lord above.
Sing, you two Johns,*
The two who lead the way ahead of me,
Two books in your hands,
Reading them aloud,
Till the great glory comes.⁴
Let him speak who has spoken,
And let vengeance fall on you
Befitting your wild words.
Let the thunderbolt strike you,
Condemn you to Hell.'

Christ Jesus on high
Came to live here below [. . .]
A thousand years have passed
Since he lived in the world;
And two thousand years before the Cross
Enoch saw visions.†
Fools do not realize
That their nature's corrupt.
You honour this world –
A marvel to you,
But a millennium of misery
Will be your life in eternity.

160

170

*   *two Johns*: Presumably John the Baptist and John the Evangelist.
†   *Enoch*: Mentioned in Genesis 5:24; appears regularly in Jewish and
     Christian apocrypha as a visionary to whom the secrets of Heaven and
     Hell are revealed.

54

Saints and Martyrs of the Faith

This is the poem to which the title 'Lament for the Thousand Children' may originally have been attached. It fits slightly better with this piece; Herod's massacre of the Innocents is not the main topic, but it is mentioned, as it is also in 'Cruel Herod' (p. 175) and 'The Stem of Jesse' (p. 178). The more general title of 'Saints and Martyrs of the Faith' suggested by Marged Haycock captures the subject matter more adequately. The poem is not exactly a litany of invocations to the saints; it is more of a catalogue providing the poet with an opportunity to play with exotic names from Scripture and ecclesiastical history, many of them written in seriously garbled form. The same fascination with outlandish names appears in other poems in the manuscript, such as the elegy for Alexander the Great, 'He Ranged the Whole World' (p. 94).

Apostles and martyrs,
Virgins, renowned widows,
And Solomon who thought on God –
Your virtues a holy path for a holy people.
And they come to me, a harmonious company,
Till my own virtues are securely protected.

A multitude of them, in their pure and holy ranks,
The shining pillars of the Church;
And all these spokesmen, they are spoken of
By those who have learned of them in holy books.   10
In the face of the cruel and cursed mob,
May my soul find sure protection.

There were many who lived – Saviour of nations –
In the chilly pains of Hell
[. . .] till the world's fifth age,
Till Christ released them from their slavery,
Saving them from the fathomless depths:
Many were led out by God's championing.[1]

20   Two thousand sons of Leah's line*
Who were two years old and under,
Killed by [. . .]
A superabundance [. . .]
Rachel's[†] fair kindred suffered this plague.
Then it came to Jerusalem.

Many the saints of Brittany,
And many who belong to Touraine;
To Tarsus[2] far beyond Rome,
To Apulia[3] and Alexandria,
Arabia[4] and India.
30   The world's divided in three:
Asia, Africa, Europa.

Many the saints of Capernaum
By the sea,[5] and of Nain,
Of Zebulon and Kishon,
Of Nineveh and Naphtali,[‡]
Tiberias and Chorazin,[§][6]

---

*   *Leah*: Wife of Jacob and ancestress of the people of Israel.

†   *Rachel*: Jacob's junior wife in the Genesis story. She is depicted in the
Gospel of Matthew (2:18) as lamenting over the massacre of the children
of Bethlehem.

‡   *Zebulon . . . Kishon . . . Nineveh . . . Naphtali*: An odd collection of
names: Zebulon and Naphtali are associated with Gallilee (Isaiah 9:1,
Matthew 4:15); Kishon is located near Mount Carmel (1 Kings 18:40)
and Niniveh is the capital of Assyria. Presumably the names are chosen
simply for assonance.

§   *Tiberias and Chorazin*: Towns in Galilee.

There was Christ foretold, Son of Mary, Joachim's
     daughter
 And we are of the crowd of this great lineage.

Many the saints of Jericho,
Of Mary's far-famed castle,   40
Hymned by the multitudes of the church at Siloam;
Of Caesarea with its round palace,
Of the Ammonites and Moabites,
And the valleys of Beersheba,
And – before there was a creed – the martyrs of
     Carthage.[7]
Heralds to the wide world
Are the speakers of Greek and Hebrew
And Latin, fervent men.

Many the saints, shining leaders,
Brave men, whose company's wonderful,   50
Full of praise in the presence of the royal splendour,
Warriors of the Beloved, his followers.
In narrow places and broad, in all times of need,
May they be a refuge for us, soul and body.

Many the saints of Nicomedia,[8]
And the isle of Ceylon.
Many the saints and blessed ones,
A flow of wine, slaughtered by men.
And the weight of their honour pleads for us.
[God] has set the saints among the stars.   60

Many the saints who have guarded the borders:
Effectus re inferior
A superare superior.
Hermon and Tabor,

* *Effectus re inferior*: Garbled Latin, probably intended to mean something
like, 'Things done here below / Because of victory above'.

Aenon's vale and Soar,
Great Carthage and Lesser,
And the islanders of the Middle Sea.

Many the saints of the Island of Britain,
And of Ireland, that lovely realm,
70   Their deeds a glorious multitude,
They believed and they served God along with us.

Many the saints longing for Heaven's court,
O God, diviner of prophecy.
In every land they held their fasts,
They lived throughout the wide world's circle.
And many the wise men who prophesied
Christ's coming, though they lived before him.
Many the saints of the East
And the company from the people of Judah,
80   The speakers of Greek and Hebrew,
And of Latin, fervent men.

Seven score and seven hundred saints,
Seven thousand and seventy score –
A great number gather in November,[9]
Made fortunate by martyrdom.
Fifteen score saints there were,
And three thousand young children.[10]
The saints of December sing aloud –
For Jesus' sake they died.[11]
90   Twelve thousand who gathered round him
Found faith through the words of John;
They pray, and they have earned their place
In Heaven, where they have come.
There were nine thousand saints who embraced
Baptism, creed and confession
To escape the pains of those living in Hellfire –
Hell which gives cold shelter.[12]

But if God has made it to be so,
Our comfort's made certain through Peter's authority.[13]
[. . .]   100
Many there were and will be,
Above Heaven and under it, many there are,
And many who believed with their whole heart,
Who believed through the will of God,
Many the world over, through the gifts you gave.
Merciful God, by the atonement you made,
Be gentle to us, wrathful God.
May I not anger you, let me be joyful.
Every lost soul cries out in grief,
Those in trouble plead insistently,   110
But those with calm minds don't croak in complaint.
I'm weary of this present world's bustle –
I shall sing when I'm in my grave
Of the wealth of God's protection,
Of the memorials made at the martyr's tomb
Safe in the commemoration of the saints.
May my sinful words bring to me
No greater things than they bring to the many
        who hear me.

------

*The following Latin text appears between lines 99 and 100 of
this poem in the* Llyvyr Taliessin, *presumably as a result of a
corrupt manuscript tradition; it has no obvious connection to
what comes before or after it.*[14]

The angels who arrived · for the Lord's nativity
To sing praises at midnight · with the shepherds in
        Bethlehem –
Are these not these angels from Heaven, · those who with
        Michael the Archangel
Advance to battle · for the souls in this world?

And are they not the same angels · who lead on before the
    confirmed,
The absolved,[15] the baptized, · until Judgement Day dawns?

When Christ was crucified, · had it pleased him,
To his aid would have come · more than twelve legions
Of holy angels · from across the whole earth,
10 Seeing the anguish · of Jesus Christ in this world.[16]
So may our succour be · likewise twelve thousand
Angel warriors standing · before the Judgement Seat,
Singing praise, who sing · what you, King of Kings, have
    done.

Cruel Herod

It is possible that the reference in this brief poem to 'betraying Jesus' may indicate a confusion between Herod the Great and his son Herod Antipas, who is recorded in Luke's Gospel as implicated in the handing over of Jesus to the Romans for execution – a confusion which appears in other mediaeval texts. It may, however, simply refer to Herod the Great's attempt to kill the infant Jesus in the massacre at Bethlehem.

To cruel Herod there came
The joy of glory –
But great sorrow was caused
At cruel Herod's doing
When he betrayed Jesus.
He shudders in terror,
The earth itself shakes,
The ground is stirred up,

Trembling falls on the world
And Christendom shivers   10
As one great jump is taken
At cruel Herod's doing –
A leap into the swamp,
Among frozen multitudes,
To the depths of Hell.[1]

The Steadfast Hebrews

This poem opens in the middle of the dramatic story of the Hebrews who have escaped from slavery in Egypt, led by Moses, and are now being pursued by Pharaoh's army (Exodus 12:37–14:31). The poem is written in the rhupunt *form, in which each line is divided in three parts; where this is not the case, it is likely that the text is incomplete. Most of the poem is taken up with the list of the ten plagues visited on the Pharaoh's people. These are loosely based on Exodus (6:28–12:51) but do not follow the Old Testament text exactly.*

The steadfast Hebrews, · Israel's children, · suffered great
    injustice:
A crowd on their trail · was drawing close · [. . .]
God permitted · vengeance · on Pharaoh's people:
Vexed by ten plagues, · before being drowned · in the sea's
    depths.
The first plague · killed the fish · in a savage manner.[1]
The second plague: frogs. · An unnumbered blight, · it stank
In houses and homes, · bedrooms · and kitchens.
The third was flies – · savage stings · full of death.
The fourth tribulation · was pains · from maggots.[2]
Then swarms of wasps · consumed · woods' and fields'
10   crops.
The fifth killed · the animals · of all Egypt's sons –
Herds slaughtered, · to the distress · of the native people.
The sixth – no lie – · running boils · leaving large scars.
Seventh was thunder, · hail and fire, · and dreadful rain,
A sweeping wind · [. . .] · on leaves and trees.
Eighth was locusts, · full of noise, · ravaging flowers.
The ninth terror, · horrific devastation: · night without end,

Deep darkness · extinguishing · the Egyptians' sight.
The tenth came at midnight: · most cruel revenge · on the
   king's people.[3]
Jesus Christ, · [. . .] · Lord Christ who falls not,   20
Thus, they are they saved, · six hundred soldiers · of the
   Hebrews' force.

57

The Stem of Jesse

The manuscript gives this poem the title Lath Moesen, *'The Rod of Moses', which properly belongs to another poem (p. 183). It looks as though the mention of the 'stem' of Jesse – i.e. the family tree of Jesus, passing back up through David to David's father, Jesse – has been confused with the 'rod' of Moses: the two words are almost interchangeable in mediaeval Welsh (and the same word is used for both in Latin). The stem of Jesse is a regular image in mediaeval hymnody and art, as in the 'Jesse Tree' motif often shown in painting, stained glass and sculpture. The text of the poem is in a poor state, with some parts of lines missing and several lines obviously corrupt, but it is a metrically skilful production.*

For all things that are now · restored in fullness · to the
    crowd of brothers,
Acknowledge with blessing · Christ the King, · never fail to
    praise him,
The fair, loving God · on Mary's lap, · where he longs to be:
The way of truth, · perfection of kingship, · source of all
    safety.
The stem of Jesse · has come at last · to Judah's people –
He is called light of all, · who suffered so deeply · for all
    their sins,
The Lord of justice, · the mountain of beauty, · his
    friendship so sweet.
And here on earth · in Solomon's temple · (so firmly
    founded),
The child of promise, · the pillar of battle, · he flames out
    fiercely;

The gate of Paradise, · God the shepherd, · reigning in
    harmony.   10
I myself have heard · from the mouth of prophets ·
    profound in learning
How Jesus was born, · how he lived out · all his days.
He offered life · to every kingdom, · life for all.
Though he caused all things – · were I to tell it – · he risked
    everything.[1]
The merciful one came · with all his fellowship · to earth's
    farthest shores
And the ocean's wastes · when your assault [on evil] · came
    down from Heaven.
Earth's open-handed Lord, · he brought Heaven here · (if
    truth be told).
Great as your anguish was, · may grace · be your gift to me,
Stem of Jesse, · grace of Jesus, · fair in your flowering.
Great was the miracle · [. . .] in all its might · through God's
    own gifts.   20
He was the judge – · both [righteous] judge · and sure-
    sighted sage,
His counsel true · for all who obey, · honest, free from sin.
He is a friend: · gently he holds · generations in their
    multitudes,
Compassionate, · [. . .] to the crowds of the righteous.
Like a sage, the king · follows in his footsteps · amid
    rejoicing hosts.[2]
So there will be, · says the Word, Mary's Son, · praise to the
    Lord,
The joyful Son · who came forth from God – · how many he
    makes holy,
From Abel onwards,[3] · a rich assembly, · an offering of
    praise! –
The gracious one · from Jesse's loins · killed, his crown
    blood-red –
Yet recognized swiftly · through the gifts he gives · as *rex* of
    humankind,   30

A new gift · that no human ear · had heard of before.

His blessing is true, · the one who upholds us · without our
    aid.

The pole star that shines · in the highest place · went ahead
    of the Magi,

As they took their way · on their precious journey · to see
    the Son,[4]

Bringing their incense · and their pure gold · from Ethiopia.

O gracious God, · God, Lord over all, · *rex* of [. . .]

Savage King Herod, · he was filled with fury · at the hidden
    Lord;

And for those who suffered, · the Lord of humankind ·
    brought loss to the land.

When God made his way · into the country · where the
    Nile's waters flow,

Herod laid hold · (his heart like a snowstorm) · on all the
40   children.

But in Nazareth town · no torment came · for the Lord of
    grace.

O world's reviver, · may I share your grace · in the land full
    of saints!

The one who governs · the hosts of angels – · he brought
    God to birth.

58

Everlasting Trinity

In this poem, God's calling of the twelve sons of Israel as the ancestors of the chosen people is presented as parallel to the calling of the twelve apostles to be adopted as sons of the one heavenly Father through the 'mothering' action of the whole divine Trinity.

Everlasting Trinity
Who made the world,
And – the world once made –
Made Adam skilful,
And – Adam once created –
Made Eve beautiful –
Blessed Israel too
He made, he who wards off anger.
A fine thing to name him,
A holy thing to praise him.   10
The twelve tribes of Israel, triumphant in praise –
The twelve sons of Israel – are the generous God's
    creation,
The twelve sons of Israel, born all together,
Twelve good souls, unspotted, born to three mothers.[1]
But only one made them: the one creator,
The ruler freely working his will.
Twelve sons of Israel the master made,
The Lord freely working his will.
Twelve sons of Israel the Godhead made,
The miracle-maker working his will.   20
Twelve too came forth
Through Jesus' birth,
One their father,

Three their mothers.
From them came blessing
And a lucky lineage.
Mary, blessed with good fortune;
Christ my strengthener,
Lord of all blessing,
Whom I invoke: may all free men invoke them.
This is how I'll prosper –
By being reconciled with you.

59

The Rod of Moses

The title properly belongs to this poem, not the one translated above as 'The Stem of Jesse' (p. 178), to which it is attached in the manuscript. It is another metrically elegant and rich composition, and skilfully weaves together narratives and themes from Old and New Testaments.

To God the Lord, God the Sovereign, mighty and merciful,
Great praise was given, guarding me through the waves'
    tumult.
The multitudes of Moses, Sovereign Lord – woe to their
    enemies!
The prince and his army met well-deserved misery [. . .][1]
They took flight through a torrent that drowned birds in
    flight.
He who draws the sun westward of all earth's multitudes –
You who guard those you love against all distress
(Apart from the armies shrieking loudly, sinking down in
    sorrow) –
He will rescue us all from the perils of Hell's pains.

To God the Lord, God the Sovereign, mighty and merciful –   10
Yours is the realm of Heaven; those who love you are at
    peace:
No slaughter, no death in your land, O God,
No-one in need, none at odds with another.
If we grasped this, we'd know how to shun what shames us.
To you songs are due, to the Holy Trinity, songs of a skilled
    man:
Poets sing to you, their love for you is limitless.

It was no harm you did when you gave Israel into David's
    hand.
Alexander, for all the great throng of his men,
Was powerless, not being reconciled with you:
20 And his armies, great legions of wicked multitudes,
When they came to the Land, their fate was lamentable.[2]
Solomon the Judge inherited the Land; he was better than
    David.
The King's son, his fellow-workers could be sure of riches.
The sons of Jacob enjoyed great riches in their Land –
They made peace, they ruled in accord with God's commands.
Righteous Abel, godly man, embraced the faith,
But his brother Cain was foul, evil-minded.
The stars are a sparkling path in the bright sky for their allies,
And one star hid the Holy Family from the wicked soldiers.
As for Moses' rod, Moses with his hosts under God's
30   guardianship,
It reddens foreheads with blood, reddens the drink of their
    lord and master.[3]
The speaking, the silent, the wise, the foolish, you protect
    them all.
Lord, where is our journey's end, where do you plan to settle
    us?
I praise the settled families in their happy homeland;
I praise the best of shelters, the canopy of Heaven.
The Lord of that realm saved Jonah from the sea-monster's
    bowels:
It was a fortunate man who preached to Nineveh's citizens.
A maid in a far land gave birth, overshadowed by God.
Ave Maria, Mary, Anne's daughter, whose prayer is so potent!
For the sake of your generosity and mercy, great King of the
40   world,
May we be welcome with you in the strongholds of Heaven.

UNGROUPED POEMS

60

Disaster for the Island

It is hard to pin down the historical allusions in this poem. In the background is obviously a serious assault on the heartland of the dynasty of Gwynedd, but there are no clues as to the exact period. The literary and metrical techniques would fit with a date around 1100, and it is just possible that the word translated as 'chief' (aeddon) could be a proper name; there was an 'Aeddan' killed in Gwynedd by Llywelyn ap Seisyllt in around 1018, but there is nothing positive to support an identification.

Disaster for the island · renowned in songs, · violence on all
    sides:
Blessed Môn, · famous for bravery, · Menai its portal.
I have drunk liquor, · wine and bragget, · with a brother, a
    protector,
An honoured lord; · he is laid low, · an end that comes to all
    kings.
The nobles grieve, · the just chieftain's nobles, · since the
    day he fell.
There has not been, · and never will be, · his like in warfare.
When this chief came · from Gwydion's land, · from Seon's
    stronghold* –
A bitter business, · four shaved heads · coming at midnight –
Warriors fell, · with nowhere to hide · in the woods, the
    wind raging.
Math† and Eufydd‡ · would make by magic · a free man, a
    skilful one.   10

---

*   *Seon's stronghold*: The Roman fort Segontium in Caernarfon in Gwyn-
    edd (*Caer Seon* or *Caer Seont* in mediaeval poetry).
†   *Math*: See note on p. 59.
‡   *Eufydd*: See note on p. 38.

In Gwydion's days · and Amaethon's,* · then there was
 wisdom.¹
His shield was pierced through, · yet, strong, loath to
 flee, · he was both strong and constant:
Mighty in the press · of his fighting, · he was no sea-trader!²
Mighty in feasting, · in every council · what he wanted was
 done.
Beloved till his death, · as long as I live · he will be praised.
Let me have from Christ · so as not to be sad · the Apostle's
 aid;
The generous chieftain – · may he receive · the angels'
 welcome.

Disaster for the island · renowned in songs, · violence all
 round.
In the young champion's presence, · stronghold of Wales, ·
 it was good to dwell –
20 A dragon-hero, · the rightful lord · of all Britain.
The king has died, · the high prince, · the earth covers him.
And the four maidens · when their feasting is over, · how
 cruel their pride!³
A cruel truth · on sea and on land, · enduring shame
That for his true follower · they could not do · the slightest
 favour.
But I'd be guilty · if I failed to celebrate · my benefactor.
Once the queen's departed, · who's to rebuke them, · who's
 to bring order?⁴
Once the chief has gone, · who protects Môn · with its great
 abundance?
Let me have from Christ · so as not to be sad · in good days
 or evil
A share in the mercy · of the land of glory, · and life
 everlasting!

* *Amaethon*: Another son of Dôn, like Gwydion and Gofannon.

61

In Praise of Tenby

*This is probably one of the older poems in the collection, orig-
inating perhaps in the tenth or eleventh century, though the
historical allusions are once again obscure. 'Erbin' is likely
to be the same mentioned in genealogies of the royal house
of South-West Wales, perhaps the same as the Erbin named
as father of Geraint in some genealogies and traditions. It is
worth noting that the poet describes some sort of repository
for books or perhaps charters of 'Britain', whose study and
supervision is part of his role. This is presumably a monastic
or clerical library of some kind, and the mention of it is a valu-
able indicator of a concern to support intellectual life in early
mediaeval Wales.*

I ask favour from God, the people's defender,
Lord of Heaven and earth, great in wisdom, most
    honoured.

There's a fine fort that stands looking out to the sea.
On that bright cliff there is joy on feast-days.
And when the sea is in a great turmoil,
There is merriment over the mead-cups among the poets.
When the swift wave is breaking against it,
They leave the green ocean for the Picts[1] to enjoy!
And may I, O God, in return for my prayers,
When I keep my vow, be reconciled with you.   10

There's a fine fort that stands by the broad waters,
A mighty castle, circled by the sea.
Now, Britain, ask who's the rightful owner!
Let it always be yours, head of Erbin's dynasty.
Within the palisade were crowds and songs,

With the eagle above the clouds and the tracks of white
    foam.[2]
Before the great chieftain, before the pursuer of enemies,
Lord of far-flung renown, men muster for fighting.

There's a fine fort set on the ninth wave,
20   With fine people lodged in it, carefree souls.
They don't find their pleasure in abusing others;
It's not their habit to be hard-hearted.
I'll speak no slander against their welcome.
Better a slave in Dyfed than a yeoman in Deudraeth![3]
A gathering of free men, feasting together,
Draws in, two by two, the best men in the world.

There's a fine fort, where all those gathered
Rejoice and praise with the singing birds.
Their songs at the great feasts are happy,
30   Songs of a lord who is generous and bold.
Before he went into the oak casket in church,
He gave me mead and wine from a crystal vessel.

There's a fine fort on the headland,
And there each one is given a fine portion.
In Tenby with its bright white gulls, I know
The companions of Bleiddudd, lord of its court.
It was my custom, each night of the feast,
To sleep near the prince who was glorious in battle,
With a purple cloak round me, enjoying my comfort.
40   So I became a tongue for all Britain's poets.

There's a fine fort that echoes with songs.
I had all the privileges I wanted there.
I don't claim my rights, I follow good manners
(He who doesn't know this deserves no feast-gift).
The writings of Britain were my chief concern
When the waves were rising up in tumult.
May it always be there, that cell I would visit![4]

There's a fine fort set on a high place:
Its feasts are splendid, its praise songs are loud.
And fine all around it, that stronghold of heroes,   50
Comes the seaspray's assault, with its long wings.
The hoarse seabirds head for the top of the cliff
Let anger be doomed to fly off over the crags,
And let Bleiddudd enjoy supreme contentment.
May this song in his memory be welcome over the ale.
The blessing of peaceful Heaven's Lord will preserve us:
He will not make us farmhands for Owain's grandson.[5]

There's a fine fort on the seashore,[6]
And there all are given the fine things they want.
Now, Gwynedd, ask [. . .]   60
[. . .] may they be yours!
They deserved the spears, rough and straight.
On Wednesday I saw men struggling in conflict,
On Thursday they suffered humiliation,
Red blood on their hair and lamenting on the harp.
Gwynedd's army was weary on the day they arrived;
On the ridge of Llech Maelwy they break their shields.
A crowd of kinsmen fell, my nephews' son among them.

Bibliography

Primary Sources

Facsimile of *The Book of Taliesin*
https://www.llgc.org.uk/index.php?id=254

Armes Prydein o Lyfr Taliesin, ed. Ifor Williams (Caerdydd, Gwasg Prifysgol Cymru, 1955)

Armes Prydein: The Prophecy of Britain. From the Book of Taliesin, ed. and annotated Sir Ifor Williams, English version by Rachel Bromwich (Dublin, Institute of Advanced Studies, 1972)

Blodeugerdd Barddas o Ganu Crefyddol Cynnar ('The Barddas Anthology of Early Religious Poetry'), ed. Marged Haycock (Abertawe/ Swansea, Barddas, 1994)

Canu Taliesin ('The Poems of Taliesin'), ed. Ifor Williams (Caerdydd, Gwasg Prifysgol Cymru, 1977). Translated as *The Poems of Taliesin*, ed. Sir Ifor Williams, tr. J. E. Caerwyn Williams (Dublin, Institute of Advanced Studies, 1987)

The Celtic Heroic Age: Literary Sources for Ancient Celtic Europe and Early Ireland and Wales, tr. J. T. Koch and John Carey, 4th revised edn (Malden, Massachusetts, Celtic Studies Publications 2003)

Facsimile & Text of the Book of Taliesin, ed. J. Gwenogvryn Evans, 2 vols, (Tremvan, Llanbedrog, Series of Old Welsh Texts, 1910, 1915)

Legendary Poems from the Book of Taliesin, ed. and tr. Marged Haycock (Aberystwyth, CMCS Publications, 2007)

Monmouth, Geoffrey of, *Life of Merlin: Vita Merlini*, ed. Basil Clarke (Cardiff, University of Wales Press, 1973)

Prophecies from the Book of Taliesin, ed. and tr. Marged Haycock (Aberystwyth, CMCS Publications, 2013)

Taliesin Poems, tr. Meirion Pennar (Lampeter, Llanerch Enterprises, 1988)

Trioedd Ynys Prydein ('Triads of the Island of Britain'), ed. Rachel Bromwich (3rd edn, Cardiff, University of Wales Press, 2006)

Ystoria Taliesin ('The Story of Taliesin'), ed. Patrick K. Ford (Cardiff, University of Wales Press, 1992)

Further Reading

Charles-Edwards, T. M., *Wales and the Britons 350–1064* (Oxford, Oxford University Press, 2013)

Clancy, Joseph, *The Earliest Welsh Poetry* (London, Macmillan, 1970)

Clancy, Thomas Owen, ed., *The Triumph Tree: Scotland's Earliest Poetry AD 550–1350* (Edinburgh, Canongate Classics, 1998)

Conran, Tony, *Welsh Verse: Translations* (Bridgend, Seren Books, 1982)

Evans, Geraint and Helen Fulton, eds, *The Cambridge History of Welsh Literature* (Cambridge, Cambridge University Press, 2019)

Ford, Patrick K., tr. and intr., *The Celtic Poets: Songs and Tales from Early Ireland and Wales* (Cambridge, MA, Ford and Bailic Publications, 1999)

Jarman, A. O. H. and Hughes, Gwilym Rees, *A Guide to Welsh Literature 1282–c.1550*, (2nd ed., rev. Dafydd Johnston)(Cardiff, University of Wales Press, 1997)

Lynch, Peredur I., *Proffwydoliaeth a'r Syniad o Genedl* ('Prophecy and the Idea of a Nation') (Bangor,University of Wales Press, 2007)

The Mabinogion, tr. Sioned Davies (Oxford, Oxford University Press, 2007)

Williams, G. J. and Jones, E. J., *Gramadegau'r Penceirddiaid* ('The Chief Bards' Grammars') (Caerdydd, Gwasg Prifysgol Cymru, 1934)

Abbreviations

AP	*Armes Prydein: The Prophecy of Britain. From the Book of Taliesin*, ed. and annotated Ifor Williams, English version, Rachel Bromwich (Dublin, Institute of Advanced Studies, 1972)
CT	Ifor Williams, *Canu Taliesin: gyda Rhagymadrodd a Nodiadau* (Cardiff, University of Wales Press, 1960)
GPC	*Geiriadur Prifysgol Cymru (The University of Wales Dictionary)* (Cardiff, University of Wales Press, 1950–2006)
LPBT	*Legendary Poems from the Book of Taliesin*, ed. and tr. Marged Haycock (Aberystwyth, CMCS, 2007)
PBT	*Prophecies from the Book of Taliesin*, ed. and tr. Marged Haycock (Aberystwyth, CMCS, 2013)
PT	*The Poems of Taliesin*, ed. Ifor Williams, English version, J. E. Caerwyn Williams (Dublin, DIAS, 1968)

Notes

HEROIC POEMS

1. *In Praise of Cynan Garwyn, Son of Brochfael*

1   T. M. Charles-Edwards, *Wales and the Britons 350–1064* (Oxford, Oxford University Press, 2013), p. 16.

2. *The Men of Catraeth*

1   The original gives 'Prydein', which in later Welsh comes to refer to the whole of Britain. But 'Prydyn' makes better sense here.

2   The proposal of a Lake District location for Gwen Ystrad depends on reading it as a mistake for 'Gwensteri', the supposed original Celtic name for the River Winster, which occurs in the first elegy for Gwallawg (p. 27). If this is the case, we should have to suppose a scribe's eye slipping to the following word in the text (*ystadl*) and converting it into *ystrad*, a common element in place names.

3   This line and the preceding one are difficult to interpret, and we have followed the emendations proposed by Ifor Williams, though they are not universally accepted by scholars.

4   'Llech Wen' is probably a place name, though this is uncertain. It does not mean 'White Stone', as it is tempting to think on the basis of modern Welsh: the rhyme in the original implies a double 'n' at the end of the second word. 'Gwen', with a long 'e', is possible as a personal name, and if so this would mean 'Gwen's Stone/Monument'.

5   As the reader will see, these last four lines form a regular refrain to the poems in honour of King Urien.

4. Here at My Rest

1   Our translation assumes that these lines are about the slaughter that precedes the feast, rather than slaughter in battle, though the latter is possible.

5. All through One Year

1   Diodorus Siculus describes ancient Celtic peoples at their feasts as sitting on wolf- and dog-skins, and served by young children. They were surrounded by cauldrons and spits cooking quarters of meat. Heroes were offered the prime cuts. Quoted in Ifor Williams, *PT*, p. 61.

6. The Battle of Argoed Llwyfain

1   *The Oxford Companion to the Literature of Wales*, ed. Meic Stephens (Oxford, Oxford University Press, 1986), p. 94.

7. Rheged, Arise, its Lords Are its Glory

1   See introduction to 'The Men of Catraeth', p. 6.
2   These lines are very uncertain textually and in terms of sense. The point seems to be that, as Gwydion inherited his abilities from his father, so shall Urien's father transmit his qualities to his son. We have rephrased the original here, in the interests of making the line convey some kind of sense.
3   'Ulph' sounds as if it might be Latin (Ulpius?) or even Germanic (some form of 'Wulf'?); cf. the name 'Uffin' in 'They Praise His Qualities (p. 87). 'Hyfeidd' may be a personal name (as it seems to be in 'In the King of Heaven's Name, They Remember', p. 27), or the name of a clan deriving from him.
4   Gododdin's name derives from the Latin name of a local British tribe, the Votadini. Neirin's poem, the *Gododdin* (see p. xix) describes the defeat of warriors from this kingdom and elsewhere by the Angles of Northumbria in a battle at Catraeth, somewhere around the end of the sixth century.

8. *Taliesin's Plunder*

1   This is presumably a reference to the Easter Vigil with its bless-
    ing of the new fire and the Paschal Candle, and perhaps also to
    the use of the branches of trees in church on Palm Sunday.

2   The reference to flat landscape here would fit with the identifica-
    tion of the site with Catterick.

3   This line is very unclear.

4   The series of lines that follow all begin with the words *Un yw*; it
    is not certain what *un* means here, but the context suggests 'fine',
    precious', 'desirable', and there is some philological support for
    this.

5   Emending *Powys* in the original to *poues*, 'rest'.

6   It is not clear where a River 'Defwy' might have been. The Teviot
    and the Tweed might be plausible: both are rather far from what
    is generally thought of as the geography of these poems, but, as
    we have seen, locations around Cumbria and the Pennines are
    not entirely out of the question.

7   This translation is speculative; the wording is very obscure.

10. *Lament for Owain, Son of Urien*

1   Ifor Williams suggests changing the word for 'joy' here (*lle-
    wenyd*) to *Llwyfenydd*, which seems to have been the name of
    one of the central territories of Rheged; in which case, the line is
    'The prince of brilliant [or beautiful] Llwyfenydd.' Either would
    make sense.

2   The manuscript has at the end of the poem *Eneit. O. ap vryen*
    (repeating the poem's first line), which may mean that the first
    line or the first two lines are intended to be repeated, or might
    be a note of an alternative title. Ifor Williams points out that fin-
    ishing a poem with the same word you started with is a familiar
    device in early Irish poetry, so that it may simply be intended as
    a closing line.

11. *In the King of Heaven's Name, They Remember*

1   At the bottom of the page in the manuscript, a hand other than
    that of the scribe has written the name '*Gwallawg ap Lleennawr*'.

2   'Hedge' here translates the Middle Welsh *perth*, 'bush' or 'thicket', which would describe the spear shafts left over from a vicious battle. The stockade in line 15 is, similarly, a reference to spears.

12. *In the King of Heaven's Name, the Hosts Are Keening*

1   Although Urien had a son called Rhun, according to the genealogies, and there was also a North Welsh king of the same name in the later sixth century, these are not likely candidates. The Welsh Triads mention a Rhun son of 'Neithon', and Neithon is identified as son of 'Senill', likely to be the same name as 'Senyllt', father of Nudd Hael.

2   Our translation here takes the manuscript's *cledifarch* as a mistake for *cledifarth*, and reads the latter as a compound of *cledd* ('sword') and some form of *dyddifarth* ('to destroy or humiliate').

LEGENDARY POEMS

13. *First Artful Command: Who Pronounced It?*

1   Lines 8 and 9 are incomplete.

2   The eagle is one of the 'Oldest Animals' which appear in Welsh legends; see *The Mabinogion*, tr. Sioned Davies, p. 204.

3   For the location and nature of these springs, see *LPBT*, pp. 62–4.

4   In Welsh folklore, Seithennyn was the gatekeeper who became drunk and allowed Cantre'r Gwaelod. *The Black Book of Carmarthen* contains a tenth-century poem, 'Pwy yw y Porthawr?' ('Who is the Gatekeeper?'), located in Arthur's court. But given the theology of the poem, there might also be an allusion to St Peter at the gates of heaven.

5   Haycock suggests that this veil may be the body of water, fire or ice surrounding Hell. It could also mean the veil of a shroud, hence death (see *LPBT*, p. 65).

6   Here, as in other places in the poems, the Latin acts as a linguistic amulet rather than a coherent sentence. Our translation depends on reading *sibilum* for *sibilem*. There may be a reference to II Kings 19:12, where Elijah, fleeing from the persecution of Queen Jezebel, hears God speaking in a 'still, small voice' – *sibilus aurae tenuis* in Latin.

7   This line and the one following are metrically irregular, using nine and thirteen syllables respectively, marking, perhaps, the switch to seven-syllable lines for the rest of the poem.

8   The poet is rhyming between the Welsh *mur* ('wall') and Latin *amandantur* ('are driven away'), with the latter word slightly miscopied.

14. *Poets' Corner*

1   This may refer to the episode in the *Mabinogion* story of 'Manawydan, son of Llyr', in which a hostile magician causes the entire population of Dyfed to vanish overnight.

15. *Taliesin's Sweetnesses*

1   See Haycock, *LPBT*, p. 92.

2   Nudd also appears as one of the 'Three Generous Ones' in the *Trioedd Ynys Prydein: The Triads of the Island of Britain*, ed. and tr. Rachel Bromwich (4th edn, Cardiff, University of Wales Press, 2014), p 5.

3   *Eynawn* means 'anvil'; if this is a personal name, it may be relevant that there was an Einion in the twelfth century who belonged to the famous dynasty of doctors working around Myddfai in Carmarthenshire.

16. *An Unfriendly Crowd*

1   Or, 'A poet – here he is!', announcing the speaker's claim to be an authentic poet unlike the others conjured up; but the lines immediately following fit better with a satirical reference to a rival.

2   This might refer to Christ or to the poet himself, Gwion reincarnated as Taliesin. The reference a few lines further on to the one 'from the depths' who took human flesh suggests the former.

3   These lines suggest either a legend of some long period of exile or a metaphor for long preparation for the poetic task.

4   This may allude to the proverbial longevity of the yew tree; but the meaning is debated. Marged Haycock proposes, 'Since it is, they went, / Since it is, they came'; but the reference to long life like that of a yew fits the general context better.

5   This is another lost allusion, unless it refers to the death of

Christ. The word translated 'innocent lad' (*gwynwas*) might be a personal name rather than a designation.

6   This is the first reference to Taliesin's connection with the figure of Prince Elffin. See p. xxxiii on the Elffin tradition.

7   The scribe has repeated an earlier line here and left out the correct one. We know there is a line missing because the following line has no rhyme.

8   These lines may be out of their proper place. It is possible – given the rhyme in Welsh – that they belong just before or after the reference to Gwion towards the beginning of the poem.

9   An incomplete line in the Welsh.

10 *Eli ac Eneas* in the original; it is very likely that 'Eneas' is a mistake for either 'Enoc' or 'Eliseus' (Elisha) – more likely the former, since the prophet Elijah and the patriarch Enoch are associated by virtue of their both having been human beings before they were bodily taken up to heaven.

11 See 'The Battle of the Trees' (p. 54) and other references to Gwydion's magical transformation of trees into warriors.

12 I.e. the cauldron that is regularly the symbol of poetic inspiration; it may be (*LPBT*, p. 159) that the two words are *fiat lux*, 'Let there be light', the first words uttered by God in creating the world.

13 The original has *yn Efrei, yn Efroec* which sounds like two variants of 'Hebrew'; *Groec*, 'Greek', instead of *Efroec* makes better sense, and better metrical sense as well.

17. *The Battle of the Trees*

1   In Welsh, the word for trees – *gwydd* – shares a root with vocabulary for knowledge and consciousness. The word *goddeu* also has a wide spectrum of meaning, including 'to aim at, to intend', as well as 'to suffer or endure'. The title might also be understood as meaning 'The Furies of Battle' (*LPBT*, pp. 199–200).

2   See pp. xxxvii–xxxix.

3   This echoes Neirin's intriguing declaration in *The Gododdin*: 'I, not I, Aneirin, / (Taliesin knows it, / Skilled in word-craft), / Sang *The Gododdin* / Before next day dawned.' *The Triumph Tree: Scotland's Earliest Poetry*, AD 550–1350, ed. Thomas Owen Clancy (Edinburgh, Canongate Classics, 1998), p 58.

4   This is Taliesin the soldier-poet's mini-vision of Hell.

5   This is a shortened line, its meaning very uncertain.

6   This line is likewise shorter than it should be, and the translation
     is very uncertain.

7   *Gwern*, Welsh for 'alder', is also the name of the son of Branwen
     and Matholwch in the Second Branch of the Mabinogi.

8   The meaning here is obscure.

9   The Welsh *kadeir*, 'chair', refers to the prize in a bardic competi-
     tion, which would originally have been a literal seat of honour in
     the royal hall. But it can also refer to the branches of a tree; and,
     as the titles of several poems in the collection show, it could be
     used for a poetic composition. There seems to be a complicated
     pun here: the pine wins the prize (*kadeir*) in a contest for the best
     branches (*kadeir* in its other sense).

10   Haycock offers several possibilities: reading *morawt* for *morawc*,
     and *vverit* for *moryt* gives the simplest meaning, 'a great army
     brings rescue', but there are other options.

11   It's not clear what kind of tree this is or why it's sickly. Haycock
     suggests that the branches are splintered by fighting; see *LPBT*,
     p. 219.

12   Haycock notes that 'clover' can be used in mediaeval Welsh poet-
     ry for trees with a sweet scent. See *LPBT*, pp. 219–20.

13   Isidore wrote that chestnuts were thought by the Greeks to look
     like testicles in their sacs. See *The 'Etymologies' of Isidore of
     Seville*, ed. Stephen Barney et al (4th edn, Cambridge, Cambridge
     University Press, 2014), p. 344.

14   This passage seems to be drawn from a stock list of the charac-
     teristics of various things, taken from Isidore (see ibid).

15   'Gwarchan Maeldcrw', in the *Book of Aneirin* (see *Canu Aneir-
     in*, ed. Ifor Williams, Cardiff, University of Wales Press, 1978,
     pp. 374–89). This poem was considered a virtuosic model for
     apprentice writers. See *LPBT*, p. 222.

16   Here the poet may be speaking in the person of Blodeuwedd,
     who was conjured from flowers by the wizards Math and Gwyd-
     ion in the Fourth Branch of the Mabinogi.

17   For an account of the elements, or 'consistencies', in the Taliesin
     cosmology, see *LPBT*, pp. 223–5. 'Nine' here may be a mistake
     for the 'seven' found elsewhere, as in 'The Great Song of the
     World', where we are given a list of earth, fire, water, air (the
     four classical elements of creation) along with flowers, cloud and
     wind.

18   Here Taliesin speaks for himself again. For 'Math, son of Ma-
     thonwy', see *The Mabinogion*, tr. Sioned Davies, pp. 47–64; in

this poem, between lines 151 and 171, the story is used as a creation myth for Taliesin.

19   Modron ('Great Mother') is the name given in the Mahinogion story of 'Culhwch and Olwen' to the mother of the imprisoned hero Mabon ('Great Son'). Are these names of supernatural beings invoked for magical purposes?

20   The text of this passage is corrupt and therefore very difficult to interpret.

21   Very hard to interpret. Haycock suggests that the whole of the passage from line 185 may refer to Christ's Harrowing of Hell and resurrection (see *LPBT*, p. 231). If the latter is correct, the 'boar' in the next line may refer to death or Satan.

22   Monstrous Cynocephali, beings with human bodies and dogs' heads as pictured on the edges of the Hereford *Mappamundi*, appear throughout mediaeval Western literature, as well as in Arthurian legend. See *LPBT*, pp. 232–3.

23   This is a particularly obscure passage, but seems to refer to the costliness of the paraphernalia of liturgical worship.

24   Virgil's Fourth Eclogue was regarded in the mediaeval Church as a prophecy of Christ's coming.

18. *Young Taliesin's Works*

1   An unclear couplet, possibly incomplete in the manuscript. The meaning may be the question of whether the thorn bush's trunk or its branches are better fuel against the cold, linking this to the lines that follow.

19. *I Am the Vigour*

1   Judas committed suicide after betraying Christ. In mediaeval times, suicides could not be buried in consecrated ground.

2   The reference at this point in the manuscript may be either to orpiment (arsenic), a metallic ore used to produce a yellow dye, or, more probably, to orpine, *Sedum telephium*, which is purple in colour. Orpine is called *Berwr Taliesin* ('Taliesin's Cress') in Welsh. The similarity between orpiment and orpine may have triggered the reference to watercress in l. 35; another member of the *Sedum* family, Biting Stonecrop or Wall-pepper, has a peppery taste like that of watercress (see Richard Mabey, *Flora Brittannica,* London, Chatto & Windus, 1996, p. 178).

3   A pun on the Welsh for watercress, which is *Berwr* or 'one who boils something'. The idea is that a strong spring looks as if it's boiling, as do the clouds of watercress growing around it. The line also contains reference to the quality of being 'pybyr' or peppery, which is true of watercress and occurs again in line 48.

4   The answer to this series of 'what connects?' riddles may be that trees in the wind lean like drunken men; the same wind blows ships carrying wine from abroad. The fun is in guessing, rather than finding definitive answers.

5   This may refer to a frame holding a cauldron over a fire, as in *Ystoria Taliesin*.

6   Haycock suggests that Gwion's river is a river of song, an image for poetry.

20. *I Make My Plea to God*

1   A slightly difficult line, but the meaning must be that the marauding Saxons will always find abundance of loot in the fertile lands of Mon (Anglesey).

2   The elements of the later mediaeval narrative of Taliesin's triumph in poetic contests before King Maelgwn of Gwynedd and the rescue of the imprisoned Prince Elffin are already taken for granted here.

3   This refers to the Second Branch of the Mabinogi, 'Branwen, Daughter of Llŷr', where Taliesin is mentioned as having taken part in this disastrous campaign and as one of its survivors.

4   A somewhat uncertain line: in the original, it could mean 'when mighty ones were wounded in the thigh', but replacing *ymordwyt* by *mordwyt* gives the sense translated here, which echoes a phrase in the text of the Branwen story.

5   *Pen ren Wleth* in the original – most likely a mistake for Pen or Penryn Penwaeth, i.e. Penwith in Cornwall, suitably distant from *Luch Reon*, Loch Ryan in Galloway.

6   The implication is that this is somewhere in the far North.

7   This refers to the Third Branch of the Mabinogi, 'Manawydan, son of Llŷr', where Pryderi is the victim of a magical abduction, presumably to the Underworld, the realm of Annwfn.

8   It is not clear whether Caer Siddi is imagined as under the sea or as a remote island.

21. *Teyrnon's Prize Song*

1   Marged Haycock takes line 59 of this poem – in her translation 'A prize poem for Teyrnon' – as its intended title, inserted in a slightly eccentric place by the scribe (an argument strengthened by the fact that it doesn't rhyme with the lines before or after it). The passage is corrupt. However, we have followed the scribe's placing of the line in the body of the poem, as it can be rendered to make some sense.

2   For more on the relationship between these names see *LPBT*, p. 300.

3   Cf. 'I Make My Plea to God', n. 5, and *LPBT*, p. 301) .

4   There is a Heilyn in *The Mabinogion*; a member of Brân's company, he opened the forbidden door on Grassholm Island, so that the lost memories of the sufferings of Brân's comrades came flooding back (see *The Mabinogion*, tr. Sioned Davies, p. 34).

5   This may refer to coastal fortresses accessible only by low tide, such as Lindisfarne, Tenby and Thanet (see *LPBT*, p. 305).

6   These lines are very difficult, but may be a traditional proverb. Here the poem turns towards prophecy, noting a lack of continuity between present circumstances and the future being predicted.

22. *Ceridwen's Prize Song*

1   This poem makes several references to the Fourth Branch of the Mabinogi, 'Math, son of Mathonwy', in which Lleu is a central character – though no son is ascribed to him in that text.

2   Here we are reading 'Dinlleu' for 'lleu'.

3   These lines allude to the exploits of Gwydion as recorded in the Fourth Branch.

4   The battle referred to is presumably an episode in the conflict between Gwydion and the southern troops of Pryderi of Dyfed, as related in the Fourth Branch of the Mabinogi, Math, Son of Mathonwy.

5   This continues the reference to the Fourth Branch of the Mabinogi.

6   This is a very difficult line. The translation accepts the emendation of *Brython* to *brithron*, so that it refers to the episode in 'Math, son of Mathonwy', where Aranrhod's pregnancy is revealed as she is made to step over a magic rod (*brithron*). If this is not accepted, the line means something like 'the greatest shame

to come from the region of the Britons was when Aranrhod was terrified' – which might refer to the magical stratagem of Gwydion in summoning up the sound of besieging forces around Aranrhod's castle, as described in 'Math'.

23. A Song of the Wind

1   *LPBT,* p. 328.
2   See *Ystoria Taliesin,* p. 79.
3   It can be found in the National Library of Wales Peniarth 50 document.
4   Our guess is that this refers to the practice of defending coastal forts by lining the sea approach with marble slabs, so that enemy anchors have no purchase.
5   Modern knowledge of atmospheric pressure has the opposite understanding, associating heat with less or weaker wind. Haycock speculates that in mediaeval culture, phases of the moon were thought to bring chaos and so were inauspicious.
6   Taliesin poems – or sections of them – often end with a description of the end of the world, as if the poem is the world itself.
7   The tenth and lowest realm was damned because it is the home of Lucifer, the angel who rebelled against God and, therefore, fell.
8   See *LPBT,* pp. 345–56.

24. A Song about Mead

1   Literally 'calends', the annual New Year feast; cf. 'They Praise His Qualities', l. 57.
2   *Elphinawc varchawc,* literally 'Elffin-like horseman' or 'knight', or possibly 'knightly supporter of Elffin'; but it is also possible to take *Elphinawc* simply as a variant of 'Elffin'.

25. A Song about Beer

1   Literally, 'not one grain.' This is where the imagery of beer making as a spiritual journey begins.
2   Welsh ale was known for having honey added to it to help the fermentation; see *LPBT,* p. 368.
3   Lines 43–7 are very uncertain. The lines sound like a refrain, untypical of Welsh poetry in the twelfth and thirteenth centuries.
4   This may refer to the grave.

26. *They Praise His Qualities*

1   This might refer to a betrayal *by* the warriors of Gwent, but the overall sense of the poem demands something more sympathetic to Gwent.

2   The manuscrupt gives the name as *Dyfyd*, which, unless it is an unusual variant of *Dafyd*, is less likely as a personal name than *Dyfyr*.

3   The same phrase is used here as in 'The Battle of Argoed Llwyfain', line 13 (p. 15), suggesting that that text was known to the author of this poem.

4   Cf. Wuffa in East Anglia and Yffi in Northumbria.

5   The phrase designates land on the other side of the north-eastern boundaries of Welsh territory.

6   If not Hardenhuish in Wiltshire, the name might represent something like 'Ard Wenhwys', suggesting a fortress in Gwent such as Caerleon or Chepstow. Gwennwys was the old name for the people of Gwent.

7   As in 'A Song about Mead', l. 21, these are literally 'calends' (*kalan*), the annual New Year feast.

27. *The Wild Horse Is Broken*

1   This poem is usually known as 'Song on the Horses', following Ifor Williams in his *The Poems of Taliesin*. We have kept to our principle of using the first line of a poem as its title, except when the scribe has given one.

2   The 'triads' are mediaeval Welsh texts which preserve fragments of information in groups of three under-headings which clarify what each group has in common. For all the extant triads, see *Trioedd Ynys Prydein: The Triads of the Island of Britain*, ed. Rachel Bromwich. This volume includes Bromwich's translation of the *Llyvyr Taliessin* catalogue of horses.

3   For the full text see A. H. Jarman, ed., *Llyfr Du Caerfyrddin*, (Caerdydd, Gwasg Prifysgol Cymru, 1982).

4   For Nwython see *LPBT*, pp. 396–7. Ll. 10–18 are extremely difficult to understand.

5   According to legend, St David insisted that his monks should pull their own ploughs, and this may be in the background here. Especially suggestive of this reading – above all in view of l. 60

– is the pun on *dichwant*, 'without desire', 'indifferent', translated here as 'heedless', but also (according to *GPC*) carrying the vernacular meaning of 'the inclination of a ploughshare forward so that it tends to cut a deeper furrow'. The 'two friends' may also be read as symbols for the rhyming couplets paced out by the poet.

6 Many of these horses are named in the *Triads*, ed. Rachel Bromwich, pp. lxxx–lxxxvii.

7 From the Latin 'Saturninus'. There is an early Welsh poem mentioning a Sadyrnin as the father of 'Morgant the Great', apparently a ruler in sixth-century southern Scotland (*LPBT*, p. 401) and possibly the same as the Morcant who was responsible for the killing of Urien of Reged (*historia Brittonum*, 63).

8 This could refer to the Emperor Constantine (whose wife Helena was identified as British in mediaeval tradition) or to one of a number of British rulers of the post-Roman period who shared the name. For some of the candidates, see *Trioedd Ynys Prydein*, pp. 318 19.

9 Two mediaeval Welsh epigrams mention Moel Hiraddug as the site of fighting (*LPBT*, p. 410).

10 The meaning of this line is very uncertain.

11 A number of monster cats came into the Welsh tradition from the Irish (see *Trioedd Ynys Prydein*, pp. 473–6).

12 The missing text makes the meaning of these lines very uncertain.

28. *He Ranged the Whole World*

1 Or 'on wings', suggesting the speed of his flight.

2 There is not much point in trying to identify the names in this passage; they are there for alliteration and sheer verbal exuberance. It is possible that *Pleth* and/or *Pletheppa* may designate the Pelopponese or even Persepolis. *Galldarus* might be the Gandhara region of Pakistan, if we take it as a mistranscription of 'Gandarus'.

3 The lines seem to refer to the land of the Amazons. The hunting is 'unnatural' presumably because it is thought to be inappropriate for women.

4 The meaning of this line is not clear, but the best interpretation is that Alexander's invasion of the Holy Land and capture of Jerusalem in 332 BCE began the process of the Hellenization –

and corruption – of Jewish worship which reached its climax under the Seleucid rulers who controlled the Holy Land from the fourth to the second centuries BCE.

30. *The Spoils of Annwfn*

1   Lundy Island in the Bristol Channel was once called Ynys Wair, and the island may have been identified with the fortress in the sea that is envisaged in this poem.

2   This suggests that Gwair had some role in the Dyfed cycle of heroic legends associated with these names, especially as Pwyll and Pryderi are depicted in the *Mabinogion* narrative as passing to and from the Otherworld at various points.

3   Geoffrey of Monmouth gives 'Prydwen' as the name of Arthur's shield (*historia regum Britanniae* 9.4), though this would not be a plausible reading here.

4   Or 'facing in four directions'.

5   In Geoffrey of Monmouth's *Life of Merlin*, 'Telgesinus' (Taliesin) mentions nine sisters who live in the Island of Apples; in the light of this parallel – and assuming that the sisters are not simply a version of the nine Muses of classical mythology – the line may represent a much older tradition about female prophetesses or magicians in the Otherworld.

6   Compare the cauldron of Dyrnwch, in mediaeval Welsh legend one of the Thirteen Treasures of the Island of Britain, which has the same property (and must be the same as the cauldron of Diwrnach mentioned in the tale of 'Culhwch and Olwen').

7   *Historia Brittonum* 13 describes how some of the early travellers who intended to settle in Ireland saw a glass tower in the middle of the ocean, whose inhabitants did not reply when spoken to. The travellers' ships are wrecked and only one vessel survives. The passage is obviously a source for this poem.

8   *Kylchwy* can mean 'circular shields', but, given the anti-clerical animus of the poem, it seems more obvious to translate it as 'girdles'.

9   The Brindled Ox appears in n. 45 of the *Trioedd Ynys Prydein*, p. 124.

10   *Caer Manddwy* is also mentioned as the site of a battle in *The Black Book of Carmarthen*.

11   Possibly what the monks guard is a saint's relic – a silver-headed bishop's staff carved in the shape of a mythical creature.

12   These lines foreshadow the later devotional poem 'Saints and Martyrs of the Faith' (p. 169), with its extravagant lists of saints.

31. Elegy for Hercules

1   Some sense can be made of this feat in relation to the more generally received legend of Hercules' labours by relating it to a version of the myth (whose date is not known), in which Hercules takes the burden of the world from Atlas, so that the latter may fetch the golden apples of the Hesperides, guarded by his daughters, for the hero. Hercules then has to trick Atlas into taking the world back onto his shoulders.

33. Elegy for Cú Roí mac Dáiri

1   *LPBT*, p. 465.
2   *Gwern* means 'alder', a wood which resists decay in water, giving the fourteenth-century meaning 'mast' (*GPC*).

34. Elegy for Dylan, Son of the Sea

1   Literally, 'who brought peace to the power of the tongs?'; but the line is difficult and might mean 'who made peace with the tenacity of a pair of tongs?'
2   The reference to Dylan in the Fourth Branch of the Mabinogi, 'Math, Son of Mathonwy' says that no wave ever broke beneath him; if this is what is in the poet's mind, the implication seems to be that, although Dylan was safe from the threat of drowning in the rolling-in of these powerful waves, he was not protected from the violence of Gofannon.

35. I Am Fiery Taliesin

1   See Patrick Sims-Williams, 'Historical Need and Literary Narrative: A Caveat from Ninth-Century Wales', *The Welsh History Review* 17, 1994–5, pp. 1–40.
2   See *LPBT*, p. 489. For an argument for the earlier dating, see John Koch, *Cunedda, Cynan, Cadwallon, Cynddylan: Four Welsh Poems and Britain 383–655* (Aberystwyth, CMCS, 2013).
3   While Ynys Wair ('Grass Island') is understood to refer to Lundy in the Bristol Channel, scholars have suggested locations for

Caer Wair as far apart as Caithness and the Isle of Wight; a location in Northumbria seems most likely in this context (see *LBPT*, pp. 295–6).

4   By representing Cunedda as related to Coel (and cf. l.13, which stresses the alliance between Cunedda and Coel's house), the legendary ancestor of Urien and the kings of Rheged, this poem skilfully integrates the interests of the North Welsh dynasty with the traditions of what was probably Taliesin's real historical context in Northern England and Southern Scotland.

5   The meaning of this line and the line following is very obscure.

6   Very uncertain. This could refer to an attack in a wood, or to men piercing the ground and descending into the grave. The word for 'weaving' (*brwydaw*) was also used for writing poetry – an intriguing extension of the image, perhaps into the thicket of words.

36. Elegy for Uther Pendragon

1   Armour is often described in early Welsh poetry as 'blue-grey', *glasar*, evoking the metallic sheen of mail and weapons, and the epithet here probably means 'glittering brightly/exceedingly'.

2   This line is extremely obscure in the original; with some (very speculative) emendation, it might be translated, 'May our God, chief light-giver, transform me.'

3   See *Trioedd Ynys Prydein*, Triad 23, and Haycock's note, *LPBT*, p. 8. We have made the emendation from *kawyl* in the original in order to give a proper name.

4   The pairing of two similar names like Casnur and Cawrnur is very typical of Welsh legendary narrative.

5   Or '[I had or I shared] a ninth of Arthur's valour'. The phrase *gwrhyt Arthur*, 'Arthur's valour', is also found in 'The Spoils of Annwfn', line 26.

6   The birds of prey are grateful to the poet/warrior for providing them with food.

7   Here the metre changes to a two-stress line until l. 39.

37. The Great Song of the World

1   For a detailed description of these, see *LPBT*, pp. 233–5.

2   In Geoffrey of Monmouth's *Life of Merlin*, ll. 788–819, Telgesinus (Taliesin) declares that the seas are divided into a hot area, a

cold area and a temperate area (see *Life of Merlin: Geoffrey of Monmouth, Vita Merlini*, ed. Basil Clarke, Cardiff, University of Wales Press, 1973).

3   Haycock suggests the emendation to *Vesperus*; see *LPBT*, p. 523.

4   We should expect a reference to Jupiter to complete the list of the planets. *Severus* might be a mistake for *Ieu verus*, 'the true Jove', or even *Ioverus*, which would be a Cambro-Latin coinage from *Iovis* (Jupiter) to chime with *Venerus*. If the reference is not to Jupiter, the name could be a garbled version of *Sirius*, the 'Dog-star'.

5   Some mediaeval writers – among them the Venerable Bede and Geoffrey of Monmouth – discussed these five divisions of the world according how useful they were to mankind. See, for example, Geoffrey's *Life of Merlin*, ll. 747–52, in which the five zones comprise an inner one too hot to inhabit, two outer zones too cold to inhabit and two temperate zones ideal for humans and animals.

38. *The Small Song of the World*

1   For the many parallels to these questions in various mediaeval collections of riddles or puzzles, see *LPBT*, pp. 528 ff.

PROPHETIC POEMS

39. *The Great Prophecy of Britain*

1   See *Armes Prydein: The Prophecy of Britain. From the Book of Taliesin*, ed. and annotated by Sir Ifor Williams, English version by Rachel Bromwich (Dublin, Institute of Advanced Studies, 1972), p x.

2   We have noted above (p. 214) that Caer Wair is often identified with Durham or a north-eastern location; the suggestion that it should refer here to Caithness – i.e. as far away as can be imagined, 'John O' Groats', as it were – is Andrew Breeze's. See Andrew Breeze, 'Durham, Caithness and *Armes Prydein*', *Northern History* 48.1, 2011, pp. 147–52.

3   Dublin was a Viking kingdom at this period.

4   The translation here is very uncertain.

5   See *AP*, p. 24.

6   If the text is indeed as early as the tenth century, this is one of the
     earliest references we have to Myrddin or Merlin. The ninth-cen-
     tury *Annales Cambriae* mention in 573 a battle at *Armterit* (*Arf-
     derydd* in Modern Welsh) in southern Scotland and its casualties,
     and then add abruptly, 'Merlin went mad'. We have no more
     details of what must have been an early form of the legend retold
     by Geoffrey of Monmouth in the twelfth century about *Merlinus
     Siilvestris*, a sage and seer who wanders in the Caledonian Forest
     after the death of his royal patron in battle. By this time, he is
     also associated with Taliesin (see pp. xx–xxi) in both Geoffrey of
     Monmouth and contemporary Welsh material, and is presented
     as a riddling bardic sage like him. Geoffrey muddies the waters
     rather by introducing the idea of two Merlins: Merlin Ambrosi-
     us, identified (awkwardly) with the 'Emrys' of the *historia Brit-
     tonum* who resists wicked King Vortigern (a distant memory of
     the historical Ambrosius who rallied the Romanized Britons to
     fight against the fifth-century Germanic invaders); and Merlin
     Sylvestris, 'Merlin of the forest'.

7   Several Welsh rulers paid tribute to Athelstan as their 'overlord';
     but note the discussion of Andrew Breeze, '"Armes Prydein"', Hy-
     wel Dda and the Reign of Edmund of Wessex', *Études Celtiques*
     33, 1997, pp. 209–22, for the argument for a slightly later date.

8   The River Dee in North Wales has been suggested, but a location
     on the upper Wye would fit better in the context of tensions with
     an expansionist Wessex.

9   See Bede's *historia ecclesiastica* 1.15 and the *historia Brittonum*,
     31–49.

10   Does this echo the description in 'The Men of Catraith', l. 20, of
     Urien's defeated (Anglian?) enemies as 'pale-faced'.

11   This line plays on the pun between *grudd* ('cheek') and *rhudd*
     ('red').

12   For the Arlego's location near Leicester, see Andrew Breeze,
     'Armes Prydein' (n. 2 above).

13   In earlier poems this word normally refers to the territory of the
     Northumbrian Angles, but this is unlikely in the present context.

14   This seems to refer to a specific occasion on which English or
     English-allied forces had attacked St Davids and infringed its
     rights of sanctuary; but we have no evidence to help us identify
     such an event. The royal house of Dyfed was allied with Wessex
     in the tenth century, and there may at some point have been a

local skirmish with anti-Wessex clerics at the shrine.

15   This line could have two opposite meanings. In the tradition of the kingdom of Powys, Germanus appears as a supporter of the royal line of King Vortigern – in which case, the revenge described is revenge *against* Vortigern's successors, those who follow his policy of alliance with the Saxons. But this would be slightly strange, as the writer seems to share the perspective of the *historia Brittonum*, where Germanus confronts Vortigern. The natural meaning of the line would then be a reference to some outrage against a religious community connected with Germanus's memory.

16   From what? The eighth-century *Annales Cambriae* give 537 as the date of the Battle of Camlann in which Arthur died; and 940 or thereabouts is a plausible date for this poem – in which case this would be an indirect Arthurian allusion. But the case is fragile, given the uncertainties in dating at both ends.

17   If Andrew Breeze is right to identify 'Lego' as Leicester, this is slightly strange; it would be more natural to look for a coastal location. But seaborne Vikings from Dublin were fighting at Leicester in 940, and this may simply be a conventional recognition of their history as seafarers.

18   *O Dyuet hyd Danet* – a better chime in Welsh.

19   This is probably a mistaken copying of the identical earlier line.

20   *Gwenerawl*, literally something like 'Friday-minded' – i.e. devoted to the crucifixion, observant of the fasting rules.

21   This is a very difficult line. It has often been taken to refer to Gelligaer in the Rhymney valley as a place of composition, but this is unlikely on many counts. Mediaeval Welsh very occasionally uses the Latin borrowing *c(a)eli* as a synonym for God ('the one of heaven'); it's possible that the copyist, puzzled by this unfamiliar word, replaced it with the more obvious place name component, *celli* or *kelli*.

40. Goronwy's Oak

1   For a full account of the wide range of 'oak' imagery in this poem, see *PBT*, pp. 25–7 and 33–4. These range from the metaphor of a tree meaning 'warrior' to Aaron's rod in the Old Testament, the staff of the wizard Mathonwy growing in a forest. In the Fourth Branch of the Mabinogi, Mathonwy is the father of enchanters Math and Gwydion. Coming to the aid of his

nephew, Lleu, who was cursed by his mother, Gwydion creates
Blodeuwedd, a woman made of flowers. She takes a lover called
Gronw Pebr, who might be the Goronwy of this poem.

2   A very obscure couplet.
3   'Cynan' is often identified as one of the heroic figures who will
    return and lead the Welsh to victory, but it is not clear which
    Cynan is being invoked here. It could be Cynan, son of Eudaf
    (named in Geoffrey of Monmouth's history) or Cynan Garwyn,
    the late-sixth-century ruler of Powys mentioned in the earlier
    Taliesin poems (above, pp. 3–5; and see *PBT*, p. 10).
4   These names are employed as a way of conveying the sense of
    vast distances. There is a suggestion that the vapour rising from
    Rhun's men will generate enough rain to drown the land. See
    PBT, p. 40, for discussion of inundation stories.

41. *Taliesin's Spring Song*

1   'Beli's liquor' is presumably a standard metaphor for the ocean.
2   This would technically be incest by the laws of the mediaeval
    Church, so the line may simply mean that there is a collapse
    of social or moral norms; the alternative is a reference to some
    specific scandal, but if so we do not know what it was.
3   The reference made at this point in our translation to the Battle
    of Brunanburh depends on amending the text from the obscure
    kattybrudawt (possibly 'the Battle of Tybrudawt' – an unknown
    and very unlikely place name) to *kattybrunawc*, 'the Battle of Ty
    Brynawc', which other early Welsh sources have as a designation
    for Brunanburh. A reference to early tenth-century events would
    follow well from the earlier mention of Anarawd.

42. *News Has Reached Me from Calchfynydd*

1   See *PBT*, p. 69.
2   The implication of this line is that Owain has been humiliated by
    Mabon's successful raid on his territory in Deheubarth.
3   This ironic question and the following answer paraphrase a chal-
    lenge issued by Mabon to Owain to retrieve his stolen cattle.
4   This is addressed to Mabon.
5   In our reading of this poem, this 'we' implicates the poet's per-
    sona in Mabon's raid on Owain's cattle in the south.
6   Mabon is such a calm and skilful cattle raider that the stolen
    herd isn't noisy.

7   Here Mabon is imagined protecting his cattle.

8   Shields were made of wood and lime-wash and sealed with wax.

9   We have treated this line as marking a shift in the poem, chang-
    ing the focus to Owain as he initiates a campaign to rob Mabon
    in revenge for his successful raid.

10 Here the poet compares the fighters with the herd of cattle who
    are slaughtered.

11 Owain's campaign against Mabon seems to be understood as a
    defence of Urien's northern kingdom against local enemies in the
    region.

43. The Awen Predicts

1   The name is the same as the 'Cassivelaunus' who appears as Cae-
    sar's British adversary in the Gallic Wars.

2   One source claims that Iago was killed at the battle of Ches-
    ter in 613 CE, where the Northumbrians defeated a force from
    North and Mid-Wales with great slaughter. 'Prydyn' is a puzzle;
    it normally refers to the Pictish Kingdom in the far North. But
    it is sometimes confused, understandably, with 'Prydein', which
    designates the whole island, and perhaps that is what we should
    read here – unless we take the line as meaning that Iago died at
    the hands of a warrior from the distant North.

3   This reading of the manuscript depends on amending the text
    from Valaon to Vlathaon.

4   Y gynhon, 'the nations', used in the biblical sense of the peoples
    outside the covenant of grace, including the Vikings and their
    Norman descendants.

44. Fine Feasting

1   The location here may be Dolbadarn Castle, near lakes Padarn
    and Peris in Gwynedd (see PBT, pp. 98 and 101).

2   The first five Norman rulers were William I, William Rufus,
    Henry I, Stephen and Matilda (though she was never crowned).
    It is not clear why Henry II would be described as ruling 'from
    sowing till harvest'. Richard I died and was buried in Normandy.

3   This must be King John – father-in-law of Llywelyn the Great,
    but a bitter military enemy.

4   That is, the Lynx's campaign.

45. *May God Lift up over the British People*

1   All three of these unknown names seem to stand for proverbially impregnable fortresses, but whether they are envisaged as near Dumbarton Rock or in Wales itself we cannot determine.

2   *Ardd* may mean a hill or high place, and *nefon* may have a connection with the usual word for 'heaven'. The implication might be that Cadwallon will create for himself a secure place in heaven, or in the pantheon of heroes whose name will survive.

46. *Long Eulogy for Lludd*

1   *The Mabinogion*, pp. 111ff., in Sioned Davies's translation. They are the sons of Beli, son of Manogan, whose idealized reign is mentioned in 'Fine Feasting' (p. 139). In the tale, the Island of Britain, ruled by Lludd, is being destroyed by three afflictions. The first was the arrival of a race called the Coraniaid (thought to be the Romans) from abroad; the invaders could hear every conversation that the wind carried. The second was a scream that was heard every May eve that made the land barren. The third affliction was that food, no matter in what quantity it was prepared, perished after the first night it was served to the king. Only when Lludd takes advice from his brother Llefelys, who rules in France, is he able to save Britain from its troubles.

2   The Welsh for 'week' is *wythnos*, that is, eight nights.

3   Once again, Cadwaladr and Cynan appear together here as symbols of heroic British resistance to invaders.

4   Low-lying, the island of Anglesey was raided by both the Vikings and British (see *Prophecies from the Book of Taliesin*, p. 138).

5   The logic here is that its peaks make Snowdonia more easily defended.

6   The sea is shameful because foreign invaders use it to reach the lands they wish to conquer.

7   This may be a sign of the disruption of the order of the seasons.

8   For the siege by King John, see *PBT*, p.143.

9   The enemies are represented as unredeemed, not true Christians.

10   These lines evoke the story in the Second Branch of the Mabinogi of how Branwen sent starlings as messengers to her brother Brân ('Raven') to tell him about her abuse at the hands of the King of Ireland; Brân subsequently crossed the Irish Sea with a

war band to release her. The suggestion is that, like Branwen, the besieged Welsh will call for reinforcements from further afield.

11 See *PBT*, p. 145. Given Seithennin's poor reputation, it fits that this is a description of an inadequate response from the Welsh.

12 The tradition that Britain was settled by a descendant of Aeneas called Brutus, so that the British were kinsfolk of the Romans, was in circulation before 800 CE and was developed into a detailed and lively narrative by Geoffrey of Monmouth.

47. He's on His Way for Sure

1 The poem returns later to the theme of the kinship between Romans and British and the Roman ancestry of British kings.

2 The poet is here envisaging warriors assembling on the frontiers of Welsh territory to join the deliverer when he returns from Ireland via Anglesey.

3 Our reading of the text here is uncertain.

4 The pallor of the English is a recurrent theme; cf. l. 20 of 'The Men of Catraeth' (p. 7) and l. 21 of 'May God Lift Up' (p. 142).

5 *Tra merin reget*, which may be either 'beyond the Firth of Rheged' – possibly the Solway Firth – or, with less grammatical justification, 'to Rheged beyond the sea'.

48. Short Poem on Lludd's Conversation

1 See *The Mabinogion*, tr. Sioned Davies, p. 113.

2 Margaret Enid Griffiths dates this poem to the eleventh century, to the time of the First Crusade (1096–9). Historians have variously suggested that 'Cafis' might refer to an area north of Kabul, to the Indus or to west Africa or Cadiz (see *PBT*, p. 179).

3 The text seems to be corrupt here.

4 The word *gwern*, Welsh for alder, also means alder swamp, and can sometimes be used for the desolate landscape of Hell.

5 A rather puzzling line, but it may refer to Welsh princes present at Athelstan's court in the tenth century, who are being encouraged to rebel against the 'overlord'.

49. A Prophecy about Cadwaladr

1 This is the first line of a couplet in the Welsh whose second line is missing, and is unintelligible as it stands.

2   An indication of social collapse, as in l. 24 of 'Taliesin's Spring
     Song' (p. 133).
3   Two incomplete lines in succession.

DEVOTIONAL POEMS

52. *I Make My Prayer to the Trinity*

1   This schema is taken from the writings of the Pseudo-Dionysius,
     whose fifth- and sixth-century writings placed pagan Neopla-
     tonism in a Christian context.

53. *A Prophecy of Judgement Day*

1   A very obscure line; our translation is conjectural.
2   Another obscure line; our translation follows the text proposed
     by Marged Haycock in her edited version.
3   Or possibly, '*Through* my wounds', i.e. forgiveness as a result of
     Christ's Cross.
4   The phrase 'great glory' depends on an interpretation of the
     Welsh *ryrys* as an intensified form of a word meaning 'splendour,
     magnificence'.

54. *Saints and Martyrs of the Faith*

1   This refers to the holy men and women of the pre-Christian
     period, who have to await the descent of Christ after his cruci-
     fixion into the depths of the Underworld. The theme originates
     in a passage of the First Epistle of Peter (3:19–20) in the New
     Testament, but was elaborated considerably in later Christian
     speculation, especially in the light of the very popular 'Gospel of
     Nicodemus' from the fourth century. The division of the world's
     history into 'ages' is a commonplace of Christian historiography:
     Christ is born after 4,000 years have elapsed since the fall of
     Adam.
2   *Thorsi* in the original.
3   *Apoli* in the original; if not 'Apulia', then just possibly a truncat-
     ed form of a name ending in '-polis'.
4   *Garanwys* in the original; but perhaps (as Breeze suggests in
     'Cruces in "The Saints and Martyrs of Christendom"', *Studia*

Celtica 42.1, 2008, pp. 149–53) this is the result of a succession of scribal errors beginning with something like 'Arabenses'. Otherwise it may be something to do with the 'Garamantes' of Libya.

5   *Maritnen.* (It is not too difficult to imagine an original *maritimam* as an adjective for Capernaum.)

6   *Judubriactus a Zorim* in the original, and completely unintelligible as such. Breeze argues (art. cit.) that a series of corruptions has left us not much more than the consonants of the initial text, and even those in a garbled form. But these Galilean names would fit nicely with the preceding line, and his suggestions make excellent sense.

7   Perpetua and Felicity, martyred at Carthage in about 203 CE, belong to the era before the classical creeds of the Church were formulated. Their names are mentioned in the Eucharistic prayer of the old Roman rite, and so would have been very familiar to an educated mediaeval writer.

8   Once again a bold but persuasive proposal from Andrew Breeze, assuming that the manuscript's *Sicomorialis* is an error.

9   All Saints' Day is on 1 November.

10 A further reference to the Holy Innocents, their number now multiplied to 3,000 rather than 1,000.

11 The Feast of the Holy Innocents falls on 28 December.

12 As in Dante's *Inferno*, Hell is conceived sometimes as a place of fiery torment, sometimes as a frozen waste.

13 A short passage in Latin follows in the manuscript; this is translated at the end of the poem.

14 Though the Latin is somewhat mangled, it retains a clear rhythmical structure, with internal rhymes. David Howlett has argued plausibly that it is a liturgical 'sequence' to be sung during the Mass ('Two Cambro-Latin Sequences from the Welsh Church', *Archivum Latinitatis Medii Aevi* 65, 2007, pp. 235–46, especially 243–6), and suggests some amendments to the text, some of which have been adopted for this version. If it is a liturgical piece, its natural setting would be the Feast of St Michael and All Angels on 29 September.

15 Reading *miserati* for *unistrati*; the former could easily be misread as the latter in mediaeval script.

16 Referring to Matthew 26:53, where Jesus says, 'Do you think I cannot call on my Father, and he will at once put at my disposal more than twelve legions of angels?'

55. *Cruel Herod*

1   See n. 12 on 'Saints and Martyrs of the Faith' (p. 172).

56. *The Steadfast Hebrew*

1   In the biblical story, the fish die when the rivers are turned to blood. The plagues as recorded in Exodus are: 1) the river turned into blood; 2) a plague of frogs; 3) a plague of gnats; 4) swarms of flies; 5) the death of livestock; 6) a plague of boils; 7) showers of fiery hail; 8) a plague of locusts; 9) three days of total darkness; 10) the death of Egypt's first-born.

2   This is a corrupt line. The fourth plague in Exodus 9:1–7 is the death of livestock.

3   This is the misfortune described in *Exodus* 11:4–9 when, on the stroke of midnight, God caused the death of every Egyptian first-born son and animal.

57. *The Stem of Jesse*

1   This line is very uncertain, as the internal rhyme between its first two parts in the Welsh.

2   This line is incomplete in the manuscript; Haycock suggests that the word *brenin* ('king') be supplied to fill out the second part of the line, giving roughly the sense of the translation here.

3   Reading *Abel* instead of *afael* in the original.

4   This line and the one preceding are very unclear. It is worth noting that the poet uses *derwydon*, 'druids', for the wise men of the gospel story.

58. *Everlasting Trinity*

1   Actually four in the biblical record (Genesis 29 and 30), but the poet presumably intends a comparison with the activity of the three persons of the Trinity in the new covenant with the twelve apostles of Jesus.

59. *The Rod of Moses*

1   This line is unintelligible in the original, and without the expect-
ed internal rhyme.

2   Compare the account of Alexander's adventures in the Holy
Land in 'He Ranged the Whole World', above, p. 94.

3   A very difficult line; we have accepted the emendation of *rudech*
to *rudeur* ('red gold') and *dalen* to *daleu* ('foreheads'), but the
meaning is still a bit uncertain.

UNGROUPED POEMS

60. *Disaster for the Island*

1   The sense of this line and the one before it seems to be that, while
once it was possible to make warriors by magic (perhaps a refer-
ence to the 'Battle of the Trees' theme), this will not now happen:
death is final.

2   'Not a merchant' rather than (as Ifor Williams proposes) 'not a
pirate'.

3   Williams assumes these are the same as the four bare-headed or
bald-headed figures of l. 8, but there is no reason to take this for
granted. They are more likely to be the daughters and heirs of
the dead king, and are obviously not disposed to continue his
generosity to the poet.

4   If *llywy* ('a fair or royal or splendid one', 'a queen') here is not a
proper name (as Williams prefers), this seems to imply a fear that
once the queen too is dead, there is no restraint on the unsympa-
thetic princesses.

61. *In Praise of Tenby*

1   *Ffichti* is the usual word for Picts, and this encouraged earlier
editors (Sir Ifor Williams in particular) to see the poem as pre-
dating the Viking raids, and so dating from before 900. This is
very doubtful: mediaeval poets were quite capable of introducing
deliberately archaic terms, and it may also be the case that *ffichti*
had become a generic word for pirates and seaborne raiders.

2   *Gran(n)wyn* may mean 'pale-cheeked, pale-faced', and Ifor Wil-
liams argues that it refers to pallid enemies in flight (another in-

stance, he suggests, of the stereotype of pale English complexions – though it is stretching things a bit to think of English forces in the far reaches of Pembrokeshire at this date). But the eagle's flight over a white-flecked sea seems more in keeping with the repeated reference to the castle's location.

3   This sounds like a proverb about the superiority of South Welsh men over North: Deudraeth is in Gwynedd (near Portmeirion).

4   The suggestion here is of a collection of texts of some kind preserved in the fortress or in a neighbouring monastery. It is tempting to think of the ancient foundation on Caldey Island, a short boat trip from Tenby.

5   This is a very unclear line, but Williams proposes taking *vrowyr* as the mutated form of an imagined Welsh adaptation of the Irish *bruig-fher*, 'cowherd' or 'farm labourer'. The sense is that the descendant of 'Owain' (possibly an Owain ap Maredudd, who appears as a ruler somewhere in West Wales in the early ninth century) will reduce the free men of Tenby to a condition like serfdom.

6   This last stanza seems to belong for the most part to another poem, and the sudden introduction of Gwynedd and its armies makes no obvious sense in the context. The prayer that ends the preceding verse would be the point at which we should expect the poem proper to end. This stanza is also found as a standalone piece in *The Black Book of Carmarthen*, with a few small variations.